PRAISE FOR *NO BEAST SO FIERCE*

'. . . The most compelling quality of *No Beast So Fierce* is that, solidly rooted in his own experiences, it explores the nature of the criminal mind with almost blinding authenticity. Bunker is obviously a man of unusual gifts honed under circumstances that would destroy most men . . .'

Los Angeles Times

'. . . A gripping and harrowing read . . .'

Daily Mail

'. . . The best first person crime novel I have ever read . . .'

Quentin Tarantino

'. . . Quite simply, one of the great crime novels of the past 30 years . . .'

James Ellroy

PRAISE FOR *THE ANIMAL FACTORY*

'*The Animal Factory* joins Solzhenitsyn's *One Day in the Life of Ivan Denisovich* and George Jackson's *Soledad Brother* in the front rank of prison literature . . . a stone classic.'

Time Out

PRAISE FOR *LITTLE BOY BLUE*

'A scalding experience – and a literary triumph in the tradition of Dreiser, Farrell and James Jones. This is an important book . . .'

Roderick Thorp

PRAISE FOR *DOG EAT DOG*

'. . . The "angel dust" of crime fiction: thrillingly violent and addictive, surging with exhilaration and fear . . .'

The Evening Standard

'Mr. Bunker has written a raw, unromantic, naturalistic crime drama more lurid than anything the noiresque Chandlers or Hammetts ever dreamed up.'

The New York Times

PRAISE FOR *MR BLUE*

At 40 Eddie Bunker was a hardened criminal with a substantial prison record. Twenty-five years later, he is hailed by his peers as America's greatest living crime writer. Those who know and understand these things become hushed at the mere mention of his name. Some call him simply, The Man . . .'

The Independent

'. . . compulsively readable piece of real-life southern Californian noir . . .'

The Saturday Times

'. . . a classic of criminal pride and indignation . . .'

The Times

'Bunker writes in straight-ahead, unadorned prose and, refreshingly, he refrains from excessive psychologizing and sentimentalizing . . . a rough-hewn memoir by a rough-hewn man.'

The New York Times Book Review

Also by the same author

No Beast so Fierce
Little Boy Blue
Dog Eat Dog
Mr Blue
Stark

Edward Bunker will be back with his final book –

DEATH ROW BREAKOUT

– in 2009. Read a story from this book online now at
www.noexit.co.uk/deathrowbreakout

EDWARD BUNKER

the animal factory

no exit press

This edition published in 2008 by No Exit Press,
P.O.Box 394, Harpenden, Herts, AL5 1XJ
www.noexit.co.uk

A CIP catalogue record for this book is available from the British Library.

EAN 978-1-84243-267-9

2 4 6 8 10 9 7 5 3 1

Typeset by Ellipsis Books Limited, Glasgow
Printed and bound in Great Britain by
J.H. Haynes & Co Ltd., Sparkford, Yeovil, Somerset

To my brothers—in and out.
They know who they are.

Dawn pushed a faint line of yellow on the city's low skyline when the prisoners, nearly five hundred of them, were herded from the jail's sallyport to the parking lot. Waiting was the fleet of black-and-white buses with barred windows and heavy wire separating the driver area from the seats. The air was filled with acrid diesel exhaust and the stench of rotting garbage. The ragtag prisoners, more than half of them black or Chicano, were in columns of two, six to a chain, a busload to a group; they looked like human centipedes. Everywhere were deputy sheriffs in knife-creased uniforms. Three deputies were assigned to each bus, while the others stood back with fat .357 Magnum Pythons dangling from their hands. A few fondled short-barreled shotguns.

Despite the smell, many men breathed deep, for no cool air entered the windowless jail, and they had already spent three hours in seventeen-foot bullpens, as many as fifty in each. Behind them the jail trustees were already sweeping the cages for the second court line of the day.

Ronald Decker was young, looked even younger than he was. In contrast to the generally disheveled clothes of nearly all the others, he wore a neat corduroy suit that had withstood three days of going to court, getting rousted awake at 3:30 a.m., standing in the jail cages, riding the bus in chains, waiting in the packed bullpen beside the courtroom, getting a twenty-four-hour continuance, returning to the jail in the evening. When the steel gates crashed, loud-speakers blared, and there was no sleep until midnight. Today it'll be over, he thought. The attorney had tried to save him from prison, but a garage with two hundred kilos of marijuana and a kitchen table with forty ounces of cocaine was just too big a bust. No matter that he, or the fat fee, had convinced the psychiatrist to report that he was a cocaine addict who would benefit from treatment. No matter that the probation officer was convinced by his "good" family that an alternative program would be rehabilitative. The district attorney, who had a legion of subordinates and didn't know one case in a hundred, sent a personal letter to the judge demanding prison. Ron grinned wanly, remembering what the deputy district attorney had called him yesterday: the "boy wonder" of drug dealers. At age twenty-five he was hardly a boy.

The prisoners climbed onto the bus, a deputy roughly guiding the befuddled winos so their chains didn't entangle as they swung around to be seated. A Chicano even younger than Ron was hand-cuffed beside him. Ron had already noticed the yawns and sniffles of withdrawals and hoped the youth wouldn't vomit the green fluid that junkies cast up when their stomachs were empty. The Chicano wore khaki pants and Pendleton shirt, the uniform of the East Los Angeles *barrio*.

Ron and the Chicano got seats, but the bus had just thirty-two and was carrying sixty-one men. The aisle filled.

"Okay, assholes," a deputy called. "Move back in there."

"Man, I ain't no motherfuckin' sardine," a black called out.

But the men were packed in. Once Ron had seen some prisoners refuse. The deputies had come with mace and clubs and the rebellion was short-lived. Then the driver had raced down the freeway and thrown on the breaks, sending the standing men crashing around. Finally, so the word came, the rebellious ones had been charged with assault on a peace officer, a felony carrying up to ten years in prison.

It was 6:20 when the bus whooshed and started moving. Other buses were also getting under way, en route to dozens of court-rooms in every region of the vast county: Santa Monica, Lancaster, Torrance, Long Beach, and more obscure places like Citrus, Temple

10

City, and South Gate. No court would convene until 10:00, but the sheriff's started early. Besides, another five hundred had to be processed for court in downtown Los Angeles.

The mood on the bus had an element of levity. It was something to be riding down the freeway when the rush hour was just beginning. Some of the chained passengers, mostly the drunks, were oblivious to the sights, while others stared avidly at everything. Some, next to the windows, stood up when a car with a woman whipped by; they tried to stare down at the best angle to see bare thighs pressed against the car seat.

Ron was too tired. His eyes felt gritty and his stomach had a hollow burning. Already thin, he'd lost nearly twenty pounds after four months of jail food. He dropped his head back against the seat and slid down as much as he could, given the chains and the cramped leg space. Through the hubbub a set of voices, easily identifiable as belonging to blacks, pulled his attention. They were close and loud.

"Listen, blood, I damn sure know Cool Breeze. Breeze, sheeit, that nigger's hotass wind! Nigger calls himself a pimp . . . an' ain't nuthin' but a shade tree for a ho. He take a good workin' bitch an' put her in a rest home. Me, I'm a mack man an' a player. I know how to make a bitch bring me *monee* . . ."

Ron smiled involuntarily, envious of anyone who could laugh and lie with such gusto in these circumstances; but blacks had had centuries to develop the knack. It was hard not to feel embarrassed when they boisterously called each other "nigger," as if they hated themselves. And pimp stories were a cliché in jail; every black claimed to be that or a revolutionary. No, he thought, "every" was an unfair exaggeration. It was stereotyping, and by doing it he was being unfair to himself, too. Yet, those he'd found in jail were certainly different from the blacks he'd done business with, musicians, real hustlers who were cool. Indeed, he'd believed everyone's stories when he first came to jail. He seldom lied about his own exploits, and because he'd made quite a bit of money, he expected to find others who'd done the same. He'd found incompetents and liars. Now he was

11

going to prison. It was a long fall from a West Hollywood high rise and a Porsche Carrera.

The courtroom bullpen was twice as large as the cage at the jail, and concrete benches lined the concrete walls, which were defaced by graffiti scratched into the paint.

"Okay, assholes," a deputy yelled as the column of prisoners filed into the room from a tunnel. "Turn around so we can get the iron off."

Ron was among the first unchained and he quickly took a piece of bench in a corner, knowing that half the men would have to stand around or sit on the floor. When the deputies left, locking the door, the room quickly filled with cigarette smoke. The ventilation shaft in the ceiling was inadequate, though most prisoners had to mooch butts. A few men handed out cigarettes, and a dozen hands were extended. One red-faced man of fifty in a plaid shirt and work boots freely passed out cigarettes and used the largesse as a wedge to vent his woe.

"I've got sixty days suspended for drunk driving and they've got me again. What's gonna happen?"

"Suspended?"

"Uh-huh."

"Then he's gotta give you at least sixty days."

"Are you sure?"

"Pretty sure."

"Oh, God," the man said, his eyes welling with tears that he tried to sniffle away.

"Check that *puto*," the Chicano addict sneered. "I've got the joint suspended, five years to life, and another robbery . . . I ain't snivelin'."

Ron grunted, said nothing. He knew that sixty days in jail could be a greater trauma for some than prison for others. What he couldn't sympathize with was the unmanly display. Hidden tears he could understand. He felt them himself. But what he felt and what he showed were different. The man had no pride.

"Save that shit for the judge, turkey," someone said. "We can't do a thing for you."

12

The quip brought a couple of chuckles, and the man rubbed his eyes with his knuckles and tried to compose himself.

The long wait began. Ron sighed, closed his eyes, and wished the judge could mail the sentence. What difference did his presence make? It was going to be the same no matter what.

After 8:00 a.m. the lawyers began visiting their clients, calling them to the barred door and talking softly. When the public defender came, carrying a yellow legal pad, a crowd gathered around the gate. Ron thought about cats in a television commercial.

"Fuckin' dump-truck P.Ds," muttered the Chicano. "All they say is "so stipulated" and "waive." They waive you right to prison . . . punks all want you to plead guilty." Nevertheless, he joined the crowd at the gate. He's exaggerating, Ron thought, but not a whole lot. After four months I know more about justice from being in jail than from two years of college. *They* don't really care about justice. "They" was both lawyers and judges. That he was disillusioned indicated how naïve he'd been to begin with.

"Okay, you drunks and punks and other assholes," a deputy said at 10:00 a.m. "When I call your name, answer with your last three numbers and get up here."

Ron paid no attention. This was the municipal court line, the misdemeanors. His court was for the afternoon. His eyes were still closed when a large key banged the bars. "Decker, front and center."

Ron jerked from his stupor and saw his attorney, Jacob Horvath, standing slightly behind the bailiff's shoulder. Horvath was tall, with long, thinning hair, flared suit, and upturned gray moustache. His hands were soft. He'd learned his trade as a deputy U.S. attorney, and now earned a dozen times that salary by defending the dope peddlers he once prosecuted. Narcotics laws and search and seizure were his specialties. He was very good, and charged a fee commensurate with his skill.

"How's it going?" he asked.

"Tell me," Ron said. "You talked to the judge."

"Not good. The trial deputy would go for the rehabilitation center, but the big boys downtown are watching this one. The judge—"

Horvath shrugged and shook his head. "And guess who's in the courtroom."

"Akron and Meeks."

"Right. *And* the captain of the administrative narcs. It's on their own time. They don't get paid for this."

Ron shrugged. Nothing would be changed by their presence, and he had accepted the inevitable weeks ago.

"I talked to your mother this morning."

"She's here?"

"No, in Miami, but she left a message to call her so I did. She wants to know how things look and told me to have you call her collect this evening."

"Just like that. She thinks I'm in the Beverly-Wilshire."

"I'll get a court order."

"Make sure it's signed and goes back on the bus. The pigs at the jail won't let me near a phone otherwise."

"Okay . . . Anyway, the judge doesn't want to bury you, but he's under pressure. I think he's going to send you to prison, but keep jurisdiction under Eleven sixty-eight. Keep your nose clean and he can pull you back in a couple of years when the heat's off."

"A couple of years, huh?"

Horvath shrugged. "You won't be eligible for parole for six years, so two is pretty soft."

"I guess you're right. It isn't the gas chamber. You did what you could."

"You were selling dope like you had a license."

"And I don't see anything wrong with it. I really don't. Somebody wants it."

"Don't tell the judge that, or anyone at the prison."

A prisoner came back in handcuffs, escorted by a deputy. Horvath and Ron stepped back from the door so the man could be let in. When Horvath stepped up to the bars again, he glanced at his gold Rolex. "Gotta go. I've got a preliminary hearing upstairs scheduled for eleven. I have to see the client for a few minutes first."

"Is Pamela out there?" Ron asked quickly.

14

"I didn't see her."

"Shit!"

"You know she's got troubles."

"Is she hooked again?"

Horvath made a face that confirmed the fact without saying it. Ron had wanted Horvath to ask the judge to let them get married, but this piece of information stopped him, sent a hollow pang through his stomach. As he nodded and turned back to the bench, he resented Horvath as the bearer of bad tidings, thinking that he'd paid eighteen thousand dollars to go to prison, recalling the promises that Horvath had made to get the money. Ron had learned since then that the business of lawyers was selling hope. Hot air was what they usually delivered. In all fairness, Horvath had fought hard to get the search warrant, and all the narcotics seized from its use, thrown out as evidence—but the warrant was solid, based on oath and affidavit, which wasn't what Horvath had said when he asked for a fifteen-thousand-dollar retainer.

Just before lunch the last pair of prisoners from morning court were brought in, new faces who'd probably spent the night in a substation, skinny youths with shoulder-length hair, peach-fuzz beards, and filthy blue jeans. They looked like city hippies, but their voices were pure Georgia farmboy. Ron wouldn't have noticed them except that they asked him to read their complaint. It said they were charged with violation of Section 503 of the Vehicle Code, auto theft. They couldn't read, didn't know what they faced, and yet didn't seem disheartened by their predicament. They were more interested in when the food was due.

At noon a deputy dropped a cardboard box outside the bars, calling all the assholes to get in line. Some crowded and jostled. Ron hung back.

"Straighten up, assholes, or I'll send it to Long Beach," the deputy called. Long Beach was where sewage went.

"That's where it belongs," someone called.

"Then gimme yours," another said.

"Knock it off!" the deputy yelled.

The men quieted and the bags came through the bars, each with salami between two pieces of bread and an orange. It was all the food they'd get until morning unless they got back to the jail early, which was unlikely for those going to afternoon court. On his first court trip, Ron had looked at the bag's contents and handed it away. Now he wolfed it down with the same gusto as the undernourished winos, pocketing the orange and dropping the bag on the floor. Litter everywhere mingled with the odor of sweat, Lysol, and piss.

Because he was the only prisoner going to this particular courtroom, the deputy handcuffed Ron's hands behind his back. They went down a concrete tunnel and reached the courtroom by a side door. The deputy took off the handcuffs before they entered. Court was not yet in session and the room was empty except for the police emissaries in back spectators' seats. One of them smiled and waved. Ron ignored the gesture, not because of a particular animosity, but because a response would have been unseemly. The young prosecutor was shuffling folders at his table while the court reporter and clerk moved around on hushed feet. A huge state seal flanked by the flags of California and the United States was on the wall behind the bench. Ron was struck by the contrast between the back-room cages of justice and the courtroom's solemn dignity. The public saw the mansion, not the outhouse.

"Take a seat in the jury box, Mr. Decker," the deputy said, and as Ron followed the instructions he smiled, thinking he had gone from "asshole" to "mister" by walking through a door. In a few minutes he'd be "asshole" again.

Horvath scurried in with perfect timing. He'd just put his briefcase on the counsel table when the clerks jumped into place, court reporter at his machine, clerk beside the chamber door.

"Department B of the Superior Court of the State of California is now in session, the Honorable Arlen Standish presiding. All rise."

As the few people stood up, the judge came through the door and mounted his throne. He was all brisk business in his black robes. He was a big ruddy man who radiated vigor. Except for tufts of white hair above his ears, he was totally bald—but his pate was tanned and marked with freckles.

Everyone sat down as the judge shuffled some papers, then looked up, first at Ron, then at the policemen, without changing his expression. He nodded to the clerk.

"People versus Decker, probation hearing and sentence."

Ron didn't wait for the deputy to motion before getting up to join Horvath at the counsel table.

"Ready for the people, Your Honor," the prosecutor said.

"Defendant is ready, Your Honor," Horvath said, glancing at Ron and winking, though it had no significance.

The judge moved some unseen papers, slipped on glasses for a few seconds to read something, took them off and looked down. Everyone stood quietly waiting for him.

"Do you have any remarks, Mr. Horvath?"

"Yes, Your Honor, though in substance it is what you'll find in the preparation report and the evaluation of Dr."—Horvath glanced at notes—"Muller."

"I'm familiar with both reports . . . but proceed."

"This young man is a classic example of the tragedy of our era. He comes from a good family, attended college, and there's no history of any criminal activity until two years ago when he was arrested with a half-pound of marijuana. Both the probation officer and the psychiatrist report that he started smoking marijuana in college and, as a favor to friends, began getting some extra to sell. In the youth culture, this isn't criminal. But things have a momentum of their own, and someone wanted cocaine, and he could get that from the same place he got the marijuana. In other words, he drifted into it without realizing what he was doing. He was also using cocaine quite heavily, which clouded his perspective, and although there's no physical addiction to cocaine, there can be a psychological dependence.

"According to Dr. Muller, Mr. Decker isn't violent or dangerous. On the contrary, the psychological tests show an intelligent, well-balanced personality, providing he is weaned from the drug dependence . . ."

Horvath went on for five minutes, and Ron was fascinated. It was weird to listen while he was being discussed. He was impressed by Horvath's plea for leniency.

The prosecutor was next. "I concur with much that counsel says. This young man is intelligent. He is from a good family. But that gives him even less excuse, because he had every opportunity. The facts don't indicate that this was a hobby, which counsel seems to imply. Mr. Decker was living in a seven-hundred-dollar-a-month apartment and owned two automobiles, one of them a twelve-thousand-dollar sports car. The amount of drugs that he was caught with are worth a hundred and fifty thousand dollars. If he needs treatment for his own drug problem—and cocaine is not addictive—the Department of Corrections has programs. Above and beyond that, this is a serious offense, and if someone with this degree of involvement, someone who has every advantage and opportunity our society provides, doesn't go to prison, it would be unfair to send those who haven't had such opportunity."

When the prosecutor finished, the judge looked to Ron. "Do you have anything you'd like to say?"

"No, Your Honor."

"Is there any legal reason why judgment should not be passed?"

"No, Your Honor," Horvath said. "I'll submit the matter."

"The People submit," said the prosecutor.

"Frankly," the judge said after a judicious pause, "this is a difficult case. What counsel says—both counsel—has merit. There is a lot of good in this young man, and yet the People have a right to demand severe punishment because this offense is so serious. I'm going to send him to prison, for the term prescribed by law, but I think that the statutory term of ten years to life may be too severe. Many years there could ruin him and not serve society's best interests . . . so I'm going to retain jurisdiction under the provisions of Section Eleven sixty-eight, and I'll ask for reports in, say, two years. If they're satisfactory, I'll modify the sentence." He looked directly at Ron. "Do you understand? If you show signs of rehabilitation, I'll change this sentence in two years." Then to Horvath. "Now this matter is off calendar, and it's your responsibility to make a motion."

"Yes, Your Honor."

Ron felt the deputy's hand tweak his elbow. Sentence had been passed and he was going where he had expected to go.

Ronald Decker began the ten-day wait for the prison bus. Since his arrest five months earlier he'd told everyone that he was going, but part of him had belived that he would avoid it somehow. The imminent reality created both anxiety and curiosity. He asked questions, listened to stories. Prison was more than a walled-in place; it was an alien world of distorted values, ruled by a code of violence. Some tales contradicted others; the viewpoint depended on the experiences of the speaker. A middle-aged forger who had served eighteen months as a clerk in the administration building while living in an honor cellhouse saw prison differently from a *barrio* Chicano who had gone in at age twenty and spent five years walking the yard and bouncing between segregation and the cotton textile mill. The clerk said, "Sure those lowriders stab each other, but if you mind your own business, nobody bothers you, except when a race war is happening. Then you stay in your cell." The Chicano said, "A *vato* can get killed quick. Every day somebody gets hit. You need to get in a gang. They run things." The clerk explained that there were four powerful gangs, two Mexican, one white, one black, and that they existed in varying strengths in every one of the prisons. The clerk didn't know much about them, and the Chicano wouldn't talk. However, a few days later the *Los Angeles Times* had an article about the fifty-seven murders and three hundred stabbings that had happened in three prisons—Soledad, Folsom, and San Quentin—the previous year. Nearly all the violence was attributable to the gangs, which, according to the article, had started up for protection during the early racial violence but were now running rackets when they weren't killing each other. The two Mexican gangs were at war, as were the whites and blacks. "Fifty-seven killings!" Ron said. "What kind of place am I going to?"

"You might miss Q and Folsom," a potbellied old con said. "But you might have trouble wherever you go. Some people can go there and fade into the crowd, but sure as shit you can't. Know what I mean?"

Ron threw the paper on the bunk and nodded. He knew.

"You'll look like Gina Lollobrigida to some of those animals who've been down for eight or nine years. Even to some who aren't animals but just hardrock convicts. The jockers will have one idea and the fairies will want to gobble you up. Shit! Give 'em a chance and all they'll find of you is shoelaces and a belt buckle." The man laughed as Ron blushed. Prison culture, he knew, distinguished between masculine and feminine roles, but he was repelled by all of it. He didn't condemn it, but it wasn't for him. He was especially touchy about it because he'd seemed to attract homosexual propositions since puberty.

"So how do I handle it?"

"Start out by not being friendly and don't accept favors. The game is to get you obligated. Don't shave too much and wear ragged clothes. Talk out of the corner of your mouth with a lot of *motherfuckers* thrown in ... and give off vibes that you'll ice the first bastard who fucks with you. It'll make 'em think about it. *Nobody* wants to get *killed*. And some people do get through with murder-mouth and nothing behind it. But they don't look like you. 'Course you could put a shiv in one and that'd keep 'em off you ... leastways them that ain't serious. But if he's got friends ... and it'd keep you from getting out."

"Thanks for the advice," Ron said. He thought of asking what the prison authorities would do if he asked for help. Certainly others were in the same situation and the men who ran the prison had responsibility. Asking for protection was distasteful, but getting buggered or killing someone was beyond distaste. He wouldn't be able to live with himself after submitting to *that*, and killing, even without penalties, would be hard. He couldn't imagine himself taking someone's life. He didn't ask, sensing that appealing to the authorities for help was taboo. Maybe he could hire bodyguards. He asked if that was possible.

"Maybe, but what'd probably happen is that they'll take your money, extort more, and then turn on you. Then again, you might find someone. Shit, I've seen twenty cartons of cigarettes buy a stabbing . . . right in the fuckin' lung."

The questions had been partly rhetorical, but later Ron lay on his bunk and thought about the price of twenty cartons of cigarettes for a stabbing. It was cheap enough—if he could afford it. One week before the bust he'd had fifty-three thousand dollars in cold cash, another twenty-five thousand dollars or more in pre-Columbian artifacts from Mexican ruins (stolen and smuggled by the same persons in Culiacán who sold him narcotics), a Porsche, a Cammaro, and a partnership in a downtown parking lot. Thirty grand was lost when the narcotics were seized. The police had seized twelve grand, and turned eight over to Internal Revenue, which claimed he still owed sixty thousand. Some policemen had kept the missing four thousand. Five thousand in the bank had gone to the bail bondsman to get Pamela out. But before she made bail, some jackal among their acquaintances had broken into the apartment, stolen the artifacts, the stereo, the color television, and his clothes. The Porsche had been sold to pay Horvath, who also got the pittance from the forced sale of the parking lot. Pamela had the Cammaro, all that remained of his empire. It had been stripped like autumn leaves in a gale.

Maybe I can't afford twenty cartons, he thought, and grunted in disgust.

Ron knew that this would be the last visit. Tomorrow or the next day he would ride a sheriff's bus to prison. When his name was called at 10:00 a.m., eight men were in the four-man cell. Every night the jail filled with drunks and traffic violators who hadn't paid their tickets. The floor was always littered with bodies, many without mattresses but too full of booze to care. In the late afternoon they were moved to the county farm to make room for a new batch. All but one were awake. The old con was reading the newspaper by light coming through the bars. The recessed cell light had been burned out when Ron arrived and never replaced. Three middle-aged blacks and a rotund Indian were playing nickel-and-dime tonk on a bunk, while two others watched. The sleeper was on the floor in front of the toilet, which Ron had to use. The wino was snoring lustily, spittle drooling from his toothless mouth. In jail vernacular he was a "grape." After a momentary hesitation, Ron stood as close as possible and pissed over the sleeper's head. Most of the stream went into the toilet, but as it expired and he shook himself, some fell on the man's face without breaking the rhythm of his snores. Ron rinsed his hands and turned around. The gate would open any moment and he had to be ready. If he hesitated, the gate would close and he'd miss the visit.

The old con had lowered the newspaper and his expression was of a privately enjoyed joke.

"What's on your mind?" Ron asked.

"See . . . it's already got you."

"What're you talking about?"

"Time in the cage, how it corrupts. Six months ago you wouldn't have dreamed of doing that—" he glanced toward the wino on the floor—"pissing on somebody, you couldn't have done it."

"He's just an old grape."

"Ah, that's what you think *now*. It wasn't what you thought *then*."

Before Ron could comment, the door slid open and the deputy at the control panel called his name. He stepped out, tucking in the wrinkled denim shirt as he walked by the faces of the cells to the front and picked up the visiting-room pass.

The corridor with waxed concrete floors and prisoners moving along right-hand walls, watched by deputies, was so quiet that soft music from recessed speakers could be heard plainly. But as he neared the visiting-room door, Ron was washed by a tide of sound, an accretion of two hundred separate conversations. A trusty took his pass, said, "E five," and put the pass in a pneumatic tube. Row E, window five, Ron thought, going to where he'd been directed. "E" Row visitors would come in a bunch when the prisoner windows were full. All phones would go on simultaneously, and go off automatically in twenty minutes. Ron sat on the stool and stared through the dirty Plexiglas, freedom inches away, wondering what kind of acid would simply melt the barrier and let him walk away. The thought was academic. Desperate moves were not his style. Next, he looked at the visitors at the windows across from him. Most were women visiting sons, lovers, and husbands, bearing the historical female burden to endure. The single impression of the throng was poverty. Prisoners came from the poor. Even the hallowed right to bail favored the wealthy. As always, he looked for pretty women. Mere sight had now become a semiprecious experience. A Mexican girl, perhaps still in her teens, with lustrous black hair to her waist, velvet skin, and fawn-like eyes, was visiting a man with the dark granite features of an Indian. Ron watched the girl's ass and thighs pressing against her jeans as she shifted around.

A fresh cluster of visitors filled the air, their faces flashing into his as they looked for the right prisoner. Pamela came quickly, plopping down with a smile. Since he'd gone, she'd returned to jeans and bra-less T-shirts, blond hair hanging straight down. She was the complete hippie chick, and without makeup she looked young. The "skinny blond with big knockers," she called herself.

Ron immediately saw the pinpointed pupils; he'd seen them several times lately, but now he didn't want to argue so he would ignore them. She carried a pencil and tablet, ready in case something needed to be written down. Each held a dead phone at the ready, smiling and feeling stupid.

Somewhere the switch was thrown on and twenty conversations commenced along the row.

"Hi, honey, why so glum?" Pamela asked, turning her mouth down to mock the mask of tragedy.

"Not glum. I'm probably going tomorrow. Two buses are scheduled."

"You'll be glad to get out of here, won't you? This is shitty—except I can visit twice a week."

"Horvath says the judge won't let us get married. I don't really know if he asked him. Fuckin' mouthpieces are lyin' bastards. They take your money and fuck you over quick."

"What about just putting down that you're married?"

"I'll try it." He needed married status to get conjugal visits. "You know you need to get fucked good to keep you in line."

She winked in exaggerated lewdness.

"Get I.D. in my name," he said. "You won't have an arrest record under that name so there'll be no trouble. They can't very well take your fingerprints. At least I'll be able to touch you when you visit there."

"I won't be able to come as often."

"I know."

"I'll call tomorrow to see if you're still here."

"I'll be glad to get it started. All these months in jail don't count."

"*What?*"

"The time doesn't start counting until I get there."

The information triggered sudden tears, which momentarily startled Ron, for although she was volatile, given to all kinds of emotional outbreaks, these tears were out of proportion.

"It's okay," he said.

"Things are just . . . so shitty." She managed a smile. "I'm going to start hustling again."

"Don't tell me about it."

"That's where you found me," she snapped, anger replacing anguish. "I mean, what the hell . . ."

"Do what you have to do, but you don't have to tell me. I've got enough trouble as it is."

"I'm sorry. I'm uptight. I never thought I'd miss a man so much."

After a pause, he changed the subject. "Oh yeah, I talked to the bondsman. He's giving back some money. Send me enough to buy canteen and keep the rest for yourself."

It was information he'd given before. Nearly everything had been said before, and there was nothing really new to say. The glass was more than a barrier to freedom; it was a line between lives. Two persons together, the condition of an entity, atrophied when they were divided. Yet he felt more longing than he ever had outside. Then she had been merely a convenience, a portion of his interests. Now she was the focus of his hope and dreams because everything else was gone. He wanted to tell her, though he'd done so in letters already, but before he could speak the phone went dead. Time was up. Men began to stand up along the row, making final, pantomined communication before a deputy began ordering them to move out. Pamela quickly wrote on the tablet and held it up to the glass. "I love you," it said, with a sketched sunflower behind it. She held up three one-dollar bills, the amount a prisoner could receive. Not needing it, he shook his head.

As Ron was heading back to the tank, face twisted with his thoughts, Pamela was crossing the parking lot to the Cammaro where a slender, light-skinned black in bell-bottom jeans and multiple strings of beads was waiting behind the wheel.

Long before daylight Ron and thirty others were stripped naked, skin-searched, given white jumpsuits, and then put in waist chains, handcuffs, and leg irons. They hobbled through the cold darkness to the bus while men with shotguns and mackinaws stood on the sidelines, mist coming from their noses and mouths. The prisoners shivered in their seats until the bus had been under way for ten minutes, its headlights finally probing the ramp to the freeway. Ron was one of the few who had a seat to himself, and he felt lucky. Pleasure comes from trivial things in jail.

For the first hour they sliced through the city on the nearly empty freeway. Ron gazed out at the dark silhouettes of the Hollywood skyline, remembering other days, wondering how long it would be until he saw freedom again. He sat near the rear, a shotgun guard in a cage behind him. Beside the guard was the open toilet, and Ron would regret having taken a seat close to it long before the day was over.

As the sun came up, the bus catapulted through the mountains. The driver turned on a radio. A speaker was nearby and Ron's mind drifted with the music and shifted from gnawing anxiety to longing. He was going to face a long, bitter experience before he "danced beneath a diamond sky . . . silhouetted by the sea . . ."

The bus ran along the coast highway, stopping at San Luis Obispo to unload some prisoners and gather others. Ron's name wasn't called and the queasiness in his stomach increased.

By late afternoon the bus had made another stop at Soledad amid central California farms, and again Ron wasn't called.

In the town of Salinas the bus took on fuel. As the driver climbed back on, he faced his passengers through the wire.

"Well, boys, next stop is San Quentin . . . the Bastille by the Bay. Our estimated time of arrival is seven-thirty tonight . . . God willing and the river don't rise!"

"Well, get the motherfucker rollin' an' quit bullshittin," one rough wag said. "We wanna see if it's bad as its publicity."

"You'll see," the driver said, swinging into his chair and starting the motor.

Earl Copen was serving his third term in San Quentin, having come the first time when he was nineteen, and he sometimes felt as if he'd been born there. If he'd ever conceived eighteen years ago that he'd be in the same place at thirty-seven, he would have killed himself—or so he thought sometimes. He was as comfortable as it was possible to be, and still he hated it.

Weekdays, Earl Copen slept late, a luxury afforded by his job as clerk for the 4:00-p.m.-to-midnight lieutenant, a job he'd had for twelve years, except for two periods of freedom, one lasting nine months, the other twenty-one months. The earlier years had been spent walking the yard or in segregation. On Saturdays during football season he got up early and went to the yard to pick up football parlay tickets from his runners. It was profitable and passed the autumn and early winter.

He came out of the North cellhouse in the breakfast line, following the denimed convict in front of him along the twin white lines under the high corrugated weather shed. Outside of it, crowded together on the pitted wet asphalt, were legions of sea gulls and pigeons. When the convicts filled the rectangle of the big yard, the sea gulls would circle overhead or perch on the edges of the giant cellhouses. Or fly over en masse and shit on everyone.

The two mess halls were inadequate to feed the four thousand convicts from the four cellhouses at the same time, so the North and West honor units ate first. They could return to the cellhouses where the gates were kept open while the other cellhouses ate, or they could stay on the yard, waiting for the gate to the rest of the vast prison to open at 8:00 a.m.

Earl removed his knitted cap as he stepped through the door, exposing his shaved and oiled head. He checked a stainless-steel tray for cleanliness, found it satisfactory, and dragged it along the serving line. A cold fried egg, burned on the bottom and raw on top, flopped onto the tray; then a dipper of grits. He pulled the tray back so the server couldn't give him the bitter dry fruit, but took a piece of stale bread. The convict servers slopped the food on without worrying whether it spread into two compartments. Years ago this had infuriated Earl, and he'd once spit in a man's face for doing it, but now he was indifferent. Nor did he pay attention to the food except when it was inedible. Usually the menu was forgotten by the time he was picking his teeth.

All the convicts sat facing the same direction at narrow tables in long rows, a hangover from the "silent" system. The tables hadn't been replaced in this mess hall because it was also the auditorium and they faced the stage and screen. He head-jerked a greeting to a pair of Chicano cooks in dirty whites who were standing against a rear wall; then turned down an aisle. Blacks turned into one row, while whites and Chicanos turned into another. When their row filled before that of the blacks, they started another. Official segregation had ended a decade earlier; the regulations now said that convicts could enter any of three rows, but nobody crossed racial lines and nobody wanted to. Racism was a mass obsession that infected everyone, and there was continual race war. So the mess hall had a row of blacks, followed by two or three rows of whites and Chicanos, then another row of blacks.

Earl gulped down the swill, mixing grits with the half-raw egg. The weak coffee was at least hot and took the morning taste of cigarettes from his mouth. He finished quickly and got up, carrying the tray. Inside the exit door sat a large garbage can beside a flat cart. Instead of banging the tray against the can to remove the garbage, and then stacking tray and utensils, he dropped everything into the can—cup, silverware, tray—in a token display that he was still a rebel.

The coffee had loosened the night's phlegm. Outside the door, he hacked and spat the goo on the asphalt and lit a bad-tasting cigarette.

Most of the North cellhouse convicts were trudging back toward the open steel doors, a few throwing crumbs of bread to the fearless pigeons on the ground, while the sea gulls wheeled raucously overhead. When the convicts were gone, the sea gulls would drive off the pigeons and gobble whatever remained.

The high cellhouses, their green paint streaked and stained, cut off the morning sun except for a narrow patch of yellow near the weather shed. The three dozen convicts who stayed out gravitated toward the meager warmth. Neither the ticket runners nor any of Earl's close friends would be there. They lived in cellhouses just now being unlocked.

Earl decided to wait in the warmth of the yard office until the mess halls emptied and he could take care of his business. The East Coast games started at 10:00 a.m., California time, and he had to have the tickets by then to avoid being past-posted. He turned toward the high-arched gate with the gun tower on top. The big vehicle gate had a smaller pedestrian gate. A midnight-to-morning guard, a newcomer Earl didn't know, stood with a list of weekend workers who were allowed to pass through. Earl took out his identification card with "third watch clerk" under Scotch tape at its top. He held it forward and spoke before the guard could check the list. "I don't think I'm on there, but I'm Lieutenant Seeman's clerk and he wants me to do some typing."

"If you're not on the list, I can't let you through."

"I'm just going to the yard office down the road."

"If he needed some work done, he should've put you on the list."

"Look, Big Rand comes on duty in a few minutes. Let me go and I'll have him call you to clear it."

The guard shook his head, his lip raised in a sneer. "Can't hear you, buddy."

"Look, be logical—"

"Logic don't cut wind here."

"Okay, pal," Earl said, turning away before he got into trouble. Eighteen years of prison had made him hate authority worse than when he was a rebellious child. And he was unaccustomed to scenes like this. He thought of having the guard transferred to Lieutenant Seeman's evening shift by talking to the convict clerk of the personnel lieutenant; and then he would put the fool in a gun tower on the Bay for a year. Some guards had been around too long for such things, but this one was a fish and it would be easy. A year ago another fish had resented Earl's roaming around at night and his obviously favored position. The guard had begun searching him and making him wait to get into his cell. When a vacancy came for a guard in "B" Section segregation, Seeman moved the fish into it. There the guard had to put up with the bedlam of two hundred and fifty screaming convicts who burned cells and threw shit and piss on passing guards. He learned that some convicts are more equal than others—that even though a convict couldn't win a direct confrontation with a guard, when that convict had worked as a clerk for a supervisor for years, he had influence. Army clerks have the same indirect power.

Knowing what he *could* do calmed Earl and made it unnecessary for him to follow through. He didn't want to spend the currency of influence on something so trivial. Yet he would make sure he had a pass to get through the gate next weekend. He went toward the North cellhouse. His cell could stand a cleaning anyway.

He passed through the first doors into the rotunda. Ahead was the locked entrance to the elevator to Death Row on a separate floor above the cellhouse. Earl turned left and went up the steel stairs to the fifth tier. The long climb several times a day was worth avoiding the evening noise from television sets and domino games. Now, however, it was quiet. Most convicts slept late on weekends.

A gray-haired Chicano was pushing a broom on the landing at the end of the tier. A hooked nose and protruding eyes had given him the nickname Buzzard decades earlier, but it seemed wrong for a sixty-year-old man, so most convicts shortened it to "Buzz." As Earl arrived, Buzz beckoned, put the broom aside, and dug five battered packs of Camels from his pockets and a football ticket from his sock. "Preacher's still asleep," he said, "and I'm going to the handball court when the lower yard opens."

Earl nodded and put out his hand. He examined the ticket before pocketing it. Convicts sometimes marked that they were playing a carton and handed in a pack. If the ticket won, there was no gain-saying what it said. This ticket was okay. Earl dropped the cigarettes inside his shirt; then noticed that no other convicts were around.

"Stand point a minute, will you Buzz? I wanna check a *clavo*."

"Sure, bro." He stood so he could watch the office five tiers below. "Make your move. You'll get a lot of warning."

Behind the cells ran a passage filled with plumbing conduits. The padlock on the steel gate had been altered so Earl could open it with fingernail clippers. He stepped inside, took a few steps, and unscrewed a pipe that looked functional but had been bypassed. A cloth-wrapped bundle was stuffed within, and inside that was half a dozen long shivs. It was the first time in months that Earl had checked them. His friends had similiar stashes around the prison. Earl rescrewed the pipe and came out, patting Buzzard on the rump. "It's okay. Gimme the key."

Buzzard brought the large spike key for the cells from a hip pocket and handed it over. Earl went to his cell and unlocked it; then slid the key along the tier back to Buzzard. In the cell, Earl took an empty gallon can from underneath the sink. The cells lacked hot water and the can was for that. Every cell had one, but by removing a tiny pin from the bottom of this one he could dump out the false bottom. Several twenty-dollar bills were flattened down. He would have to move them to a safer place this evening.

He shaved, starting with the top of his head and working down to his jaw and chin. Then put oil on his skull and lotion on his face. Next he made the bed and swept the cell, and finally straightened up the shelves. They were shuttered with paintings of sunflowers. The cell was just four and a half feet wide and eleven feet long, but he had everything arranged for comfort. A thin glass-topped table was beside the bunk, and a tiny shelf with slots for cup and toothbrush was next to the sink. A shelf for books was on the wall between the top and bottom bunks, though he'd arranged through Lieutenant Seeman that nobody would be moved in.

Two thousand convicts packed the yard by 8:30 a.m. Most of them sought the widening strip of sunlight. The blacks, however, congregated along the North cellhouse wall, an area nicknamed "Nairobi." A decade of race wars had made it impossible to relax without a territorial imperative. Theirs caught the afternoon sun. Half a dozen guards with clubs stood around, reinforced by riflemen on catwalks suspended from the roof of the weather shed or attached to the outside of the North cellhouse.

When Earl came out of the rotunda, he immediately turned left to avoid walking through several hundred blacks. The last racial killings had been six months before, but there was no use taking a chance for no purpose.

He weaved through the crowd, looking for the runners who picked up tickets in the other cellhouses. He found them at the far end, near the canteen lines. The crowd provided cover as they handed him the rubber-band-wrapped bundles. Each one told him how much action was there, and the total was slightly over one hundred cartons, which was somewhat less than he'd expected for the last week of the regular season.

When Earl started to walk away from the throng, someone touched his arm from behind. He turned to face his oldest friend, Paul Adams. Paul had already been to San Quentin once when Earl, who was waiting to come for the first time, met him in the county jail. Now Paul was the elder statesman of Earl's "family." Actually, Paul was just four years older than Earl, but white hair, potbelly, and time-worn face made him look a decade older than he was.

"Where's the Bobbsey twins?" Earl asked.

"The twin maniacs. They're down on the lower yard with Vito and Black Ernie. We got a hot one goin'—some fool named Gibbs has some narcotics and we're plottin' on ripping him off."

"Gibbs! Isn't he that Hoosier with the crewcut in 'A' Section?"

"That's the dude."

"He's slammed down. That's restricted except for meal unlocks. How do we get to him?"

"That's what I came to find you for. Let's go down and get to scheming."

"Can't think of a better way to pass a boring Saturday in San Quentin."

The two convicts moved toward the yard gate, which had been opened to let the crowd pass to the lower recreation yard, to the handball courts and gym. The pair occasionally nodded to convicts they knew, or slapped someone on the back while passing. To the uninitiated observer, the yard looked like an anthill, but despite the sameness of the clothes—and the fact that they'd all been convicted of a crime—there was infinite variety and conflict. Indeed, some-times murderous hatreds smoldered for years like hot coals beneath cool ashes, flaming into murder at some small provocation, or when the balance of power shifted. So although Earl was at home, it was in the way that the jungle animal is at home—cautiously. He had no enemies here who posed a threat, at least none that he knew, though some might have been threats if he didn't have the affec-tion of the most influential members of the most powerful white gang, and friendship with the leaders of the most powerful Chicano gang. Of course that marked him in the eyes of the militant blacks— but it was better than being powerless.

"You goin' to the movie tonight, Paul?" Earl asked.

"I was thinking about it. The flick's supposed to be good."

"*The Graduate*, huh?"

"Uh-huh."

Paul also worked at night, one of the crew that hosed down the big yard after the evening count. It gave him the opportunity to enter the mess hall-auditorium early.

"Save a row of seats," Earl said. "I think I'll go."

They passed through the arched gate and started down the long flight of worn concrete stairs. In the distance they could see an inlet of San Francisco Bay beyond the wall; and beyond the inlet the windshields of cars crowding a highway reflected the coldly bright morning sun. It might as well have been a thousand miles away.

"I got a good book you might like," Paul said. "*At Play in the Fields of the Lord.*"

"Who wrote it?"

"Some dude named Matthiessen. I never heard of him before, but it's not bad."

"Bring it to the movie."

"I got another one you might like . . . but I haven't got the patience to wade through it. Marcuse's *One-Dimensional Man.*"

"Lemme try him, too. I've been hearing his name for about a year, but I've never read anything by him."

The vast lower recreation yard, in addition to a baseball diamond, handball courts, and full gymnasium, held the laundry and some shops in Quonset huts. The sunlight, which was blocked by the buildings in the big yard, shone bright here, but it gave little warmth.

Some convicts were jogging the circle of the recreation field, while others gathered in clots here and there. The usual group of country boy singers were getting their guitars ready beneath the high wall, while the jazz group unlimbered instruments next to the laundry.

The quartet that Earl and Paul sought was hunkered in a circle beside a Quonset hut: two Mexicans, Vito and Black Ernie, the first a close friend, the second merely okay; two whites, T.J. Wilkes and Bad Eye Wilson, both under thirty and physically dangerous with and without weapons. T.J. could stretch on a bench, legs straight, and lift five hundred pounds off his chest; Bad Eye did a thousand pushups and ran five miles every day. They were the most influential members of the Brotherhood, and they adored Earl and Paul.

Long before the two older convicts were within earshot, Vito saw them, said something, and the others swiveled their heads to watch them approach. When Earl arrived, T.J. uncoiled and squeezed an arm around Earl's shoulders. "Sit on down here, boy," he said, "an' help us scheme on gettin' them narcotics."

"How much has he got?" Earl asked.

Black Ernie answered, "Half a piece. It come in on a visit a couple days ago and he kept it cool, just selling to some dudes over in the South block."

"He won't have half an ounce now," Earl said.

"He's got a couple, three grams left," Paul said. "When Ernie told us, we sent a runner in to see if we could buy some . . . told him we had a couple hundred dollars. He sent word that was just what he had and to send the money in."

"An' that, folks, is just where we are now," T.J. said.

Earl grinned, his hard-angled face turning warm. "So okay. I know you motherfuckers had a reason to send for me. What is it?"

"Ah, brother," T.J. said, "you'd have gotten fixed if you all was layin' in the hospital with a broken dick." He hugged Earl again, and although the older man was an inch taller and weighed one hundred and ninety pounds, he felt like a rag doll in the grip of a grizzly bear.

"I believe *that*," Earl said, "but in the heat of a scheme you didn't call my name just because you love me."

"Hunch on down here," Bad Eye said. "We'll run it to you. Ernie brought it to us because it's a white boy . . . and the motherfucker didn't throw us our end. We're the motherfuckers that be fightin' when the rugs start wasting people around here." Bad Eye's face was flushed and he was blinking rapidly, a mannerism of his whenever he was angry, and he tended to anger whenever the clique was into something tense.

"We've got to get him out of the cellhouse," Paul said. "We can't get in there. One of us might sneak in, but it's a restricted section and this crew here carries too much heat."

"You want me to get him out?" Earl said.

"You can do it," Bad Eye said. "You're the juice man around this camp."

"Uh-huh . . . And what if you crazy motherfuckers kill him!"

"We ain't gonna do that," T.J. said. "Hellfire, we're jes' gonna talk to the ol' boy—in the North block rotunda."

"Here's how we figure it," Paul said. "We'll make up a bogus money package, some lettuce or green paper in cellophane and Scotch tape. I'll send word that we're gettin' him out—or that *I'm* gettin' him out—and then I'll lure him into the rotunda. The fellas here can ease in behind and rob both of us. The sucker trusts me . . . not enough to *give* me anything, but enough to show up. You can't be one of the robbers," Paul added to Earl. "He knows you and me are together from when he hit the ticket last month and I paid him off."

The group watched Earl, and although he had some misgivings, there was no doubt that he would help. He would have preferred to tell them to wait, that he was being sent a load of heroin by someone they knew in Los Angeles, but none of them were interested in what might happen in a week or two; they wanted it now. Almost equally important, they wanted some action, something to ease this boredom, and prison limits the choices in that area.

"When do you want to do it?" Earl asked.

"As soon as we can," Vito said. "I need a fix."

Earl went back up the stairs two at a time, but instead of turning right into the big yard, he went left down the road between the education building and library. The yard office was a hundred yards from the arch, a five-year-old building with front and rear office and toilet. It was redwood and glass, designed thus because too many beatings had taken place in the old solid-walled office it replaced. A fence ran from in front of it across the road. Beyond was the plaza in front of the chapel, the custodial offices, and main gate.

When Earl entered, the Indian day clerk, Fitz, was at the typewriter. A solid convict who was personable unless drunk, Fitz looked at Earl and winked. "Pretty early for you, ain't it?"

"Business."

Through the glass wall Earl could see Lieutenant Hodges in the rear office. Hodges disliked him and the feeling was reciprocated.

Big Rand, the three-hundred-fifteen-pound guard who ran the office, sent yard officers on escort details, and otherwise coordinated activities, jerked open the washroom door. "I heard you out here, Copen, heard every word."

"Well, tell your mother about it," Earl said. "Assuming you can get the bitch out of the whorehouse."

Big Rand tried to puff his face into a mask of rage, but when Earl gave him the finger the guard began grinning. Earl glanced through the glass to the rear office. "Cool it," he said. "You forget who's the lieutenant today. Remember, he kept your big ass in a midnight-to-eight gun tower for three years."

"Yeah . . . the cocksucker," Rand said.

"C'mon outside, Supercop. I need something done."

"I know this is trouble," Rand said, but followed Earl into the sunlight.

"There's a guy in 'A' Section I want pulled out for fifteen or twenty minutes. His name's Gibbs, but I don't know his number. We can get it off the spindle."

"Whaddya want him for?"

Earl shook his head and made a face of disgust.

"Jesus, Earl," the giant said in defensive plaint, "I wanna know so I can protect myself in case . . ."

"In case what?"

"You kill the guy or something."

"Fuck, I don't do any shit like that."

"Not anymore, but—"

"Okay, if any questions come up, you called the guy to interview him for a janitor's job at the office. The guy's on restriction because he doesn't have a job."

"We only use niggers as janitors."

"So you're a bigot now? Won't hire a white boy?"

Rand made a "sss" sound and slowly shook his head, a surrender in what had been a game more than a test of wills.

"Wait about ten minutes before you call over there," Earl said.

"What if he shows up?"

"Interview him for the job."

"What's his name?"

"Gibbs. They'll know his number over there."

Rand stepped back to the door and stopped. He pointed a

threatening finger. "I'll bet this has something to do with dope. I'm gonna bust you someday."

"You'll bust your mother. You'd rather jump in a pit with a grizzly bear than fuck with me."

In mock rage, Rand kicked the door frame. "You'd better show some respect. I'm Supercop."

Earl ignored Rand and began walking away.

"Inmate Copen!" Rand bellowed. "You'd better be here for work early. I wanna see you."

Earl kept walking but glanced back. Rand was in the doorway, both arms extended, and he was giving Earl the finger with both hands.

Ten minutes later everyone except Paul was at the northeast end of the big yard; they were all watching the other end where Paul would come through the throng near the canteen after meeting Gibbs at the South cellhouse entrance. To a casual spectator they would have looked languid, but Earl saw the flared nostrils, tight lips, eyes bright with concentration. This was a big score in prison terms, and Earl had no doubt that any one of them would kill Gibbs to get the heroin if there was a chance of getting away with it. What strange icons men worship, he thought. How fucked up we get in this place— and I want it as bad as they do. Heroin is the only dope that takes away prison's misery.

"Gimme a cigarette, Homeboy," Bad Eye said to Vito.

"I'm dry . . . just a poor Mexican trying to get high." He was slender, with striking green eyes and a bright white smile. Earl liked Vito; everybody liked him.

"How big is this *vato*?" Vito asked.

"He's big," Ernie said; he had a shoelace in his hand and was snapping it nervously. "We oughta get some steel."

Earl made a deprecating sound. "Shit! If five of us need iron for one dude, even if he's King Kong, we better go ask Stoneface to lock us up for protection."

Black Ernie winced at the rebuke.

T.J. spoke. "Yeah, we don't need to carry a felony for this fool. We just fake. He's big . . . but he's weak as soggy toilet paper."

Paul Adams appeared, moving quickly from the thickest part of the crowd. He was alone.

"Check him," Vito said. "Old folks has the coldest stroll in town."

Earl grinned, for Paul's walk epitomized the 1940s hipster: a hand in one pocket, the other swinging high with a snapping motion, the shoulder dipping and rolling.

"Where's the guy at?" Ernie said, voice shrill. "That old motherfucker better not have fucked this up."

Earl watched T.J. and Bad Eye look at Ernie, who never noticed the narrowing eyes. Vito did and winked at Earl, saying silently that Ernie was a fool and should be ignored. He's a fool, Earl thought, but those youngsters are bigger fools. They'll feed him his heart if he fucks with Paul. And if they can't, they've got fifty more who will.

When Paul arrived, his usually doughy complexion was florid. "He's coming in a minute. You dudes come in right behind us. And don't start laughing. This is serious shit."

"Serious as a heart attack," Bad Eye said.

Earl was going to stand lookout. When Paul moved away from the group, Earl went ten yards the other way and stretched on the concrete bench fastened to the East cellhouse wall, crossing his legs and bracing himself on one elbow.

Suddenly Paul started moving back toward the crowd, and Earl saw Gibbs emerging. The two met, exchanged words, and came toward the North cellhouse door. Gibbs weighed over two hundred pounds, but his belly bounced against his shirt and his movements were ungainly. He looked as square as Paul looked hip.

Earl watched Gibbs's eyes to see if they were focused on the waiting group, who were ignoring the walking men and feigning conversation among themselves. They didn't stand out because of the other clusters of convicts. Gibbs wasn't even looking around. He was listening to Paul.

Earl scanned the yard for guards; none were visible except one on the gun rail, and he was a hundred yards away and looking in another direction. As the two men neared the open steel door, Paul put a hand on Gibbs's shoulder and held back a pace to let the man enter first. The instant he disappeared, the four thugs began moving, and Earl got up to arrive just behind them. As they slipped through into the semi-darkness, Bad Eye pressing to be first, Earl took a position outside the door. There was risk that a guard might start to come out of the cellhouse or Death Row.

A young black appeared beside Earl, moving quickly and glancing over his shoulder. Earl would have felt the same way if he'd met four known black militants in a blind spot like the rotunda.

Earl leaned to his left and peeked around the door into the gloom. Paul and Gibbs were against a wall, the four bandits crowding them, with Bad Eye and Vito holding right hands inside their shirt bosoms as if they had shivs hidden there. Paul was holding up his hands in supplication. T.J. snatched something from him and pocketed it—the cellophane-wrapped paper.

Through the yard gate came the gangly figure of Sergeant William Kittredge, walking slightly behind and to the side of a tall black convict whom Earl recognized; he had stabbed a white tier tender in the East cellhouse during a race war six months earlier. Sergeant Kittredge was obviously taking the man from the visiting room back to segregation in "B" Section and would not come toward the North cellhouse rotunda. A few seconds later, Earl heard the splat of flesh striking flesh, and then grunts and shuffling feet. Before he could look inside, a figure flashed past him, followed by a grasping, burly arm covered with red hair. The arm missed and Gibbs was loose in the yard, running in a ludicrous pigeon-toed gait, his shirttail flapping behind him.

Running was forbidden and the quick movement immediately attracted the attention of a gun rail guard. A police whistle bleated. Sergeant Kittredge froze and turned as Gibbs ran toward him—and saw the four thugs scurrying along the cellhouse wall. He also saw Earl—and Earl knew it, so instead of walking away he entered the cellhouse. After all, he lived there.

The bottom tier was active, especially around the television set where the Army-Navy game was about to start. Fear gnawed at Earl's stomach. They could all spend a year or two in segregation over this, and it had been a long time since he'd been in the hole. Kittredge had seen all of them, and if Gibbs was questioned by Lieutenant Hodges . . . Earl next felt anger, wondering what the fuck had gone wrong in the rotunda. Had Gibbs balked? Unlikely. Someone had punched him when it wasn't necessary, had scared him too much, and he'd panicked.

Earl went to the front row of the television seats where his place was saved by Preacher Man, a chubby thirty-year-old member of the Brotherhood who handled the North cellhouse tickets. Preacher was bundled in a heavy melton jacket zipped to his throat, and a black knit cap was pulled over his ears. It was Preacher's usual mode of dress and, also as usual, he needed a shave. Earl gave him all the tickets he'd collected on the yard, which was the reverse of the usual process, and told him to hold them until later. Sensing something amiss, Preacher wanted to know if help was needed. Earl shook his head and went back through the rotunda. He stopped in the shadows to peer out. Kittredge, Gibbs, and the black were gone. Nothing was happening. The sergeant would have had to keep going with the black, so there would be a delay before the repercussions started.

The gang had scattered. Earl prowled in the direction they'd gone and found Paul.

"What happened back there?" Earl asked.

"Ernie trying to be a bully. He smacked the chump in the mouth and the guy broke and run. He was scared shitless. Ernie couldn't wait for the chump to dig it out of his sock."

"We shot a blank, then?"

Paul made a face of disgust and nodded. "We might wind up busted, too . . . if Kittredge saw us."

"He saw you. Where'd Gibbs go?"

"They got him, took him to the hospital."

"So where's everybody at?"

"Vito split to the West block, Ernie's with his friends, and the

Dynamic Duo went to the gym. Bad Eye is madder'n a mother-fucker. He's cussin' a blue streak. T.J. is phlegmatic as usual, but you know how he is. He can be murderous and you never know it. If we go to the hole, Ernie might be in trouble."

"He's just a fool who wants to be a killer. It isn't worth a killing and the risk because he's a fool. What the fuck . . ."

Earl fell silent, knowing that although he and Paul had as much influence as anyone over the two young men, it wasn't enough. Conditioned by a lifetime of violence, he was willing to use a knife if he felt threatened, or if it was a question of saving face, but he didn't believe in revenge unless it was necessary to avoid ridicule. He was capable of violence while disliking it; T.J. and Bad Eye both thought of violence as the first answer to any problem. T.J. was less quick but more relentless; Bad Eye was more explosive but could be reasoned with after the first blaze of temper. Earl didn't care about Ernie, a loud-mouthed braggart whose ambition was to be a big shot in prison's violent world, but Earl did care about his friends.

"It might come out okay," he said. "Kittredge is Seeman's protégé and he likes us okay. It depends on whether Hodges gets our names. If he does, we better pack our shit for 'B' Section."

"What can the guy tell 'em? He can't tell 'em we tried to rip him for some dope—he doesn't think it was me anyway and he doesn't know any other names, I don't think. If he says we were pressuring him, what the fuck, *he* stays in the hole and gets transferred. We might get ten days, but here they gotta cage the prey because there are too many predators."

Earl snorted, nodded, seeing the irony. Gibbs would be in protective custody for months until he was transferred to a softer prison. The officials couldn't make transfer too easy or they'd be overrun with men asking for protection just to get out of San Quentin. During those months of isolation, Gibbs's food would be spat in, his face spat on, and he would be despised as a coward—for being a victim.

The public-address speakers blared: "Copen, A-forty-two forty-three, report to the yard office immediately!"

Earl squeezed Paul playfully on the shoulder cap. "Well, I'm gonna find out what the score is."

"I'll be waiting right here."

Sergeant William Kittredge was waiting on the road beyond the yard gate, leaning against the wall of the education building, a sly grin on his face. He was bouncing a red ball the size of a jawbreaker up and down in his hand, and Earl knew it was a balloon containing two grams of heroin. The powder was packed down, the balloon knotted and the end snipped off.

"You guys lost something, didn't you?"

Earl shrugged. "Not that I know of."

"What about this here?" Kittredge held the balloon up between his thumb and forefinger.

"I never saw it before," Earl said, careful to keep his voice modulated. Kittredge might take too vehement a denial as an insult to his intelligence, while something coy would be an indirect admission.

"That's not what I heard."

Earl didn't reply. It was better to wait till he knew Gibbs's story.

"Let it hang. I'm not telling Hodges what I saw, but when your boss comes on duty, I'll see what he wants to do. Meanwhile, come on down to the office so you can type a memo."

"Where's Fitz?"

"On a visit. Anyway, I want *you* to type this one." Earl walked beside Kittredge to the yard office, where Rand was doodling on a yellow legal pad. The lieutenant was not in the rear office. The memo had been roughed out. Earl polished the grammar and spelling as he typed:

TO: THE CAPTAIN

SUBJECT: GIBBS, 47895

At 9:50 a.m., this date, while on duty as yard sergeant, the writer was escorting an inmate from the visiting room to "B" Section when a gun rail officer blew his whistle on the Main Yard. I turned and saw inmate GIBBS, 47895, running from the direction of the North cellhouse rotunda. I took the subject into custody and continued to "B" Section; then took Gibbs to the hospital clinic where he was treated for a cut mouth (*see medical report*). At that time he handed me a red balloon knotted into a ball and containing a beige powder. Gibbs claims it is heroin, and that he was given it by three inmates, two white and one Mexican, whom he can identify if he sees them but cannot name. They wanted him to take it into "A" Section for delivery to "Bulldog," apparently LADD, 12943. When he refused, he was assaulted and ran out. According to Officer Rand, Gibbs had been called to the yard office for a job interview. Gibbs was placed in administrative segregation pending hearing by the Disciplinary Committee. Contents of the balloon have not been given a field analysis as of this report.

Now Earl knew Gibbs's story—and that Kittredge believed it. Refuting it was impossible without confessing the truth, and that was out of the question. He handed the report to Kittredge, who signed it and put it in an envelope.

"There are better ways," Kittredge said. "I could bust the whole fuckin' mob of you."

Earl saw Rand behind Kittredge, and the big guard was holding a finger to his lips. The admonition was unnecessary.

"You run things around here," Earl said. "You can lock everybody up every day of the year."

"Okay, Earl, okay," Kittredge said. "What I'm trying to tell you is to get your friends to lighten up. That fucking gang is getting too far out of line. Every day the captain gets a dozen snitch letters about those maniacs. There must be a hundred letters that Bad Eye killed that colored guy in the lower yard last year."

"What about that white boy they killed in the East block? And the four that got stabbed in the school building? And the bull that they killed in the hospital?"

Without saying it in so many words, Earl was subtly reminding

Kittredge that since the beginning of the racial wars a dozen years ago, and especially since black convicts had begun killing white guards, there was an unspoken alliance between some of the guards and the white convict militants. Before the guards began falling, most of them had been even-handed; now many looked the other way at what white convicts did.

"So okay . . . he's not locked up, is he? But the associate warden doesn't need much evidence to get him . . . and the others."

When the big yard was crowded with lunch lines, Bad Eye came up to Earl and Paul. Seconds later, Ernie appeared out of the throng. When Bad Eye heard the story, he expressed fury at the "stinkin', lyin', stool-pigeon punk," and vowed to make sure something happened to Gibbs wherever he was sent. Earl kept silent, planning to talk sense to his friend when he was calmer. Bad Eye had come to San Quentin eight years earlier, when he was eighteen, for a ninety-dollar gas-station robbery, but instead of becoming mature, he was wilder, like a bull enraged by pain. "Fuck," Bad Eye said. "Another bust and I'll never get a parole. I wish I could escape. Earl, help me bust outta here."

"You're gonna get a parole next year. This is going to be okay. Just hold your temper and be patient."

"I didn't blow it," Bad Eye said, pointedly looking down rather than at Ernie. He hadn't greeted Ernie when the latter joined the group.

Ernie's earlier toughness was now diluted by fear of the possible lockup. He nagged with questions about Kittredge, whom he didn't know. Earl reassured him that he was safe, and hid his contempt. He detested falseness, and Ernie was a pussycat trying to be a leopard, though he would probably murder someone from behind if he had ten-to-one odds. To get rid of the man, Earl advised him to go to his cell so he wouldn't be seen with them.

Bad Eye went to tell T.J. what was happening, so Earl and Paul found themselves pacing the length of the yard alone. Walking in this fashion was a habit of years. Friends would gather if they stood in one place, but if they kept moving, they were left alone. Earl's and Paul's friendship had begun eighteen years ago in the county jail when Earl was going to prison for the first time and Paul for the second. Now Paul was on his fifth term, and where he had once been slim and dark-haired, he was now fat and gray. They knew each other's faults, but this didn't mar their friendship; sometimes they argued heatedly, but without lasting rancor.

"Well, brother," Earl said dolefully, "we're having another wonderful day in jail."

"Yeah . . . no work and no taxes and plenty of excitement. If we didn't have some *wrong* to do now and then we'd lose all our initiative. This one got fucked up good."

"It looks like we skated. You'd better start cooling it; you could get a play from the parole board next appearance."

"I was thinking that when I saw Kittredge looking at us. A nickel should be enough for car theft."

"Hold it! You weren't just joyriding. They found a ski mask and there ain't no snow in L.A., plus some gloves . . . and a pistol. You should get a parole, but don't rationalize so close to home. I know you."

Paul laughed. "It's still just a car theft."

"Yeah, I figure I've got two or three left, depending on how politics are. Nine years is a long time, even if you say it fast. The trouble with being a criminal is that you get two bad breaks—mistake, luck, whatever—and you've blown a couple of decades. I'll be nearly forty when I get out and what else can I do to catch up except put a hacksaw blade to a shotgun and run off into a bank or something?"

They walked a lap in silence. Usually Earl contracted his world to what was within the walls. Excessive fretting about the outside drove men insane. He cut himself off from everyone he knew outside because they could do nothing for him except make his time worse than it was. If he counted on them, he would be disillusioned, for after a few years in prison, you were as forgotten as a man in a coffin under the earth. During his first term, after matriculating from reform school, he'd taken all the school courses available, graduating from high school and even getting a semester of college credits. He'd completed the vocational printing course, too. None of that had gotten him a job, nor had it made him feel comfortable except among the kinds of people he'd known all his life. He recognized that he was, indeed, a habitual criminal, with a metabolism that demanded he gamble his freedom, even his life, for real freedom— freedom from a life of quiet desperation. He would get one more chance, and he would take it. He'd gone too far and lost too much to quit the game now.

"When is that dope bag due?" Paul asked.

"Maybe this week. We'll know when the mule gets a visit tomorrow."

"Dennis must be doing okay out there."

"He always makes money and he usually lasts a few years. He's been out less than three months and he's sent back about five grand worth of dope. A couple bags to Folsom, too. I sent word if he wanted some money and he said he'd freeze if I tried to pay him."

"We can use it when it gets here. I owe Vito's clique twenty papers."

Earl laughed. "You've been sneakin' around on me again."

Paul answered with lips pursed into a cone and opened his very blue eyes in a parody of innocence. Responsibility of any kind was beyond him, but he was a good friend nonetheless. The one quality that mattered to Earl was loyalty. It outweighed a thousand other flaws. He gave it and he wanted it, and his close friends gave it to him and to each other.

As they approached the North cellhouse, they heard a brief roar of voices from within.

"That fuckin' game," Earl said. "All of 'em play the ticket, so I'd better see what's happening with the scores—and make sure sleazy ass Preacher doesn't run in a couple of bogus tickets with winners."

"I'll see you at the flick if I don't see you after count."

"Bring those books."

Earl went in and took his seat. Preacher had a checklist of games on the ticket and scores, some partial, some final. Although Earl hadn't checked each ticket, he had a good idea of how they ran. From the scores he could see that he was in no danger of being bombed out. He sat down to watch the game, knowing that nearly every ticket had picked Navy because they were a seventeen-point favorite and he'd listed it on the ticket at thirteen. Ten years of running a ticket told him that traditional rivalries often ended much closer than handicap form indicated. Navy was ahead by fourteen and he forgot Kittredge, Gibbs, and Seeman. Two minutes before the end Army scored, the convicts groaned, and there it ended. When Earl stood up in the front row, he faced the crowd, yelled "Hurrah," and clenched his hands over his head. Most of them had lost a couple of packs, but not enough to bother them, so many laughed. Earl liked being known and respected, but moments later as he trudged up the steel stairs toward his cell, the thrill of winning disappeared. He'd won—a lot of tobacco.

At 4:20, when nearly all the convicts lined up in the yard and then returned to their cells for count, Earl went to the yard office. At count time it became a hangout for sergeants and lieutenants coming on and going off duty. Sometimes closed-door conferences were held in the back room, and Earl eavesdropped by going into the washroom, locking the door, and putting an ear to the wall. Today Hodges and a couple of sergeants were in the back room, but the conversation Earl wanted to hear was taking place fifty yards away, beside the plaza fish pond outside the chapel. Kittredge was talking and Lieutenant Bernard Seeman listened stolidly, nodding occasionally. Seeman was a heavy-shouldered man in his midfifties, starting to get a belly, and he wore his billed cap tilted to the side like a Navy man; he'd been a submarine bos'n for twenty years. Earl crossed his legs on the typewriter stand, seemingly uninterested while he watched through the window.

When the count cleared, a bell clanged from atop the building with the main gate. Before the tones died, convicts and guards spilled from the custody office across the plaza, the former heading toward the road to the mess halls, the latter making a beeline for the sallyport. The yard office disgorged all but one guard, and other guards hurried by in a stream, carrying coats and lunchboxes. Those with seniority counted the nearest cellhouses so they could get away a couple of minutes earlier.

Usually Earl went to eat early, but today he waited for the conversation to end and his boss to head toward the mess halls. Seeman stopped at the open Dutch doors. "You and your mob be over here after chow," he said.

"Who's that?"

"Bad Eye, T.J. Wilkes, and Vito Romero. There's another one, but Kittredge doesn't know who he is."

"Then I sure don't."

Seeman smiled, his square weathered face showing good humor. "Hell, I didn't think you did."

"Somebody'll have to clear 'em out of the cellhouses."

Seeman leaned his head over the door and looked at the old man behind the desk. "Take care of that, Colonel, will you?"

"What time do you want them?"

"Six twenty is okay. Earl will tell you who." The irascible Army retiree nodded, but his face expressed distaste at taking orders from a convict. The colonel was kept away from groups of convicts where his martinet tendencies could cause trouble.

At 6:20 in December it was dark, though the ubiquitous prison lights left few shadows.

"Close the door," Seeman said.

Earl shut the door to the outer office and stood beside it. Vito was stiff in the chair across the desk, while T.J. and Bad Eye braced their rumps on window ledges. T.J. was at ease, but Bad Eye was wary and angry; he reacted to all unpleasantness with anger.

Seeman's hat was off and his steely hair was pressed to his skull. "I'm not asking questions because I don't need to hear any lies." He looked around at their expressionless faces. "The story I heard seems pretty far out even for you desperadoes." He took an envelope from the desk and dumped the red balloon on the green desk blotter. Earl was surprised. Regulations said that all contraband was to be placed in the associate warden's evidence locker. Earl also felt the sliver of an evanescent idea, and in hindsight would realize he knew the truth at this moment.

Seeman looked at the balloon as if it were a crystal ball; then glanced up at Vito. "What's it worth on the yard?"

Vito blushed, looked down, and tossed his shoulder. Seeman looked at each face, ending with Earl, who spoke: "Thought there weren't gonna be any questions, boss."

"Oops, that's right. My apologies. Besides, I know Mr. Wilkes here doesn't know about this."

"All ah know 'bout is some white lightnin'," T.J. said.

"Just an old country boy, huh?"

T.J.'s face lit up. "How'd you know, boss?"

Seeman's pale eyes blossomed with laughter. "Okay, quit the bull-shit," he said. "I'll talk." He told them that he and Kittredge liked them, but other lieutenants and the associate warden didn't, and they should think about getting out of prison instead of all this bullshit inside. He was going to let this go because if he locked them up, someone would kill Gibbs wherever he was sent. He wanted them to forget Gibbs if he forgot the situation. He didn't expect an answer, but he'd watch what happened.

Earl liked Seeman, considered him a friend, though he would never dare admit it. Seeman gave him free run of the prison at night and never asked questions; in return, Earl made sure that all paperwork going to the administration was done correctly. But he knew that some of the license given tough white and Chicano convicts by certain other guards was because of the racial conflict. Blacks had killed several guards in the three tough prisons during the past two years, and guards who had once been mild bigots were now outright racists. Certain of them would frisk a white or Chicano convict, feel a shiv, and pass the man by. It was an unholy alliance, alien to all of Earl's values. All his life the police had been his enemy, and if he had a political creed it included Marxism.

People would never be equal, but the difference should be between a twenty-thousand-dollar home and a fifty-thousand-dollar home, not between a rat-infested hovel and a half-a-million-dollar estate. And the difference should be decided by ability. So he was inclined to the Left, which favored the oppressed blacks. On the other hand, here in San Quentin the guards, while searching cells, found poems describing the joy of bayoneting pregnant white women, and six years earlier, when the racial conflict had only involved small groups of Black Muslims versus Nazis, blacks had escalated matters by sweeping down a tier and indiscriminately stabbing every white man they saw. Now both sides did it whenever the war was renewed. There were huge gangs, and Earl, though not officially a member, had as much influence as anyone on the White Brotherhood, especially since T.J. and Bad Eye were its unofficial leaders.

Seeman, though hated by the black convicts, was not a racist. Rather, he was politically conservative; he saw the militant rhetoric of revolution, with its emphasis on Mao and Che, as a declaration of war on the United States.

It was an odd friendship—the former submarine bos'n who epitomized Middle America and the hard-core convict so ravaged by moral confusion that he believed in nothing except personal loyalty.

Lieutenant Seeman was still talking, and the convicts listened expressionlessly. All of them spoke the same language, but to these men moral abstractions were babble. He ended with a warning that they should rein in, that too many complaints were getting to the higher officials. He told them that if they had any problems, he would do all he could.

Nobody answered. If they wanted something, they would go through Earl, just as he would go through other clerks. Seeman stood up, put on his hat, and put the balloon back in the desk drawer.

Earl's eyes widened when he saw that Seeman was leaving. Seeman was indirectly *giving* them the balloon. His eyes met Earl's as he came around the desk to usher the others out. "Be cool, Earl," he said. "You're going to get out in a couple more years."

As Seeman followed the convicts through the front office he told the colonel that he'd be at the movie. Ten minutes later, Earl followed, the balloon making a tiny bulge in his pants pocket.

Some December days in the San Francisco Bay area exhale pure spring, and this was one of them, a Monday between Christmas and the New Year. The sun had burned off the freezing morning fog, and although the lower recreation yard was still crisp, it was dazzlingly bright. Earl sat shirtless on the worn bleachers along the third base line, finishing a joint in the nearest thing to solitude the prison allowed. A red bandanna was tied around his forehead to keep the sweat from his eyes, though it had dried ten minutes after he left the handball court. A still soaked glove lay limp beside him, and his legs ached from the hard hour of exercise. He played poorly but loved the game. He couldn't bring himself to jog or do calisthenics, because he quit the moment he began breathing hard, but when there was competition he kept going until his body screamed in protest and he had to bend at the waist to draw a good breath. Winter closed the handball courts for months at a time, so he played whenever they were open for a few hours. He sucked on the joint, muttering "dynamite shit" inanely, and the aches went away. He was reluctant to make the long trek to the big yard, and then five tiers to his cell to get a towel to shower with. "Too beautiful a day to be locked up," he muttered, liking the bittersweet ache of longing for freedom. It told him that he was still human, still yearned for something more than being a convict. He still hoped . . .

He'd decided to follow Seeman's advice and avoid trouble by avoiding the situations. He was keeping to his cell during the day, reading a lot, and when something happened, it was over before he heard about it. One of the Brotherhood had killed a man in the East cellhouse, and the next day during the lunch hour two Chicanos had ambushed a third and cut him up pretty bad. If he'd died, it would have tied the record of thirty-six murders in a year; the record for stabbings, one hundred and seven, had already been broken. T.J. and Bad Eye worked in the gym, and he saw them only at the night movie when the Brotherhood filled two rows of reserved benches. Earl would have come out during the day if heroin was on the yard, but the prison had been dry since he'd gotten an ounce three weeks earlier. Pot, acid, and mini-bennies were abundant— through the Hell's Angels—but Earl was not interested. In a paranoia-laden atmosphere, he couldn't risk being spaced out.

Earl did know about a strike that was to happen the following morning, but it was known by everyone, including the warden. Someone had illegally used a mimeograph machine to run off thousands of copies of a bulletin calling on all convicts to either stay in their cells in the morning or not leave the big yard at work call. The first demand, an end or a modification of the indeterminate sentence—a term anywhere between a year and eternity until the parole board decided—was something Earl fiercely agreed with. It was the cruelest torture never to know how long imprisonment would last. And the demand that prison industry wages be raised above the present *maximum* of twelve cents an hour was also reasonable. But then the writer had turned irrational, demanding that all "Third World" people and "political prisoners" be released to the various People's Republics. This absurdity would attract whatever coverage the press gave the strike and blunt any consideration thoughtful people might give to the other demands—not that many cared about what went on in prison. A strike was futile, yet at least it showed that the men had not surrenderded. It would bring a lockdown of everyone while the leaders were rounded up, clubbed, and segregated. "And I'd better go get some cigarettes, coffee, and food to last until the unlock. Four salami sandwiches a day won't make it."

As he stood up on the top row of bleachers, he saw two convicts climbing toward him at an angle. One was Tony Bork, a chunky young con who was the East cellhouse plumber, not a tough guy but personable and known as a "stand-up dude." He had in tow a slender youth in the stiff, unwashed denim of a newcomer. Even without the clothes, Earl knew the youth hadn't been long in San Quentin, for although he often saw faces for the first time after they'd been around for months, this one he would have remembered. He was too strikingly good looking and young looking, especially because of a clear, pale complexion set off by dark blue eyes that were serious but inexpressive. There was nothing effeminate about him, but there was an extreme boyishness that by prison standards would be considered pretty. Pretty was a bad thing to be in San Quentin.

"Hey now, big duke of Earl," Tony said. "I need a favor. Rather, my friend here does. A show pass." Tony glanced at the youth. "Ron Decker, Earl Copen." A nod of acknowledgment did the work of the usual handshake.

"Are they running the show lines yet?" Earl asked.

"They were getting ready to when we came down."

Earl picked up his sweatshirt and handball gloves and started down the bleachers. Bork and Decker fell in beside him. As they walked, he struggled into the sweatshirt.

"You haven't been here very long, have you?" Earl asked.

Ron shook his head. "Three weeks. Tony tells me you're good at law."

"I used to fuck with it. No more. I don't believe in it. Smith and Wesson beats due process."

"What do you mean?"

"Besides being funny"—Earl smiled—"I mean that law is bullshit. Judges don't have any integrity. They'll spring some big shot on a point of law, but when some poor Hoosier in here has the same point, they shoot it down."

"But when Smith and Wesson won't do anything, the law might be all there is. I don't want to impose, but I'd like you to look at my case. I'll pay you."

56

"When I get some time," Earl said, not noticing that his brushoff made Ron blush.

"What fuckin' movie are they showing today?" Earl asked. "It's a Monday."

"Blood-donors' movie," Tony said. "I'm on the list but Ron isn't."

Earl glanced at Ron from the corner of his eye and felt bad that he'd stalled him so coldly. "What kind of thing did you want to know about your case?"

"The main thing is the judge said he'd call me back and modify my sentence in a year or two. Some guy in the bus said the judge loses jurisdiction and can't do it."

"He used to lose jurisdiction, but six months ago a court of appeals ruled that if he sentenced you under Eleven sixty-eight he can call for reports and review his sentence."

"That's what he sentenced me under."

"What kind of beef?"

"Possession of narcotics for sale with a weed prior."

Earl made a silent whistle and looked at Ron more closely. "Ten years to fuckin' life, with six to the parole board. You'd better hope he modifies."

"Don't I know it."

As they reached the top of the stairs, the sound of country and western music from the loudspeakers poured over them. The last line of convicts was going into the mess hall, and the guard checking passes wasn't one Earl could influence. "C'mon to the yard office. We'll get a pass from that big sissy." When they neared the yard office door, Earl took Ron's I.D. card to get his number. He left them outside. Without saying anything to Big Rand, who was dangling a string before a cuffing, scrawny kitten (one of hundreds in the prison), Earl sat down and typed a pass; then dropped it on Rand's desk for a signature. The big man ignored it, continued playing with the kitten.

"Hey, you want me to throw that cat in the Bay?" Earl said, knowing Rand just wanted attention.

Rand picked up the pass. "Two weeks ago—Gibbs, remember?"

"Oh, man, that wasn't nothing."

"Nothing happened, but a whole bunch of shit could've happened."

"Whaddya think—I was gonna snitch on you? Sign the mother-fucker."

"Who is this asshole?" Rand leaned in his chair so he could look out over the Dutch door, dubiously eyed Ron and Tony. He knew Tony Bork and his wasn't the name on the pass. Rand curled a fore-finger and Earl leaned forward. "You're trying to fuck that kid, aren't you?" Rand accused.

"You got a dirtier mind than these convicts, Rand. You really do."

"Well, who is he?"

"A good white brother. Are you gonna sign? I've got business. I wanna get to the canteen to stock up in case there's a lockdown over that strike."

"We'll get you out if—"

Earl cut him off with an upraised hand. "Uh-huh. I'm a convict. If the joint's slammed, I'm slammed."

"I'll make sure you get something to eat."

Earl didn't protest, though for a moment he was surprised. Rand (Seeman, too) could be savage to convicts he disliked, especially blacks. He wore a swastika medallion under his shirt.

Rand signed the pass slowly, making a deliberate childish scrawl, and then handed it to Earl with a grin.

"I should have signed it myself," Earl said, but he took it and went out, giving it to Ron. "I'll walk with you. I've gotta get some food and dirty magazines in case they have that strike. We'll be locked down with nothing to do but abuse ourselves, and I've forgotten what broads look like."

Ron laughed, showing good white teeth.

When they reached the big yard, Earl paused long enough to make sure the pass wasn't questioned; then he went toward the heavy crowd outside the canteen. Others were also stocking up.

Half an hour before the main count lockup, Earl entered the big yard. Half a dozen of the Brotherhood, including Paul, T.J., Bird, and Baby Boy, were gathered in the afternoon sun near the East cellhouse wall. When Earl walked up, T.J. reached out and brushed the slick-shaved skull.

"Where's Bad Eye?" Earl asked.

"On a visit. You know his folks love their baby boy." The conversation was about the strike. Nobody thought it would accomplish anything, and Baby Boy was angry because he liked to work and was going to the parole board in two weeks. Yet there was no question of them breaking a strike, even one they disagreed with. "Wha ... what we oughta do," said Bird, a small, tight-muscled man with a big nose and a choleric disposition, "is burn the motherfucker down. I'd go along with the niggers on a riot where we get in some licks. They just talk revolution . . ."

"Yeah," Baby Boy said, "they wanna go back to Africa or wherever, send the fuckers."

"Them people over there don't want 'em either," T.J. said. "I was readin'—"

"Fool!" someone said. "Quit lyin'. You know you can't read."

Earl scanned the yard. It was becoming crowded with convicts being herded from the lower yard before lockup. Near the edge of the shed he saw Ron Decker talking to a Puerto Rican whose name Earl didn't know—but who he did know for a glue-sniffer and loudmouth troublemaker. A couple of the Puerto Rican's clique were hovering nearby. The conversation was heated, with Ron gesticulating, and the Puerto Rican suddenly jabbing a finger at his chest. The good-looking youth spun on his heel and walked away. Earl saw Tony waiting some distance away.

The whistle blew and the swarming convicts began to form lines. Earl headed against the tide toward the yard gate. A closed-door conference took place during count, and Earl locked the washroom door and listened. The warden had gotten word from the stool pigeons (probably in exchange for a transfer, Earl thought) that several dozen inmates, mostly black, planned to crowd around the big yard gate just before it opened, knowing that even convicts willing to work wouldn't cross such a line. The lieutenants were being briefed by Stoneface Bradley, the pockmarked associate warden. Extra personnel would be on duty. Those trained for the tactical squad would be held in the plaza until needed, and the highway patrol would lend a dozen sharpshooters to beef up fire-power on the wall. But they would try to break the strike before it began by opening the yard gate an hour early and running the cons directly from the mess halls to work, or to the far side of the yard away from the gate so they couldn't gather and create a bottleneck.

As soon as the count cleared, Earl went to the yard, watched the lines come from the cellhouses to the mess hall until he saw a willowy young black with a *café au lait* complexion who belonged to the Black Panthers. It was a certainty that he was involved in the strike plans, or at least knew who was. Earl also knew the man wasn't a racial fanatic. When he came out, Earl waved and walked over and told him what he'd overheard. "For whatever it's worth," he finished. The black thanked him.

As he turned away, he saw Tony Bork getting a cigarette lit by another convict nearby. Earl gave a brief wave and started to leave, but Tony beckoned him. The yard was dark except for the floodlights, and convicts were streaming by them en route to the cellhouses.

When Earl stepped over, lowering his head slightly because he was taller than Tony, the plumber put a hand on his shoulder. "My friend," Tony said, "the one I introduced you to today, he's got prob-lems—"

"I guess so," Earl said, snorting. "Some cocksucker in Sacramento should get a foot in his ass for sending him here ... among the animals."

"Somebody cut him in to Psycho Mike—"

"The Puerto?" Earl interrupted.

Tony nodded. "The glue-sniffer, yeah. And he's scheming on the guy. Did him a few favors, bonaroo clothes, et cetera, before Ron knew the score. The youngster woke up to what's going on, and he's trying to back off, but Psycho's on the muscle now and he's got that little clique."

x

60

"Is that kid Ron a broad?"

Tony shook his head. "No, man, but you know that goes. He doesn't have any henchmen or—"

"What about you? You trying to turn him out?"

"You know I don't play that shit. I like him and I'm giving him moral support . . . but like I go to the board real soon and I've got a good shot at a parole. Besides, I'm no tough guy."

"So you want to cut me into the action, is that it?"

"Somebody's gonna get him, or drive him into protective custody, or make him kill somebody. Why don't you pull him?"

"I need a kid like I need a bad heart. A pretty kid is a ticket to trouble . . . and I'm too old to ask for that. Shit, I haven't even booked Tommy the Face in two years. I'm turning into a jack-off idiot."

"He's ten times smarter and classier than the shitbums around here. I was thinking about that blond youngster that Psycho Mike's boys grabbed off the bus last year—ran a gang bang, made him pluck his eyebrows, and then sold him to that old pervert. The kid wound up in the psych ward."

"Fuck it. It's none of my business. If a sucker is weak, he's got to fall around here. I came when I was eighteen and nobody turned me out. I didn't even smile for two years."

"Things were different then . . . a dude could represent himself by himself. There weren't gangs then. He's not a killer, but he's not a coward."

Earl shook his head and refused to listen further, but when he turned away he found his jaw muscles tight as he remembered what Tony had described. Raised in reform schools, used to places without women, Earl like everyone else with such a background was not against queens and pretty boys. After several years without a woman, a surrogate could arouse just as intensely. But Earl *was* against force, and even more than that, he loathed the practice of buying and selling young boys, a phenomenon of recent years. For a moment he thought of asking Ponchie (whom he'd known all his life), or Grumpy or Bogus Pete, all of the powerful Chicano Brotherhood, to jerk up Psycho Mike. Not that it would do any good; with Mike gone (that was easy), others would move in.

"What the fuck do I care?" he muttered, seeing Paul's figure working with a broom on an open gutter across the shadowed yard. He went to see if Paul had word of any narcotics. It would be easier to go through tomorrow if he was tranquilized on heroin.

Late in the evening, while the clack, clack, clack of cell doors being locked reverberated through the cellhouse, Ron Decker stretched on the top bunk of his cell. An elbow propped up his torso as he lay on his side, while spread in front of him, as if for reference, were Pamela's letters, her Christmas card, a battered collegiate dictionary, and a photo of her against a background of a field of pinkish wildflowers. The last letter, on pale yellow stationery with a hint of perfume, he studied while he wrote. He adored her letters, for she had a flair for mood and nuance and sometimes included a page of evocative poetry. Sometimes the letters made him imagine an entirely different person than he remembered, and he blotted out memory to respond to the letter writer. Ron was uneasy with the written word. He was well enough educated, but lacked experience in transmitting thoughts with the pen. He'd written more since his arrest than in all the previous years of his life. He wanted to make his letters a journal, and the one he was working on tried to convey what he was seeing and experiencing. He described San Quentin's hideous look, but he could not tell her of the wholesale violence and paranoia, nor of the expected strike. A letter with upsetting information would be returned by the censors. He did tell her that the classification committee had assigned him to the furniture factory, and he was to report in the morning. He was unhappy with the idea of sanding varnish from chairs all day, but there was nothing he could do about it for a while. He told her that he had a personable cell partner, without amplifying that it was a forty-five-year-old queen. He told her that he was disillusioned by the personalities he had found, that he'd expected at least some who were intelligent, but here were the underworld's stunted failures, muggers, gutter junkies, gas station robbers, and those who committed moronic rapes and murders. Master criminals didn't seem to exist. He wanted to tell her about the young men raised in reform schools that so deformed their psyches that institutions and institution values were their whole life and whose status was built on violence. He wanted to tell her about racism that went beyond racism into obsession—on both sides—and how it was affecting him to be the object of murderous hate just because he was white. It aroused fear, and a kernel of hatred in response.

None of these things could be written, so he finally signed the letter. He was putting it in the envelope when the public address speaker blared: "*Lights out in ten minutes!*" He swiveled on the bunk so he could put the letter on the bars for the last mail pickup. Then he jumped down. Jan the Actress, so called because he'd lived as a woman for ten years long ago, was cross-legged on the bottom bunk, fingers flying and yarn trailing as he worked on an afghan that would sell for ninety dollars in the visitor's handicraft store or for five hits of acid, twenty joints, or two papers of heroin on the yard.

Ron stepped to the back of the cell and got his toothbrush, his eye catching his reflection in the mirror. It was odd to see his hair so short and combed straight back—but without a part; someone had told him that some would think a part was sissified. He'd laughed at the ignorance but followed the advice.

Jan the Actress pulled a cardboard box from beneath the bunk and began depositing the knitting gear. "How's the problem with that Psycho Mike coming?"

Ron spat out the toothpaste foam. "Tense. He wanted to know why I was shying him on . . . and something about owing him."

"I could've told you he was bad news."

"He was friendly at first . . . and I didn't know anybody. I should've known."

"What happens now?"

"I'm going to stay away from him."

"What if that doesn't work? He's got some friends and it could get rough."

Ron shook his head. He wasn't afraid of Psycho Mike, not really—and yet in a way he was. And it was demeaning to be worried about someone so stupid. That he would go along with what Mike wanted (he stopped short of fully imagining it) was unthinkable. He already knew what he would suffer if he went into protective custody, and rejected that idea. He was willing to fight if necessary, but could imagine what little chance he had against a clique. If he used a knife—Tony had offered him one—it would be resolved, but he balked at that choice for two reasons: it would at least mean a denial of modification by the judge, and even if he got away with it, the vision of running steel into human flesh was revolting. When he finished his ablutions, Jan was waiting to use the sink. The cell was less than five feet wide, and the space beside the bunks was so narrow that they were chest to chest as they passed. Jan's fingers brushed at his crotch and he reflexively shot his ass back. "Damnit!"

"Try it, you'll like it," the queen said, the time-worn parody of a woman's face screwed up with a smile and desire.

Ron quickly jumped onto the top bunk, his legs dangling over the side. "This is supposed to be a place of tough guys. Everybody is some kind of pervert. Wow!"

Jan had turned to the mirror, trying to make thin hair cover lots of pate. "No, they're not. More the pity."

"It sure seems that way."

"Just because you're young, tender sweetmeat."

Ron blushed furiously. When the lights were out (though it was not really dark because lights outside the cell threw a bar-waffled glow inside), Ron could see the blackness of the Bay beyond the cellhouse, and beyond the blackness twinkled the lights of the Richmond hills. It was an insult to put the ugliness of a prison in such a beautiful setting. It increased torment to be walking dead amid so much life. He had another thought and stuck his head over the edge of the bunk where he could see the featureless paleness of Jan's face. "Say, I was thinking about having some guy look at my case today . . . some older dude with a shaved head, Earl Copen. Know anything about him?"

Jan's giggle was quick. "Do I know Earl Copen? Honey, he was my cell partner years and years ago when I came here. For a few weeks. He ripped me off."

"Ripped you off. Him, too, Yuk."

"Oh, he's another convict. He waited until the lights were out and—"

"Spare me the details."

"You're not interested in my love life?"

"Not especially."

"Earl was just a kid then. He was one step ahead of the wolves himself, but he was a wild sonofabitch. Stoneface, the A.W., was a lieutenant then, and I remember Earl turned his desk over on him and spent a year in the hole. And I remember some wolf eyeing him with *that* look—"

"I know the look."

"Earl asked him what he was looking at . . . and the guy told him, 'I wanna fuck you.' Earl told him that if he kicked his ass he'd let him. The guy was a light-heavyweight prizefighter and Earl was skinny as you. They were supposed to meet in the back of the block after breakfast. When the guy came in, Earl was on the fifth tier with a big water bucket, the kind the tier tender uses to fill up gallon cans. It weighs about seventy pounds when it's full of water. I don't know if it was. Earl dropped it, and it would've put the guy's head down around his asshole if it'd landed, but it barely missed and shattered his ankle. Earl came running down the stairs with a claw hammer to finish him, but that fucker managed to get out, broken ankle and all. He was scared to come out of the hospital. Earl could have fucked him by then."

"He didn't strike me that way—crazy and all."

"Oh, he's beautiful people. I talk to him. He's intelligent and seems burned out. When you reach your mid-thirties, you tend to slow down. That's old for a convict. He's tired of doing time."

"I saw him with some youngsters up against the wall. Is that his gang?"

"Probably part of the White Brotherhood. That's not his gang

. . . not anybody's. They don't even think God is boss. I've seen a lot of dangerous men here, but never a bunch of them ganged together."

"What about the Mexican Brotherhood?"

"The same. Maybe worse. There's more of them. But they get along with Earl's friends. Those kids—hell, some of them are nearly thirty—love Earl. Paul, too."

"Who's Paul?"

"The guy with the white hair, looks about fifty."

"I haven't seen him." When he rolled back and pressed his head to the pillow, Ron decided to keep away from Earl Copen. Jailhouse lawyers were abundant. Earl was too unpredictable. All I need is a serious disciplinary report, Ron thought. The judge'll toss the key away.

When the morning bell wakened Ron, the land outside the cell-house windows was covered with fog. The edge of the shore, twenty yards away, was totally invisible. The fog wouldn't go over the cellhouses into the big yard, but the lower recreation yard would be blanketed. The factory area was beyond the wall of the lower recreation yard; it had its own wall.

Ron dressed and washed quietly, for Jan never got up until the 8:30 lockup, arriving at work half an hour late. He was clerk to the supervisor of education, who came in at 9:00, so nothing was ever said. Neither did Tony Bork go to breakfast, so Ron stood by the bars and waited to eat alone, wondering about the rumored strike, wondering if a "fog line" would be called, closing the lower yard to everyone.

The mess hall was abnormally quiet, the customary roaring voices a low hum, exaggerating the clatter of utensils against steel trays. It seemed as if fewer men than usual were eating. Ron's tier was among the last to sit down.

Ron gulped his food, dumped his tray, and stepped into the cold gray morning light. A row of guards waited just outside the mess hall door, nightsticks in hand. Perched on the gun rail above the yard gate stood a guard and a highway patrolman, one with a riot gun, the other with a tear-gas grenade launcher. Ron stopped, surprised. "Industries workers down the stairs," a tall sergeant said, moving his head to indicate the open gate. "Everybody else across the yard."

In less than five heartbeats Ron's eyes panned across the yard to where nearly two thousand convicts waited. The crowd broke in an L shape where the East and North cellhouses joined. The blacks were, as usual, along the North cellhouse wall. Ron didn't know if he should go through the gate or join the throng. One might make him a strikebreaker, bring retaliation from other convicts; the other could get him in trouble with the officials.

"Get moving," a guard said to him—and at that moment three convicts stepped from the mess hall behind him and turned without hesitation to go out the gate. Their exit brought no jeers or catcalls from the crowd, so he lowered his head and followed them.

The fog met him on the stairs. The figures ahead turned into vague outlines and disappeared altogether. He couldn't see the prison walls. He followed the road around the lower yard; the industrial area gate was a quarter of a mile away. No guards were in sight; even on bright days when there was no trouble, the gate had several.

Now he turned and followed the road along the base of the wall, feeling strange in the blinding landscape. Two convicts appeared, trudging toward him, caps pulled over their ears, hands jammed in their pockets.

"Hey, white brother," one said as they reached him, "you might as well go back. The niggers blocked *this* gate."

The other one laughed, the caw of a crow, showing gaps where teeth should have been. "The fuckin' bulls got slick and opened the yard gate early. The rugs got slicker and blocked this gate. With the fog and shit, it's worse for the bulls."

"Nobody's going to work?" Ron asked.

"They're waitin' down there 'bout a hunnerd yards, waitin' to see what happens. The people blockin' the gate are after that."

"I think I'll go see."

"I learned to get away from hot spots. Some shit is likely to kick off down there. I wanna miss it."

"Don't stay too long. Stoneface is gonna be mad as a Jap. He'll be wantin' to kill somebody, an' convicts all got the same color to him."

"It's the color of shit," his friend said, and they went off through the fog toward the big yard.

Curiosity and excitement flecked with fear grabbed Ron as he went forward upon the back of the crowd. From beyond he heard a voice with a Negro accent screaming, "They can *kill me!* I ain' no mammyfuckin' *dawg!*"

Ron stepped to the left, where a fence bordered the opposite side of the road from the wall. There was room to push through and he did, coming to the front ten yards away.

Across a space from the crowd was a tightly knit group of about fifty. Most of the faces were black, but a few whites were there. Some of the strikers had baseball bats and lengths of pipe. One roly-poly black was in front of the strikers, exhorting the workers: "Whatcha gonna do? Get on over here. We all together. Don't be scared!"

A white convict beside Ron shook his head. "I'd go over there if it wasn't all spooks. My fuckin' partners would turn on me if I did."

Ron looked along the summit of the wall. A single guard in great-coat stood in silhouette, his rifle hanging like a half-mast phallus. Did the officials know that was happening? What would they do?

The cold was insidious. Because there was no wind, it did not cut; rather, it ate slowly like acid. Ron began to shiver and chatter. He wished something would happen, wondered if he should trudge back to the yard.

A flurry of movement in the workers' crowd made him stand on tiptoe and crane his neck. A chubby middle-aged Chicano was pushing through with a yellow card held overhead. He walked resolutely toward the strikers. The yellow card was a checkout slip that had to be signed by his work supervisor before he could leave the prison on parole. "*Yo vaya . . . la lebere esta mañana.*"

The front rank of strikers opened like lips to swallow the man without protest, and a moment later the innards churned and crunched and Ron heard the splat of blows and a gurgled scream. His excitement fell away, replaced by horror. "Oh God, they're . . . killing him." He fought away nausea.

"He shoulda waited," the con beside Ron said. "I'd have waited. Now he's goin' out the back—in a box."

The crowd around Ron suddenly crushed into him, split by some force he couldn't see. Then he did. Men in helmets with Plexiglas masks were wading through, swinging long clubs. One man went down. He wasn't a striker but blood spurted from his head as he drew his legs up. The guards were in formation.

The young convict beside Ron leaped to the fence. Ron was thrown against it. He struggled, turned, dug his fingers through the holes in the wire and scrambled up. The baseball field was on the other side. The fog provided a hiding place of sorts.

Earl's cell on the fifth tier was a perch overlooking the yard. Just before 8:00 a.m. he looked out. The herd of convicts against the cellhouse walls stood quietly. He spotted his friends halfway down. They'd gathered together in a moment of possible trouble, but it seemed that trouble was passing by. Earl put on his heavy coat and gloves and went out of the cell.

As he came out of the rotunda he met other, more timid men, coming in. But Earl had looked and it seemed okay. He ran his eyes along the gun rail. Half a dozen guards were there, weapons held casually except for a sergeant—a weightlifter with a Thompson submachine gun at port arms.

Earl walked along the rear of the crowd until he saw Baby Boy's red hair. Then he pushed through to where his friends were.

All the other convicts were quietly serious, but the clique was grinning and laughing, coming alive in the threat of chaos, which Paul was reducing to absurdity.

"All they want is a white ho an' a Cadillac. That's sure as hell reasonable after all white done did to 'em . . . Check that bull." He pointed to a chubby rosy-cheeked guard facing the crowd fifteen yards away. The guard couldn't decide how to hold his club, at his side, across his chest, behind his leg, in one or two hands—and he kept glancing nervously at the protective cover of rifleman. "Fool don't know whether to shit or go blind," someone added.

Bad Eye caught Earl's attention and put two fingers to his mouth, asking for a cigarette. Earl started to reach into his pocket when the flatulent report of a rifle echoed, followed by a hollower firearm, either a shotgun or a tear-gas gun using a shotgun charge. The two thousand men on the yard fell instantly and utterly silent, frozen, as hearts leaped to a faster beat and atmosphere pulsed with tension. The chubby guard fell back a step, and riflemen shook off their casualness.

Even Paul was quiet.

A figure came hurtling through the gate, jerked to a walk, and tried absurdly to be nonchalant. The guards started to close on him, but then others came and the guards let them through.

Two blacks came up out of the fog, one guiding the other, whose hand held a blood-sopped rag to his forehead. They turned left, heading for their brothers. Two guards went to cut them off, but a massed spontaneous moan that turned into a roar stopped them— a wall of sound. And as they hesitated, the black crowd broke forward, surrounding the arrivals while the guards fell back. The riflemen braced their weapons on their shoulders, squinted along sights, but the blacks stopped.

Earl's heart pumped like a bird's wings. Bodies surged against him, blocking his view. He saw some whites and Chicanos run from the gate into the crowd, and seconds later got word that a Chicano had been stomped to death by the blacks.

The racially divided crowd now pulled apart, like organisms mutually repelled. Earl almost fell, but T.J. grabbed his belt and kept him erect. The sound of voices was like the lowing of cattle before a stampede.

Moments later the spilled gasoline of madness was ignited. A *whump* sound from a tear-gas launcher and grenade arced down between the crowds, sending them farther apart as it exploded, gyrating and spinning as it gave off its fearful fumes. Again Earl was buffeted so that he had to fight for balance. It was like struggling to keep his head above water in a stormy sea. The motes reached his eyes and fluid began to run from them and from his nose. "Cocksuckers . . . bastards," he cursed silently.

Like some mindless beast driven without purpose, the twelve hundred Chicano and white convicts swung in a clockwise motion so that they were against the mess-hall wall. Driven by the tear gas from the North cellhouse wall, the blacks were where the whites had been along the East cellhouse. The two groups, twelve hundred whites and eight hundred blacks, faced each other across a hundred and fifty yards of open space.

A hundred convicts were jammed against the East cellhouse gate, trying futilely to get in away from trouble.

"*Lockup! Lockup! Mandatory lockup!*" the loudspeaker blared.

"Open the fuckin' gates," someone near Earl said. Both sides were now spread out. Earl's friends stuck together and his fear became fury. He was certain the officials had deliberately turned a strike into a racial confrontation.

A window of the mess hall crashed out. Then another. Men were yelling in fury. Stacks of stainless steel trays were being passed to the raised hands of whites and Chicanos. Then came other things that would serve as weapons—mop wringers, pieces of the dish-washing machine, heavy wooden ladles used on the kitchen vats.

Across the yard the blacks were ripping benches apart to get hunks of lumber. Earl did nothing, knowing the groups would never get at each other across the no-man's-land. The rifles and subma-chine gun would erect an insurmountable barrier of death.

A convict pushed against Earl to leap to the window to get some-thing. He landed on Earl's foot when he came down.

"Asshole!" Earl snarled, ramming the heels of his hands into the man's chest and knocking him back. The convict bumped into someone behind him and kept from falling. His face was already contorted with rage at the blacks. His curse at Earl was drowned in the churning, screaming crowd as he tensed to spring. He had a piece of pipe in his hand and lunged. Earl stepped back, raising an arm, intending to rush under the swing if he could. He wished he had a knife. The convict rushed without seeing T.J., nor did Earl see him until the powerful weightlifter swung the flat of a stainless steel tray as if it were a baseball bat. The man rushed into it, and his feet kept going as the tray curtained his face. His shoulders hit the ground first, and it was a few seconds before the blood came from his squashed flesh. His legs trembled in spasms.

Bad Eye came from somewhere and planted a steel-toed brogan against the man's head, as hard a kick as he could deliver. T.J. gave him the accolade of a pat on the back.

The tumult made it impossible to talk, but they pushed through the crowd toward others of the Brotherhood a few feet away, leaving the supine figure to be walked on—or to die for all they cared.

The two crowds were screaming at each other, brandishing makeshift weapons.

Bad Eye cupped his hands to Earl's ear. "We'll get the black mother-fuckers this time. All they've got is some sticks."

Earl said nothing, but looked again at the riflemen. The two crowds started to surge toward each other and the submachine gun hammered three short bursts, tearing up chunks of asphalt in stitches. Then the rifles volleyed. Bullets swept down the open zone and the crowds froze and fell back. The gunfire silenced the screaming.

One black was twisting on the ground. Obviously a guard had shot into the crowd instead of in front of it. The black was holding his thigh and trying to get up. Two blacks started forward to help him, but a bullet whipped over their heads to drive them back.

Some of the hysteria had drained away. Glazed eyes began to narrow, madness was replaced by questions about what to do, what was going to happen.

"Attention in the yard! All inmates by the mess hall will go the the lower yard."

The answering bellow of defiance was a shadow of a few minutes earlier. Some men yelled and shook their fists, but they would have done the same if told to stand fast or go home.

The tear-gas grenades flew over the men, landing under the shed beyond the fringe of the crowd. The gas drove convicts crashing into others, sending a reverberation through the crowd and jamming bodies together again. The route of escape was through the gate. They couldn't go down the road because the visored tactical squad was waiting with clubs and mace, so they surged down the stairs, some falling until another body stopped them.

They were herded like cattle into the thinning fog. All was gray under the lightless sky; the walls looked soft in the fog, lined by faceless silhouettes with rifles. The lower yard was big, and the convicts spread out like water on a plain. Everyone searched for a friend, sensing that this was a dangerous situation, for no guards were on the ground and those on the walls were too far away to see what was going on. It was a chance to settle old grudges. The law of brutality was replaced by no law whatsoever.

The Brotherhood gathered near the wall of the prison laundry. Or at least most of them, about thirty men, all younger than Earl and Paul, but all with wizened, bitter faces and hard eyes. Most were dangerous, though a few were faking, using the Brotherhood for protection. Those who counted among them respected and listened to Earl and Paul as much as to anyone. They had to listen to T.J. and Bad Eye.

The temperature was below freezing. Because there was no wind, it took a while for the cold to seep in, but soon the convicts were stomping their feet, trying to keep warm, and vapor issued from their mouths and nostrils. Faintly they heard the loudspeakers in the big yard order the blacks into the cellhouses to lockup. "Typical shit," someone said. "Let the niggers go in while we freeze our asses off."

"Sheeit!" Paul said. "What you bet them redneck bulls ain't clubbin' the shit out of 'em?"

"The bulls're scared of 'em," Bad Eye said.

"That's where hate come from, baby—fear."

"And Whitey's slicker," Earl said bitterly, thinking how the officials had turned a strike against them into a race riot by the simple expedient of separating the two groups and letting nature run its course.

"Fuck 'em," Bad Eye said. "I hate niggers *and* bulls—but the bulls ain't no threat to kill me just for walkin' around, and the niggers are . . ."

74

"The boy's got a point," Paul said. "Ya'll sho nuff a smart young motherfucker," he said, grabbing Bad Eye's arm and shaking it playfully. "How'd you get so smart?"

Earl was unable to dispute Bad Eye. It was impossible not to be a racist—whatever one's color—where blacks and whites murdered each other indiscriminately. Nevertheless, he was bitter about tomorrow's headlines that would scream "*San Quentin Racial Disturbance.*" Not a word would be printed about the protest of conditions. He lit a cigarette, hunched his shoulders, and stared out across the canyon of the yard.

Flocks of sea gulls swooped, soared and circled overhead, emitting shrill cries. The twelve hundred shivering convicts were now quiet, spread across the baseball field, most of them in left field, the farthest point from the wall with the armed men. The laundry where Earl's group stood was in deepest center field. The building hid them from another wall. More guards with weapons were hurrying along the skyline. Maybe three dozen were positioned for a clear shot.

Some convicts had pulled the benches from the third-base dugout and were starting a fire.

Earl saw Ronald Decker standing with Tony Bork behind second base. The young man's hands were jammed in his pockets and he was jumping up and down to generate circulation. Twenty yards beyond him, apparently unnoticed, was Psycho Mike and three of his sullen-visaged henchmen. They were squatted, bringing clenched rags to their mouths—shoe glue, Earl knew—and glancing in Ron's direction. Earl knew what they were thinking. They were working up courage for a ripoff.

On sudden impulse Earl pushed away from the laundry wall and walked to Ron and Tony, who saw him coming and told the younger man. Ron had open, candid eyes; he didn't try to look tough as did so many young men in prison, as Earl himself had in his day. As Earl came up to them, he looked beyond, gazing at Psycho Mike expressionlessly; but the combination of the gaze and his action conveyed the message. "C'mon over by the laundry," he said to Tony. "It's warmer."

Tony looked to Ron, who shrugged. As they started toward the laundry, Earl looked over his shoulder at the glue-sniffers, cocking his head sideways and jutting his chin pugnaciously.

The clique of tough young convicts eyed the newcomer; they would have raised an eyebrow except that such an expression wasn't in their repertoire. "Don't be so *mean*, Earl," one said, the voice unrecognized, making Earl blush and some others smile. He didn't want to discomfit the youth, but Ron apparently hadn't caught the implication.

"Nobody would believe this," Ron said.

"Nobody cares."

"They killed that man—kicked him to death—for nothing."

"He was a damn fool for trying to cross a picket line of berserk niggers."

Ron shook his head. He was shivering and had his hands stuck under his armpits. "How long will they keep us here?"

"God knows. They're thinking about it." And Earl was thinking that Ron was pretty. "Were you down here?"

Ron told what he'd seen, as if describing it could erase some of the horror still within him. Earl listened, liking the precision and economy of Ron's words, without the convict's usual obscenity every few syllables. The manner of speech indicated a keen, logical mind.

Simultaneously Earl watched Psycho Mike and his gang, but they had gone to where a crowd had gathered at the fire and weren't looking toward the laundry.

"This is really a study in stupidity," Ron said.

"What's that?"

"The races at each other's throats to give the guards an excuse for target practice."

"I had about the same thought—but it's not that simple, not just black and white, to make a poor pun. It's something nobody can control . . . and nobody can stay uninvolved. I'll run it down to you sometime . . . what I think."

Baby Boy came over to Earl. "Say, bro," he said, "check the play.

Ponchie's boys are gonna down somebody." He gestured to the field where a tall pale Chicano was slipping through the scattered crowd toward the dense group around the fire. His cap was pulled low, his coat collar up, and he moved in a furtive way. Flanking him were two others. The trio was obviously stalking someone.

"Maybe we should see if they need some slack," Bad Eye said. "They're our allies."

"They don't need no help," T.J. said.

Ron sensed the heightened tension and stared in the same direction, toward the crowd at the fire, trying to pick out who was going to be assaulted.

"Bet they nail Shadow," Earl said, touching Ron's arm. "That tall skinny dude in the white pants. He burned them for some money . . . made a bad move. They've been layin' to catch him."

The middle Chicano with the cap, his head down to shield his face, paused ten feet behind the back of the victim, pulled a long knife from beneath his shirt, and ran forward on tiptoe. Three strides and the weapon came down, buried to the hilt in the man's back. Ron grunted involuntarily, as if he'd felt the blow. The victim was driven forward into the fire, his hands extending reflexively to stop his fall. The two backup men were looking around, their hands inside their shirts. The stabber had spun away the instant he delivered the blow, began walking nonchalantly, sort of wandering, but heading toward the laundry. Ron lost him, looked at the man fighting his way back from the flames and hot coals, the taped handle of the knife jutting from between his shoulder blades.

The men around the fire had pulled back, away from trouble.

Ron expected the man to fall. He had to be dead. But he got to his feet, began walking in a circle, a hand groping unsuccessfully to reach the thing in his back. Then he suddenly began walking away, off the baseball diamond and toward the stairs in the direction of the hospital.

"Unnnnh," Earl grunted. "That's the weirdest thing I ever saw. He's got fourteen inches of blade in him."

The man who'd done the stabbing passed by the Brotherhood, grinned, gave a clenched-fist salute, and kept going. Ron saw a gang of Chicanos farther along the laundry wall who were waiting for their associates.

"That wasn't how to collect," Ron said wryly. "He can't pay them in the morgue."

"He can't pay anyway. He's broke. And there's no small claims court so it's a lesson to others."

Ron said nothing.

A pale sun hinted through the overcast without noticeably raising the temperature. Now three fires were burning. Some of the clique wanted to break into the laundry to get warm or to find fuel so they could start a fire on their own.

Stoneface had come to the wall, a battery-powered bullhorn in hand. "*Attention in the lower yard! All inmates will form in the left field grass—*"

A halfhearted Bronx cheer was the reply. The men were playing out their roles, their hot fury long since chilled. They were ready to go to their cells—and many stirred to follow the order.

They didn't have a chance. Stoneface gave a signal. Without warning, the rifles and shotguns began firing and the bullets fell like rain. The shotgun pellets percolated patches of lawn. Some men were swatted down, as if struck by an unseen fist, and the others dived for the ground though it offered no protection.

A window above Ron's head disintegrated and a rattle like a handful of pebbles came from nearby. He found himself on the pavement, and Earl was chanting, "Shit, shit, shit. . . ."

The gunfire echoed from the walls. It seemed to go on forever, but it actually lasted just thirty seconds. When it stopped, the silence exaggerated the moans of the injured and the cries of frantic sea gulls beating through the mackerel sky.

Every convict except one was face down on the earth, and the exception was running doubled over holding his belly where he'd been shot.

Stoneface raised the bullhorn: "*You have thirty seconds to form on the outfield grass.*"

No defiant yells answered the order; men were hurrying, but under their breaths they cursed and their eyes were filled with bitter hate.

The tactical squad, highway patrolmen, and other guards had been waiting in the wings. They carried clubs, pick handles, shotguns, and cans of mace. As they closed around the convicts, Stoneface spoke again, ordering them to strip to their underwear. Everyone complied; the choice was between that or more bullets. A dozen men were still down on the grass and dirt, some moving, some not. One was missing the back of his head. The sea gulls were swooping down to scavenge what had sprayed from his skull.

Now the convicts were driven up the stairs in a line—or a chaotic stream. It was a driven stampede of seminaked bodies. Guards and patrolmen were on the flanks, jabbing with clubs and shotgun butts. The guards, terrified earlier by the mass beast, now gave vent to the rage engendered by that terror. Many who were usually decent turned brutal. Any convict who faltered was immediately attacked.

Earl lost his friends and his senses. He struggled to keep his feet and push forward. Once he slipped to a knee on the stairs and a highway patrolman's shotgun butt crashed into his spine, making him yelp involuntarily and sending him upward despite the pain. He wanted to fight, but it wasn't worth the consequences.

In the cellhouses the men ran single-file up the stairs to the tiers. The police swung clubs as they went by. When one went down, he was beaten for faltering.

Earl got into his cell, fell on the bunk, panting and sweating. After a few minutes be began to laugh. "It sure as fuck broke the monotony," he said, laughing again.

An hour later the San Francisco radio stations gave news bulletins the convicts could hear on their earphones. Officials reported that four inmates had been slain and nineteen injured in a racial altercation between neo-Nazi white inmates and black militants. The situation was now under control with all inmates in their cells. Ringleaders were being isolated, and there would be an investigation.

All during the afternoon and evening Earl heard security bars being raised and cell doors being unlocked, and then the dull sound of blows and falling bodies. Sometimes pleas of "No more," or from guards, "Asshole troublemaking nigger . . . how tough are you?" And more blows.

A hundred men were rounded up, three quarters of them black. Some went to the Adjustment Center, others to "B" Section segregation. The two hundred prisoners already in "B" Section heard the beatings and went berserk, smashing toilets by lighting fires underneath the porcelain and kicking it; the toilets collapsed. They hurled the chunks through the bars. They burned mattresses, tore bunks from bolts on the walls. One young queen and his jocker in adjacent cells used the bunks to dig through the five inches of concrete separating them. Guards couldn't go down the tiers to count because the convicts hurled jars against the bars, spewing out glass shrapnel. Firehoses and tear gas were turned on them—"B" Section was a mass of burned, waterlogged mattresses, broken beds, shattered windows, singed paint, fragmented toilets, and miserably wet convicts. Only the Queen and her jocker were happy.

No food was served the first day. Late the following afternoon, two cold sandwiches were passed to each man. This went on for two more days, and then the prisoners were unlocked for "controlled" feeding twice a day, fifty men at a time, under the watchful eyes of many guards. Black and white convicts eyed each other with every feeling except affection, but the security was too tight for any incidents.

The next morning a few convicts in key job assignments were let out. Earl was still under the blankets, drinking coffee and smoking, when Lieutenant Seeman appeared outside the bars, hat cocked, hands jammed into the deep pockets of a long green coat.

"Hey, bum, ready to go to work?" Seeman asked, simultaneously looking up and down the tier. Seeing nobody, he fished a carton of

Camels from his coat pocket and pitched it through the bars onto the bunk.

Earl sat up, took the cigarettes, but said nothing; no thanks were called for. "How many are coming out?"

"Just a few today—captain's clerk, kitchen workers—a few of them the officer's dining room crew. Fitz, of course. But I can pull you out if you want."

"Naw, boss. I'll wait for tomorrow. It'd ruin my image to be among the first unlocked after what happened down there."

"Wasn't that a—" Seeman finished with a snort of angry disgust. "If they had an investigation . . . Kittredge and I were just going to go down. We knew everybody was frozen and *wanted* to go in. I was so goddamned mad I almost forget myself. I mean . . . hell, I can see coming down as hard as necessary if someone needs it, but shooting into unarmed men who weren't doing a goddamned thing except burning a couple of wooden benches . . . I better be quiet or I'll get mad again."

"I'll come out tomorrow if there's a few others. What're you doin' here during the day?"

"Making lots of overtime. A lot of people are doing it the last few days. A prison can't run without convicts working."

The men who ran the prison from air-conditioned offices beyond the walls, the men with faces never seen by the convicts, decided that the weekend was a good time to unlock the cells. The press had forgotten the riot within days, and now two weeks had passed. The honor cellhouses and necessary workers had been on normal schedule for several days without trouble. The known agitators were in segregation. *Bonnie and Clyde* was the scheduled weekend movie, and the officials knew that nothing pacifies a convict more than a good movie.

Ron came out for breakfast with everyone else. Jan the Actress had been going to work after three days of lockup, and Ron had enjoyed the daylight hours of solitude. He'd ceased minding about the lockdown, though if it had gone on for months, he would have. Even before the Monday of madness, he had preferred cell time accompanied by books, letters, and thoughts to the crowded yard, where he felt out of place and on display. The mass violence had reinforced his aversion, not so much when it happened, because the episode was too swift for more than survival reaction, but rather after the shock evaporated and he knew the security of his cell. The animalistic screams, the racial epithets, rose anonymously from the honeycomb of cells and made Ron think of wild beasts snarling in their cages. His contempt for stupidity and his sympathy for the oppressed condition of black people in America had both been overwhelmed by fear. During the lockup, he had to pass along the tier between groups of young blacks. He could feel their hatred as if it were radiant heat. He averted his eyes, stomach upset, and in the cell's sanctuary his fear was the acorn from which grew the oak of hate—and he disliked feeling that hate. He disliked the entire idiocy of prison and tried to hide from it.

On Saturday, however, he came out. Staying in would have attracted attention, probably from the guards, who would think he had trouble, certainly from convicts who would sense his fear, evaluate it as weakness and try to exploit it. When he entered the yard from the mess hall nearly four thousand convicts milled in the canyon between the cellhouses. The pale green walls were washed in a hot butterscotch sun. His eyes squinted and tried to focus in the glare. He'd expected a tense silence after the weeks of lockup, especially since the last meeting of black and white convicts had been so furious, but instead he was engulfed by the sound of hilarity, the voices had the timber of a party, and rock and roll music came from the speakers. The faces were bright and animated, though somewhat pasty from weeks of lockup. Friends who hadn't seen each other during the lockdown slapped each other on the back, hugged, and laughed. The only visible signs of the recent trouble were three extra riflemen and the voluntary segregation of the blacks on the northeast quarter of the yard.

Ron moved with his eyes down, avoiding collisions, looking around for a familiar face. Everyone else seemed to have a friend or to belong to a group. Ron had brought a paperback book along in case he didn't find one of his few friends. Jan the Actress stood in the sun with two other queens. Ron circled the trio. He was also watching for Psycho Mike and his gang; again in the hope of avoiding them.

"Hey, young 'un," someone called right beside him. He turned and there was Earl Copen five feet away. The older convict was seated on the concrete abutment to which the weather shed's pillar was attached. He wore a faded navy blue sweatshirt, its sleeves raggedly amputated above the elbow. He needed a shave everywhere but on his head. The chin stubble was gray, but the bare skull gleamed from a film of oil. His ugly face had an infectiously warm smile, and his eyes were alert. Ron instantly recalled his resolve about Copen, and the stories Jan had told. Simultaneously, his sense of lonesomeness evaporated. He went over. Earl seemed the most relaxed person in the prison yard.

"See you survived the shitstorm," Earl said.

"It was shaky."

"This the first time you've been out?"

"Uh-huh. I didn't mind it, though. What's out here?"

"Just hairy-assed convicts." Earl looked at him more closely. "You need some sun."

Ron looked down, ignored the comment. "When did you get out?"

"Fuck, last week. Me, I'm an honor inmate."

The laconic way Earl spoke rather than the words gave his speech humor, human warmth. In coming months Ron would learn that Earl had several vocabularies and selected the one he wanted according to whom he was talking to and what it was about. He could use this soft, twangy voice and exaggerate it to buffoonery—or, he could give off the obscenely vicious radiations of a rabid doberman. When he talked about law or literature, he used perfect diction, a mellifluous voice, and precise phrase selection. Relaxed and friendly now, he was interested in the younger man, but not too much. He was offhand rather than intense. When he learned that Ron was assigned to the industrial area—at two cents an hour—he asked if he liked the job.

"Christ, no! But that's where classification put me. What can—" Ron tossed a shoulder to end the explanation.

"If it's worth a pack of Camels, go to sick call on Monday. Ask for a convict clerk named McGee. He's just inside the door in the clinic ... a big dude about forty with gray hair. He'll get you a medical lay-in for thirty days. Actually, for a carton a month you never have to work. But it's best to get something. Where you work is half the secret of doing easy time."

"The other half?"

"Where you live."

"What's the guy's name?"

"McGee. Ivan McGee."

The old con and the youngster stood talking in the shadow of the shed, indistinguishable from the teeming four thousand, two voices lost in the sea of sound. Ron was articulate when he had something to say, but he was not by nature loquacious, and in this unfamiliar environment he had become even more reticent. Not until later did he realize that Earl had him talking easily, about his case, about Pamela, about his situation. Forgotten was the discomfiture, the sense of being out of place. Earl seemed interested in his success in narcotics trafficking, and he told with some pride how he'd started selling ten-dollar bags and expanded until he was rich within a year. It was delicious to recall those days of glory. He knew that he'd made more money as a criminal than ninety-eight percent of those around him, men he now had to fear. Earl's face indicated his interest. Once he corrected Ron about prison ethics. Ron used the term "inmate," Earl cut in: "Uh-uh, brother. An 'inmate' is a weak, sniveling punk. It's an insult. 'Convict' is the term that solid dudes prefer." This correction was the first tiny lesson, gently given, the forerunner of many.

The lower yard opened and the press of bodies lessened as men went down to sit in the bleachers, lie on the grass, play handball and horseshoes, or strum guitars. The canteen lines were running. And men came from the crowd around the canteen carrying pillowslips of commissary.

Paul Adams and Bad Eye came up. The latter had two brown bags from which the tops of milk cartons peeked out. Paul had an open quart of buttermilk and a sack of tortilla chips. He and Bad Eye glanced at Ron with momentary curiosity, nodded a greeting. He remembered them from the lower yard during the riot, but didn't recall Bad Eye's name. Paul's he remembered; the whitehaired man stood out among the youths even more than Earl did.

The new arrivals aborted the conversation. Ron hadn't realized how much he was enjoying himself talking to Earl. He now experienced a momentary pique.

Earl offered Ron the sack of chips and buttermilk, but Ron made a wry face and turned them down. "Buttermilk, blah."

"There's sweet rolls and regular milk," Bad Eye offered, indicating the sack.

"No, thank you," Ron said.

"Go ahead," Bad Eye said, voice rising.

"Hold on, young 'un," Paul said, pursing his mouth and shaking his head. "You always wanna force a dude to take a gift. Maybe he isn't hungry."

"I'm not," Ron said.

"Don't turn it down if you are," Bad Eye said. Then to Earl. "C'mon, we gotta get to the gym. Brother T is holding some weights and there's some brew in the equipment room. He'll be madder'n a Jap if we don't show pretty soon."

"Wanna smoke some grass?" Earl asked Ron.

"No thanks. I would, but I've got to see somebody up here in a few minutes."

"Suit yourself." He slapped Bad Eye on the back and they turned to go.

Watching the figures leave, Ron felt a mingled sense of loss and jealousy because they belonged and he didn't. For lack of anything else to do, he wandered under the high weather shed where a dozen convicts had spread newspapers and laid out scores of paperback books for the weekly exchange. They would also sell them for a pack of cigarettes for two, sometimes only one, depending on the title and condition.

Ron was looking down at the books when someone touched his shoulder. He turned—and so did his stomach. Psycho Mike faced him, the swarthy face devoid of expression except for the maliciously glittering eyes. Ron fought back the surge of dismay, knowing that any sign of weakness would magnetize aggression. The surprise wiped out his resolve to bluff, and then fight if necessary.

"You been duckin' me, *ése*," Psycho said.

"We were locked up until this morning," Ron said.

The Puerto Rican nodded, but he hadn't been listening, didn't care; his mind was locked on its own intentions. The crowd was close around them, and he was keyed up and fidgety.

"C'mon, *ese*. I wanna talk to you. You got a problem."

Psycho Mike jerked his head and made his way through the crowd, but watched Ron from the corner of his eye in animal wariness. Ron followed unprotesting, thoughts twisting, conscious of weakness in his legs, resenting the peremptory order and yet afraid to balk. Maybe he could avoid trouble.

They approached the mess hall wall where there were fewer convicts. Some of Psycho Mike's friends were spread along the wall, faces set in permanent masks of toughness, watching the two men approach. Psycho Mike stopped just beyond the hearing of his friends.

"Some guy's talkin' bad about you," Psycho Mike said.

"Who's that?"

"Some white dude in the West block . . . says you're a rat."

The word fell like an electrical charge, as terrible an accusation to a convict as a death sentence, and virtually the same. "That's crazy! It isn't true!" Then indignation was overcome by fear. "I don't even know anybody here," he croaked.

"I don' know, mon . . . but we gotta see him . . . get it straight. Like, if you are a rat and you been hurtin' my name by hangin' around me . . ." The words trailed off into silent threat while he nodded his head for emphasis.

"Well . . . it's a mistake. How do we see him? I don't want my name fucked over."

"We'll go over to the West block after lunch. I told him I'd bring you." The words were cold with menace.

"The West block is out of bounds. Can't we get him out here on the yard?"

Psycho Mike shook his head. "No, we gotta go over there after lunch. The regular bull on the mess hall gate gets relieved and doesn't know who lives over there."

Ron's sightless eyes were on his shoetops, and his lips sucked together as if they'd been touched by a persimmon, but the expression hid his overpowering sense of being trapped. His hands were jammed in his pockets and were wet with sweat. Temporarily forgotten was his loathing of Psycho Mike.

Convicts sauntered by, going about their own business, and Mike's cohorts eyed the conversation they couldn't hear. Ron looked up, and despite his dilemma, or perhaps because it made him more acute, he was struck by the drab monochromatic colors—dull green buildings, dead blue denims. The lack of sun made everything gray.

They stood speechless for a minute, Ron looking away but aware of Psycho Mike's stare. Then police whistles blew, indicating it was time to form up lines for lunch or clear the area. Those who weren't eating could go to the other side of the yard or the lower yard. A guard came along, shooing convicts like chickens.

"Let's go eat," Psycho Mike said.

Ron accepted the trek to the West cellhouse, but he rebelled against eating with the man. "I don't feel like it. I'm going to walk around the lower yard, get myself together. I'll meet you after lunch."

"Up here. You be up here." The threat beneath the order was open.

As Ron went down the stairs he looked over the field where bullets had rained the last time he'd seen it. Now a cheering crowd of several hundred convicts watched an intramural football game. Cleats dug into grass stained with blood, and Ron was amazed at how quickly convicts forget. He heard music from a jazz group. In the distance Mount Tamalpais was crowned with cumulus.

Ron didn't know what to do. He had no reason to doubt Psycho Mike's story, though it was utterly unreasonable. He didn't know anyone in the West cellhouse. He wondered if the narcotic agents had set him up. They'd offered him a soft deal if he cooperated and were enraged when he'd refused. No, that was crazy. It was just a mistake and would be corrected when he saw the man. Yet what if the man persisted? Ron knew the code required him to make the man retract or else do him violence, in a kind of trial by force. Without a retraction or a stabbing, the accusation would be taken as true. He would be a reviled outcast and someone—a twenty-year-old psychopath craving a reputation—might run a shiv into his spine. He could go to the yard office and ask to be locked up, but that would be taken as a confession.

He found himself at the gymnasium door when what had been lurking in the back of his mind surfaced. He'd put the story before Earl, ask advice. He wouldn't ask for help, but he knew that he was hoping for it.

The gymnasium, the prison's newest building, had a guard inside the door checking privilege cards. As Ron held his card out for inspection, he scanned the vast room. Tall, supple blacks in red gym shorts were playing half-court basketball. Chicanos and whites were watching games inside the two four-wall handball courts. The weightlifting platforms were filled with workout groups, each one with three or four men. Ron saw T.J., remembered the craggy face from the laundry during the strike. Now the weightlifter was bare-chested, his muscles pumped up and flushed with blood. His massive arms were marred with jailhouse tattoos. He was sitting on the end of a padded bench, two other men with him. He sprawled back, raised his arms to where a rack held an Olympic weight bar, on each end of the bar five forty-five-pound wheels. It totaled well over four hundred pounds. The two assistants lifted the weight from the rack and held it until T.J.'s extended hands had a grip. "Okay," he said. They let go. The weight came down, went back up with seeming ease, descended again, and then rose slowly, the great arms quivering for a second until the elbows locked firm. The two men took it away and put it on the rack. Ron exhaled, realizing he'd been holding his breath.

"Get on, Superhonky," an onlooker said, bringing a grin and a wink from T.J. as he swung up to his feet, arms extended from his sides, the blood vessels on his shoulder caps swollen into hard ridges.

Ron went up on the platform, through the groups of men. T.J. saw him coming and gave an impassive nod of recognition.

"Where's Earl?" Ron asked.

"They're all up in the equipment room," T.J. said. "An' they're up to no good." When Ron hesitated, T.J. jerked with his head and pointed with his eyes toward a wide mezzanine at the far end of the gym. A third of it was wired off with heavy mesh and here were stored football and baseball uniforms. The rest of the mezzanine was a television viewing area.

Skirting the basketball court, Ron went up the stairs and rattled the door by banging on the mesh with the heel of his hand. The inside of the area was invisible because the uniform racks were set to hide it.

A slender Chicano, shirtless and barechested except for a dangling medallion, appeared from behind the uniforms. His visage was thin, ferretlike, but his hazel eyes were ready for quick laughter. Before Ron could speak, the Chicano called back over his own shoulder, "Earl, that youngster is here."

The reply was inaudible, but the Chicano unfastened the lock and opened the door. Behind the uniforms was an area with a Ping-Pong table and chairs. Half a dozen convicts were spread around, and a sweet alcohol odor came from a plastic mattress cover on the table. It was loaded with liquid and the pulp of oranges and its folded mouth stood upright. Paul Adams was dipping a gallon can inside and pouring the contents into a plastic tumbler. He handed the can to the shirtless Chicano who'd opened the door.

"Hot Vito, baby," said Bad Eye from a corner. "Don't get too drunk. You're too smooth to lose your senses."

"Man," Paul said. "Hot V's got a prick like a horse. You'd better not mess with him. Show him, V."

Vito grinned impishly but said nothing. He was too busy drinking.

Earl Copen was on a chair tilted against the one solid wall, a coffee jar filled with home brew in his hand. "Yeah, remember Vito put that sissy in the hospital with a split asshole last year."

"You motherfuckers got dirty minds," Vito said.

Bad Eye was at the brew sack. He glanced to Ron, who stood just inside the room. "Want some? It's pretty fuckin' good hooch."

Ron shook his head, feeling ill at ease and out of place. These were volatile men, and half-drunk more unpredictable than usual.

Yet there was apparently no resentment at his presence. Nobody looked at him with hostility. He caught Earl's eye and motioned that he wanted to talk. Earl thunked the chair down and followed Ron outside. The room was noisy behind them.

"I'd like to borrow a knife," Ron said without preamble.

"Whoa!" Earl said, holding up both hands. "Not so fast. I can't give you a piece if I don't know who it's for. I gave one to a guy once and he stabbed a couple of my friends in the Mexican Brotherhood. And they might've wanted to kill me if they found out . . . even though I didn't know. What is it? Psycho Mike making trouble?"

"No, not him directly, but—" And Ron told the story, at first hesitant and stilted, but then in a rush. Earl listened with the wisp of a smile, but his eyes drew narrower and the flesh around them flickered.

When Ron finished, he became aware that Bad Eye's face was at the wire on the door, like a fish at the glass of an aquarium. He'd been listening unnoticed.

"I know I've got to stop that kind of talk," Ron finished.

"Think he's needin' a knife, Bad Eye?" Earl asked.

"Yeah . . . to stick in that greasy Puerto Rican for tryin' that stale ass game."

Earl looked Ron directly in the eye. "They want to trick you over to the West block. There's just one bull in the whole building. They were going to pull you in a cell and rape you."

Ron colored, furious at such treachery and embarrassed at his own gullibility.

"It's no big thing," Earl said. "Lemme go talk to the dude."

The burden on Ron was lightened, but he didn't want to involve Earl, and he didn't want to be obligated. Not knowing what to say or what he wanted, Ron didn't answer.

"Stay here," Earl said.

"I don't want you to fight my battles for me."

"I'm not, man. If I thought I was going to have trouble, I wouldn't go. But he's playing a game and I've been playing games around here for eighteen hard years. It's easier if you're not on the scene."

"I'm goin'," Bad Eye said.

"Fuck you," Earl said with an affectionate grin. "You're drunk and you get too extreme even when you're sober. We don't want a war over some bullshit."

"He might not like you gettin' involved."

"I'll take Superhonky. And Ponchie, if I can find him—just to stand in the background and look tough. If we're gonna have some trouble, you'll be there—'cause I know you ain't gonna let nothin' happen to me. I raised your ass."

When Earl went down the mezzaine stairs, Bad Eye asked Ron if he wanted to go inside. Ron declined.

Inside, Bad Eye repeated the story to Paul and Vito.

"Is Earl tryin' to fuck that kid?" Vito asked.

"Naw," Paul said. "He might think he wants to, but he won't turn him out. Earl hasn't got any dog like that in him. What's happened is that kid's found a friend."

"Shit!" Bad Eye said. "Earl's an old snake in the grass."

"Hold it! He befriended you when you were just a shaver."

"I was a tush hog and a bully when I was a baby."

"Okay, tush hog . . . but it's still not a smart move for Earl. Someone that young and good-looking is a time bomb around here. There's a lot of animals here. There's some crazy motherfuckers here—"

"We're crazy as anybody," Bad Eye said.

"Right . . . but you know there's nobody *that* strong here. We don't know every maniac. I mean . . . you know what I mean."

They knew—any fool can kill you.

Psycho Mike and his retinue were among the last to leave the mess hall. Despite the bright day, their jacket collars were turned up. They slouched along in arrogant toughness.

But a viper gives no warning, Earl thought, and a coral snake is pretty. He was standing nearby, leaning on a steel pillar of the shed, while T.J. and Ponchie stood twenty yards away in feigned nonchalant conversation.

Earl strolled casually toward Psycho Mike's group, thinking that these kids had seen too many motorcycle movies. He kept his hands exposed to show he wasn't armed—though he wouldn't have put his hand under his clothes even if he was; that showed the hole card. He was thinking that he would have to be delicate, imply the threat without showing it, be careful not to upset insecure egos. He wanted to get through without violence—not that he was afraid of violence when necessary, but he *did* want to get out of prison one more time without having to break out.

Psycho Mike's eyes were on him; his face was hard and he'd noticed Earl's allies, though they were giving no indication that they were involved.

"Excuse me, Mike," Earl said. "I need to talk to you." He angled between Psycho Mike and the gang, separating them, and then eased away a few steps. Mike stepped with him, warily.

"I heard about that guy in the West block putting a jacket on Ron."

"So, *ése*?"

"So it's bullshit."

"He's gotta do something about it. It makes me look bad."

"I know it isn't true . . . and the kid is ready to cut the guy's head off. He's got a shiv." Earl paused, noted the flicker of surprise in Mike's eyes. "Personally, I don't want to see him get in trouble. Both of us are his friends. We can go over and see the dude . . . do *whatever* has to be done. Maybe you're not that involved . . . I dunno. If you're not, tell me who the dude is and T.J. and Ponchie and me'll go see him."

Earl spoke with such sincerity that Psycho Mike was confused. He couldn't be sure it was a ploy, and his scheme shriveled up. He was not afraid of Earl, whom he didn't really know and thought was too old to be tough, but he knew of T.J. and Ponchie and the White and Mexican Brotherhoods. Psycho Mike's ego would have required that he make a stand in a straightforward power play, but Earl's strategy left him an out.

"Whaddya think?" Earl asked.

"We don't have to do that. I'll see the guy and pull him up. I thought something was funny 'cause he's from Sacramento, not L.A. He's got Ron mixed up with somebody."

"I'll really appreciate that, bro," Earl said. "I'd hate to see serious trouble over nothing."

Psycho Mike grunted noncommittally. He'd been outmaneuvered and was certain Earl had the same plans he had for the youth. Why else would a hardrock con put himself out on a limb for a pretty kid?

Earl didn't know what his intentions were about Ron, nor why he'd become involved. He would have snorted derisively at the mention of altruism and become irritable if accused of trying to make the kid a queen. At the moment, however, he was giddy from relaxed tension. He walked down the stairs between his friends, patted Ponchie on the back and thanked him for coming along. They'd known each other since juvenile hall but were in different groups, and Ponchie was under no obligation to get involved in Earl's problems.

"You didn't need me, *carnal*. You could bust a foot in all their asses."

"Maybe . . . but sometimes it's better to be a fox than a lion. You being there cinched the domino that we'd skate without a shit-storm."

When they reached the lower yard, Ponchie went off toward where some Chicanos were gathered around a trio with guitars singing *rancheros*.

"That guy's all right," T.J. said.

"Solid and game," Earl said. "But he gets wilder as he gets older. He was cooler when he was twenty-two."

"Fuck, they made him a mad dog in these places. Happens all the time."

"Sometimes you're pretty perspicacious, old country boy."

"What the hell does 'pers-shit' mean?"

*   *   *

When they pushed through the gymnasium door and turned right, they saw Paul, Bad Eye, Vito, and Ron being marched down the mezzanine stairs by three guards, the last guard carrying the sack of home brew over his shoulder. Some of the other convicts in the gym stopped to watch the bust. A few scattered catcalls rang out, but they were more for form's sake than out of real indignation.

As prisoners and guards crossed the basketball court and headed toward the door, Earl and T.J. had to step aside to let them pass. Paul was first, strolling hip, as if the guards didn't exist. He shrugged as he passed. Vito was next, still smiling mischievously. He winked. Bad Eye, however, was flushed and glowering. "These assholes say I'm drunk," he said as he went by. Ron was last, his face grim, but he nodded recognition with the shadow of a smile.

"That other mess is square," Earl said to Ron.

"Don't talk to 'em, Earl," the guard with the sack said, a pudgy little sergeant with tufts of booger-encrusted hair coming from his nose. He was notorious for his halitosis and for snitching on other guards. He loathed influential convicts like Earl.

T.J., who shared a cell with Bad Eye, said, "Well, damn, leastways I can jack off in peace for a few days."

"Yeah, they'll be out in a week. I wonder why they busted Ron. He wasn't even in there when we split. He wasn't in the jug."

"Man, you're gettin' like a father. He can do a week in the hole. What the fuck. It'll do him good."

"Yeah, I guess." But Earl was thinking of Ron's court situation, that the judge was going to call him back, and although this was a trivial infraction, it was a bad way to begin. Moreover, the intercession with Psycho Mike seemed to have created responsibility; having helped once, he was obliged for some reason to help again— if he could. If it was only some other fuckin' sergeant, he thought. He could influence some old-time guards, and others could be influenced by Seeman. But some would take pleasure in thwarting him, and would like to lock him up if they could catch him.

T.J. had wandered to the weight platform where he got an eyewitness report of the bust. Someone must have snitched because the sergeant and two guards had headed directly for the equipment room. Ron Decker had been sitting at the head of the stairs, and as the guards crossed the gym, he'd gotten up and knocked on the wire. He'd been arrested as the lookout.

Earl snorted and shook his head. "It was a classy move, but futile. They couldn't have stashed that much booze in thirty seconds."

"He did what he was supposed to. I kind of respect him."

"So did the Light Brigade . . . Aw, fuck, maybe I can do something, not for the fellas. They're dead."

"I oughta hit you in your chest. You're schemin' on that boy . . . an' you're goin' to a lot of trouble. We can just rip him off. He sho' nuff is purty. I wouldn't mind . . . ummmph."

"Now, boy, you ain't gonna do that," Earl said, but his tone erased any order from his words. T.J. loved Earl, would do anything for him, including murder, but to be ordered by anyone to do or not to do something was an automatic cause for rebellion. Earl was the same way, but the years had smoothed his rough edges; he could usually hide his feelings from the guards, and his friends didn't give orders. All of them had the same view of authority.

"So what're you gonna do, suck his prick?"

"He couldn't come anything but honey, pretty as he is."

"You've got enough time in where you've got a license."

"It's always all right if it's true love and you don't get caught and ruin your image." Earl barely thought of his words; they were part of a standard routine about prison sex. It was a jocular credo that after one year behind walls it was permissible to kiss a kid or a queen. After five years it was okay to jerk them off to "get 'em hot." After ten years, "making tortillas" or "flip-flopping" was acceptable, and after twenty years anything was fine. So the banter said. It was not a true reflection of the ethos, which condemned anything that didn't ignore male physiology. It did, however, reflect a general cynicism about roles played in the privacy of a cell. Too many tough guys were caught in *flagrante delicto*.

Earl thought about what might be done. Fitz would type the disciplinary reports in the yard office. After the sergeant signed, he or Fitz could steal them back. It was often done on small offenses where the particular guard didn't check the results of the disciplinary hearing. Sometimes the clerk just "misplaced" them, so if there was an outcry, he could simply take them out of a drawer or discover them lost in other papers on his desk. The flaws here were twofold: *This* sergeant would check to see what had happened, and all four men were in segregation.

Maybe Seeman could talk the sergeant into quashing the report? No, the sergeant was under Lieutenant Hodges's supervision.

"What we need is a postponement," Earl said; then noticed that T.J. was gone. Looking around, Earl saw him burying punches into the heavy sandbag. He wore no gloves and his knuckles would soon be raw meat. Nobody would mistake him for Sugar Ray Robinson, but his hands were blurs and the punches devastating.

When T.J. came back, he asked, "What now?"

"Got any dope?"

"Nope, no dope. Some weed, but they want to sell it—to *us*. That's insultin'. I'd rather sniff some glue."

"You and Paul and Bad Eye."

"Let's go outside and play some handball. I can beat your big ass at that—especially when you're all puffed up."

"You do okay for an ol' man. But I'll kick your ass today."

"Okay, Muscles, get your glove. Be on the court when I get back."

"Where you goin'?"

"I got an idea to get Ronnie out of—"

"*Ronnie!* Sheeit!"

"Fuck you," Earl said, grinning as he pushed out of the gym.

97

As Earl came around the corner and saw the yard office, he remembered that Big Rand was on vacation for a week. The guard had confided that he was going to Tahoe without his wife to meet a secretary from the outside administration building.

"I wish the big slob was here," Earl said to himself. Instead, Joe Pepper, nicknamed Deputy Dog by the convicts, was on duty. Rather, his feet were on the desk, soles worn through. He was all cop in attitude, but not that dangerous because he was lazy and dumb. He thought Earl Copen was a model convict.

As Earl went inside he saw the bad-breathed sergeant at the desk in the lieutenant's office, scribbling his report on a yellow tablet. Fitz was typing and didn't see Earl, who looked over the day clerk's shoulder and saw he was working on minutes from the last Indian Cultural Club meeting. Earl leaned over and said, "Let's go check the fishpond."

Fitz stayed out of trouble because he didn't want to jeopardize his chances for parole. He wanted to get out and help his people. But he took vicarious pleasure in Earl's intrigues. He put the cover on the typewriter and took a slice of dry bread from a drawer. He'd do his daily chore of feeding the fish while they talked.

The pellets of bread plunked into the water, drawing the goldfish tribe, while Earl told him about his plan, clarifying the last touches in his mind as he talked. When he finished, he asked, "Think it'll work?"

Fitz nodded. "Probably. Things could go wrong, but they'd be bad luck. It's really pretty slick. He'll check the results, but he'll never go back and see it's a different report. If he does, we're in deep shit. Try and stall the typing so he signs just before he goes off duty. But if you can't, fuck it. The captain's clerk will be on the lookout for it."

"You leave early," Earl said. "I'll come in at three."

In "B" Section the guards conducted a perfunctory body search, scarcely watching as the four convicts stripped and went through the ritual dance of showing cranny and orifice. One by one they were put in the first four holding cells on the bottom tier. In Ron's cell there was a filthy striped mattress on the floor with two blankets in a tangle on top of it. Both the light fixture and the toilet had been torn from the wall, leaving scars of bare concrete around the holes. There was just enough light coming through the bars to be able to see. The top of a gallon can was covered with a magazine—the toilet. The sink was still in place, coated with grime. They must've forgotten it, Ron thought. He'd heard that the men in "B" Section had burned and destroyed their cells during the first night of the strike.

As soon as the guards left, convicts came up to talk to Bad Eye, Vito, and Paul. They were men in segregation who were let out to work. Ron folded the blankets into a pillow and lay down. He could hear voices, snatches of words and frequent laughter. He wondered why he didn't feel worse. He expected to be terribly depressed, but instead he felt empty. Maybe so much tension for so long sapped the capacity for emotions.

"Hey, Ronnie," Bad Eye called.

For a moment Ron hesitated, disliking the diminutive; then Bad Eye called again and he answered, "Yeah."

"Are you all right?" Bad Eye asked.

"I'm okay."

Several convicts walked by the cell, including some blacks with mean expressions. None said a word. In the jail they had usually tried to test him in some way, and even in prison a couple had approached him—and he met them with cold aloofness, seeing that it was really hostility rather than friendship. Now they just glanced in and kept going, and he sensed it was because he'd been arrested with Bad Eye and the others.

A shirtless convict appeared, his bulky torso a collage of blue tattoos, many drawn as roughly as a first-grader's picture. He pushed through a stack of magazines with a pack of cigarettes and matches on top. "Here you go, brother."

"Where'd these come from?"

"From the Brotherhood—me. I'm with T.J. and Bad Eye. They call me Tank. How's Earl?"

Ron wondered how the man knew that he knew Earl. "He's okay."

"Good dude. Got a lot of sense." When everything was through the bars, Tank leaned against them and asked for a cigarette. "I didn't bring any for myself."

Tank lit a cigarette and asked how long Ron had been in San Quentin. It was a conversation of introduction, slightly stilted but not uneasy. Then, somehow, Tank was telling his story. He'd escaped from reform school, where he'd been sent for chronic truancy, and stole a car. He was sent to a youth prison where he'd killed a man and been sentenced to death. After a year on Condemned Row, he'd gotten a new trial and pleaded guilty for a life sentence. He was now twenty-five years old, had been in jail for eleven years, the last six in segregation in Folsom and San Quentin. There was a forthright, almost childlike naïveté in his manner. A year ago the casual references to murder would have nonplussed Ron, caused a pang of fear. Now he felt sorry for the young man, who was his own age and both wiser and dumber than he, who knew nothing of life but prison, whose desires concerned prison, whose idea of freedom was to get out on the big yard with his "brothers." He seemed to include Ron automatically in that circle, and somehow it made Ron feel good.

"Do you need anything else?" he asked.

"The mattress is filthy. Are there any sheets?"

"You're not supposed to have 'em down here on the bottom floor but I'll bring some. Put the blanket over 'em. I'll bring some coffee, too."

When Tank left, Ron flopped back on the mattress, feeling happy. He knew it was ridiculous to feel so good in the hole. Yet for the first time since his arrival, he felt accepted. He didn't yet blend, but he felt stronger; it was good to have friends, to be liked, to belong, to have someone do something as simple as bringing cigarettes and coffee.

A while later, when the workers were locked up for count, he talked to Paul, who explained that they would go to disciplinary court in the morning and would probably get five days.

The evening meal was cold, but Ron was hungry and got it down. Then he leafed through the magazines, mostly old *Playboys* with the pictures of naked ingenues razor-bladed out. Several articles were interesting. He put his head against the bars to get the striped light on the pages.

"B" Section was continuously in an uproar. Conversations were screamed from the fifth to the first tier, usually by means of a relay man. One had to yell to be heard in the next cell. Ron tried to block out the cacaphony and hoped it would quiet down later. He jerked, surprised, when someone ran up to his cell, blocking out the light.

"Here," the convict said, putting his hand through the bars and dropping something on the concrete floor. The figure was gone before Ron could see who it was. The "something" was a note wrapped in Scotch tape. Ron disgustedly began ripping the tape off; it was probably a sick proposition from some pervert. He'd already gotten such a note in his regular cell, asking him to tie a towel to the bars if he was interested.

When he saw it was from Earl, he grinned at his own paranoia. It said:

> Make the D.C.
> read the report out
> loud and plead not
> guilty. Tell Paul I
> signed him up for A.A.

Ron tore the note to pieces and turned to flush them before he saw the hole where the toilet should have been. He dropped the note into the can, which he held in one hand while he pissed into it. "If they want to fish it out of there, they're welcome." He wondered what Earl's instructions meant. He didn't bother to relay the rest of the message to Paul. It wasn't worth fighting the din around him.

After 10:30 the noise dropped a decibel or two, and from the morass of sound Ron began to recognize certain voices by timber and catch snatches of conversation. Above him, perhaps on the second tier, he picked up a gumboed black voice saying he'd like to kill all white babies, while his listener agreed it was the best way to handle the beasts—before they grew up. A year earlier Ron would have felt compassion for anyone so consumed by hate, and whenever whites casually used "nigger" he was irked. Now he felt tentacles of hate spreading through himself—and half an hour later he smiled when a batch of voices began chanting: "*Sieg Heil! Sieg Heil! Sieg Heil!*" The chant drowned out everyone else for ten minutes, and when it finished there was a temporary calm in the storm of sound.

"Brother James," a Negro voice called. "Can you hear them white beasts?"

"Yeah, brother . . . their time's comin'."

"Your Aunt Jemima mammy's time is comin', coon."

"Listen to the beast, brother."

"He won't give his name. What's your name, honky?"

"Call me *Massa*, uncle," the voice said in gross parody of a southern sheriff. It elicited a cluster of white laughter.

Ron's fear-filled hate of the nearby black was suddenly overcome by disgust. This was sick. Two hundred men occupied the terraced cells, each cell as identical as the compartments of a honeycomb. Each man was worse off than a beast in a zoo, had less space—yet all these men did was hate and revile others who were equally outcast. Yet he knew he would say nothing, could say nothing, or the whites would tear him apart—and as for helping the blacks, he'd seen a white hippie in the jail be friendly. He'd been beaten and raped. It was an endemic disease, and he was catching it.

Eventually Ron fell into a troubled sleep, thinking of Pamela, while the voices went on until the wee hours of morning.

On the floor of "B" Section was a cinder block building that served as an office. The structure had had windows once upon a time, but too much falling glass had caused them to be replaced with sheet metal. The Disciplinary Committee met in the office.

Ron and Bad Eye stood with a guard outside the door. Paul and Vito, who had already received seven-day sentences, were totally unconcerned as they went back to their cells.

A voice from within called, "Decker."

Ron started to enter, but the guard stopped him and patted him down for weapons. In Soledad a convict had stepped into the Disciplinary Committee, pulled a knife, and dived across the desk to kill a program administrator.

Three men sat behind a table, solemn as prelates in their cheap, unfashionable suits. On the table sat piled manila folders, each one containing a file. Ron's name was on the thinnest file of all.

"Sit down. Decker," the center man said; his head seemed to grow neckless from his narrow shoulders. It was topped by thin gray hair cut high above the ears. His face was sallow and brown liquid eyes were magnified behind wire-rimmed glasses. A nameplate on his coat pocket said "A. R. Hosspack, Program Administrator," and he was obviously in charge.

As Ron edged around to sit gingerly on the straight-backed chair, he smelled cheap cologne. It was especially intense because he'd already become unaccustomed to such smells.

A black lieutenant beside the program administrator found the right manila folder, opened it, and passed it to the center. The third man was younger, with much longer hair; he had no nameplate.

"We have a disciplinary report here," Hosspack said. "Do you want us to read it?"

"Please," Ron said.

"You're charged with D-eleven-fifteen, use of stimulants or seda-tives. 'On Saturday, February 1, while on duty as lower yard sergeant,

103

the writer made a routine patrol of the inmate gym and found inmate DECKER at the top of the mezzanine stairs near the equipment-room door. On entry to the equipment room, the writer found several inmates drunk and in possession of five gallons of home brew (see supplementary reports). The writer believes Decker was keeping lookout.'"

Ron was astounded. Missing was the crucial fact that he'd pounded on the door and warned those inside. Earl had somehow . . .

"How do you plead?" Hosspack asked.

"Not guilty. I—" He let it hang.

"But the report is accurate," said the third man. "You don't find anything false in it, do you?" His voice had an effeminate shrillness, a bitchiness, as did his hand movement as he spoke. Ron was to learn that most convicts, themselves grossly masculine in every phrase and motion, thought he was a queen.

"It's accurate, but I wasn't a lookout. I was just up there to watch television when they turned it on." Ron spread his hands palms up, for emphasis. He nearly believed the lie. "There's no connection with me and whatever was going on."

The black lieutenant seemed to nod, as if believing. Hosspack hadn't looked up while Ron spoke. The program administrator was reading the file. "You've only been here a month," he said, sliding the file to his younger colleague. "You're doing a lot of time."

"Yes, sir," Ron said.

"Step outside," Hosspack said. "We'll discuss it."

Ron stepped out and closed the door.

"What happened?" Bad Eye asked.

"No talking," the guard said before Ron could answer. So Ron tossed a shoulder to show he didn't know.

In less than two minutes his name was called and he went back in, sitting down when the lieutenant nodded at the chair.

"We're going to find you not guilty," Hosspack said. "We just don't have enough here to do otherwise."

Hosspack shrugged off the gratitude, dropped his pencil on the table, and webbed his hands behind his head, all the while studying Ron from behind the glasses with his liquid brown eyes.

"How old are you?" Hosspack asked.

"Twenty-five."

"You look younger. Are you having any trouble? Anybody putting pressure on you?"

For a second Ron wondered if they knew about Psycho Mike, but realized Hosspack only knew how things were likely to be in prison. Ron shook his head. "No, sir."

"That's strange," Hosspack said.

"We've got a lot of animals here," the black lieutenant said. "They'll eat you alive."

"I do my own time," Ron said, knowing *do your own time* was the ultimate prison maxim for both convicts and officials.

"You know what we're referring to, don't you?" said the younger man.

"I've been warned about it ever since I was in jail." Smiling, he added half-facetiously, "I think it's exaggerated."

"No, it isn't exaggerated," Hosspack said. "I've worked twenty years in these places and I've seen thousands of cases. Don't accept favors . . . get obligated."

"I've heard about that, too," Ron said, thinking of the old con in the jail.

"There's also the San Quentin cross," the lieutenant said. "First you get a friend. He doesn't make advances. Then you get pressure from somewhere else, maybe a gang. They want to start trouble with you so you think you've got a violent situation. You can't come to us, you think, so you go to your friend and he comes in like a knight in shining armor . . . puts his life on the line, so you think. Now he puts it to you—drop your drawers or he'll throw you to the gang."

Ron flushed, embarrassed, angry, strongly resenting their attempt to make him appear weak and helpless. "Don't worry," he said. "Nobody's going to make a punk out of me, and I'm not running. If you want to help, take me out of the furniture factory."

"You have to stay there six months," the younger man said. "Nobody likes it there, but you're not at home."

"Let's not get into collateral matters," Hosspack said. "My warning was because you got picked up with some real jewels—*in case* you know them. Bad Eye Wilson is volatile as sweating dynamite. Vito Romero would shoot piss if he thought it would get him high, and Paul Adams . . . he was useless when I came to work here, and he's got worse every year since. It's definitely not the group you want to associate with to keep your nose clean and get out of here." He paused, waiting for a response that was not forthcoming; then turned to the lieutenant. "Anything else?"

"There are some good programs here," the lieutenant said. "You can waste your time or make it pay. You can take a trade, go to school, join some groups. We're not here to fuck you over. If you have any problems, come see me. I'm here to help if I can."

Ron nodded as if he was seriously accepting the advice, but he wanted to ask about the unprovoked murderous fusillade and beatings in the lower yard. Had those things been "help"?

"That'll be all," Hosspack said, nodding that Ron could go. One hand on the doorknob, Ron turned. "When do I get out?"

"As soon as they notify control to make you up a cell move ducat."

When Ron stepped out, Bad Eye stood erect from where he'd been leaning against the wall. "What happened?"

"Not guilty."

"Damn, that sure was a lot of talk for that."

Ron shrugged, but as he walked back to the cell, stepping around the countless pieces of trash that turned the floor into a ghetto alley, Bad Eye's comment made him feel guilty. He hadn't meant anything, but the convict code had a streak of paranoia. Just as a judge needed not only probity but the appearance of probity, a convict needed not merely to be solid, but to have an unquestionable appearance of solidity. Convicts did not indulge in long conversations with officials if they could be avoided.

The cell gate slammed and was locked. Paul called over, "What happened in the high court?"

"They acquitted me."

"You didn't do anything . . . Say, they'll spring you in a few minutes. Tell Earl to send us some smokes and coffee."

"Does he know how to get them in?"

"Oh, yeah, he knows. He has his boss bring them, and nobody fucks with Big Seeman."

Ron folded the blankets, stacked up the magazines, and waited. A few minutes later he could hear Bad Eye cursing, his voice becoming louder as he approached between two guards. The door clanged shut and he called to Paul, "That motherfuckin' Hosspack and that nigger Captain Midnight . . . didn't even crack about the drunk beef. They kept asking about that killing, the one I got cut loose on. Hosspack said he wouldn't have cut me loose . . . I'd bust this fuckin' cell up except there's nothing left!"

"Don't let 'em provoke you," Paul said.

"Provoke me! Them motherfuckers *retained* me. They'll *review* in ninety days! I'll be in this cocksucker a year!"

Ron was silent, but he wondered how anyone's sanity could withstand a year in "B" Section; yet he knew that some men had been locked in there for several years.

Ron Decker turned away from the pass window at the custody office to face the sunny plaza. Half a dozen convicts loitered on the chapel side of the fishponds while the sound of organ music drifted from within. Earl was on the fishpond wall. In a sweatshirt with torn-off sleeves and many holes he was not the Beau Brummel of San Quentin. His head was smooth and shiny in the yellow sun, but a stubble of gray beard was on his jaws. Ron started over, unable to restrain a smile of jubilation at his new friend—and then he wiped it away, wondering if Earl was really a friend. When he got there, Earl reached out to shake hands, and then simultaneously embraced him. For a second Ron froze, unaccustomed to such gestures between men, and also thinking of all he'd heard about Earl. But there was no time to dwell upon it now.

"What happened to the others?"

Ron told him, and Earl grinned until he heard about Bad Eye.

Then he dropped his eyes and shook his head. "They're dirty, sanctimonious whores. They're making a real madman out of him, and then they'll kill him because of what they made."

Ron was impatient to ask, "That report . . . how did you—"

"Shhh," Earl said, looking around, feigning worry about eavesdroppers. "That's top-secret shit. Really wanna know?"

"Sure I want to know."

"That's good 'cause it's too slick not to brag about." So Earl told him about stealing the original report, typing a second with a few changes, and then forging the sergeant's name.

It was so simple as Earl explained it, yet it seemed unbelievable that a convict could do such things. It didn't match what Ron thought he knew about prison before he got there.

"A damn fool would learn to get around if he'd been here long as me." There was something touching in Earl's wry self-disparagement, his awareness of the triviality of such accomplishments. "Let's go to the yard," he said. "We're not supposed to loiter around here."

As they went down the road, they met Mr. Hosspack pushing a handcart with the files toward the front gate. As he passed the two convicts his limpid eyes flicked from one to the other. He looked at Ron and nodded several times, a silent "Uh-huh, now I see you were lying all along." He ignored Earl.

"He told me to stay away from your friends," Ron said.

"I'll bet he did. He doesn't hate me, not personally, but he thinks I ain't worth two dead flies and should be locked up the rest of my life, and from his viewpoint he may be right. He doesn't do half the things to me that I'd do to him if I had the chance."

When they entered the yard, Ron felt even more conspicuous than before. If his youthful good looks contrasted with the milieu, the contrast was exaggerated by his companion, who was at the other end of the spectrum. Ron either saw, or imagined he saw, convicts look at him and then at who he was with; they seemed to be *knowing* looks. These fuckers are like hicks in a small town, he thought.

Across the yard they saw Psycho Mike going the other way. "When you see him," Earl said, "walk on by and don't even look at him. And in general, watch where you go around here. San Quentin has a lot of blind spots and a goodly share of maniacs. I don't want to cut some fool's heart out if it can be avoided."

"Why . . . why are you doing all this?" Ron blurted.

"I don't really know."

"I'm not a punk . . . not gonna be your kid."

Earl's ugly face lit up; when he smiled it was complete and radiant and wiped away the ugliness. "What about me being *your* kid?"

"You're crazy."

"Just lonesome. I take in stray dogs and cats, too. We'll discuss the dynamics later."

Monday began as a typical San Quentin day, so overcast that all light was gray, and even without clouds it took until midmorning for the sun to climb over the buildings. By noon it would be bright, and by twilight it would be glorious, but by then the convicts would be in their cages unable to enjoy it.

The 8:00 a.m. siren whined out work call. The yard gate rolled open and it was as if a dam wall had collapsed. A lake of convicts poured out en route to the industrial area. This was the first day of full work since the strike, and the faces reflected pleasure at going back to looms, saws, and forklifts. Ron had heard several complaints about the loss of wages; six cents an hour bought a jar of cheap powdered coffee and a couple of cans of Bugler tobacco at the end of the month. Many convicts needed nothing more. Many had no means except the factory to get even that.

Ron had expected tension, possibly a hush as the siren recalled the bullets and brutality. But no one seemed to remember the deaths and beatings. Minds were wiped clean as a blackboard under a wet rag. In ten minutes just a few cons were still on the yard, the cleanup crew meandering around with long-handled dustpans and tiny brooms, dabbing at orange peels and empty cigarette packs. The sea gulls descended.

Ron crossed to the South cellhouse, showing his hospital pass to the guard at the door, a heavy steel door studded with rivets.

Convicts pressed out as Ron entered, plunging into the hospital clinic that resembled a bus depot at rush hour. Milling about were dozens of convicts in denim, and collectively they looked as healthy as a football team. A few cons in green blouses moved in and out of examination rooms to the left. At a half-door convicts lined up to get their medical cards and then stood in two other lines to see the pair of doctors. Rather, there were two doctors and one line. One was being boycotted. The doctor's hair, head, and clothes were so askew that he gave the impression of standing in a cyclone. He yelled and gesticulated in a vain try to get convicts to enter his line. One young, skinny black with a woolly Afro was caught. By gestures one could tell that he had a back complaint. In less than a minute he was waving his arms and screaming; the doctor was screaming back.

A cluttered desk stood on a platform just inside the door, but nobody was behind it, and the convict clerk assigned to it was the one Ron was supposed to see. He looked around the throng for a convict in green blouse with a "a dome bald as a baby's butt except for some red above the ears ... and John L. Lewis eyebrows the same color." The man thus described passed so close that Ron missed him until he was at the desk, two cartons of cigarettes in one hand and a medical card in another. A second convict followed him, stopped beside Ron but ignored him. The clerk threw the cigarettes into a desk drawer, ran the medical card into the typewriter, wrote a few lines quick as a machine-gun burst, and jerked the medical card. He inserted a smaller card and typed again. The whole thing took less than a minute. "Okay," he said to the convict beside Ron, "take this little card for the bull to sign."

"Are you sure it's cool? I can't stand a beef."

"That's the two-carton diagnosis, duodenal ulcer, and you get milk three times a day."

"I go to the board."

"Look, the doctor signed the order. It's legal as the Supreme Court."

Ron watched as the convict took the card to the guard, who signed it without glancing at what it said. Ron looked back to the man behind the desk. "Say, are you Ivan McGee?"

"'Tis I, lad. What can I do for ye?" The round red-veined face lost in excess flesh held the same predatory eyes Ron had seen in so many convicts, eyes that were simultaneously fierce and veiled.

"Earl Copen told me to see you about a thirty-day lay-in."

"You're a friend of Earl's?"

"Uh-huh. And they've got me stuck in the furniture factory."

"I can see why you want a lay-in. I suppose Earl will arrange a job change before you need another."

A light flashed in Ron's brain, an awareness of how convicts would view the favors Earl was doing for him. He could see this speculation in McGee's eyes now, and for a moment he wanted to rage out. It was everywhere, and it was sick—and humiliating.

"Got a medical card?" McGee asked.

"No."

"Never been to sick call?"

"No."

McGee filled out a blank medical card, using Ron's I.D. card for name and number. "You sure are a fish," he said. "The ink ain't dry on that number yet." He pulled out the card. "A shoulder separation should keep you idle for thirty days."

"Isn't that painful?"

"Not the way we do it." Grabbing some forms and the medical card, McGee beckoned Ron to follow him through the clinic and up a corridor into the hospital proper. A grill gate blocked the middle of the corridor, watched over by a middle-aged guard in a chair, who opened the gate as McGee approached.

"He's with me," McGee said to the guard, waving the documents to indicate Ron.

"Where to?"

"X-ray."

The X-ray department was in a corner of the second floor. The whole hospital was a separate world from the cellhouses and big yard. It was even outside the walls, though it had its own fence topped with concertina wire, and the ring of gun towers watched over it, too. The floors were polished, and the convicts they passed smiled a civilized "good morning."

In the X-ray department two convicts were playing chess. One was white, the other black. It startled Ron.

"We need a shoulder separation here," McGee said.

"We're here to supply the necessary," the black convict said.

Seconds later, a twenty-five-pound dumbbell was produced. Ron was told to hold it while standing in front of the X-ray machine.

"Just let it dangle," the white convict said. "It's below the photo, but the shoulder will look pulled loose. We call it a York syndrome."

When Ron and Ivan McGee were going downstairs, Ron asked, "What do I owe you?"

"Nothing."

"Man, I owe you something!" Ron said.

"If you insist, get me a couple joints. But you don't have to. Earl and me go way back—"

"What do I do now?"

"Just go to the yard. It will be on the movement sheet this afternoon."

Ten minutes later Ron was on the yard with nothing to do. It was still empty and only a few minutes after 10:00. The lunch lines didn't form until 11:00. Four young convicts were near the canteen, sharing two pints of ice cream. Ron recognized them as part of the group from the laundry wall, Earl's group, but it was not his place to join them. He had nothing else to do so he went to the yard office.

"Earl," the huge guard bellowed when Ron asked. "That no-good fuckin' dope-fiend sonofabitch better never show up if he knows what's good for him." The guard jerked a gas-billy from his hip pocket and slammed it on the desk. It dented the wood. "Oops," he said, glancing back toward the lieutenant's office and putting some paper over the blemish. Then to Ron, he said, "Pay me no mind. I'm crazy. Earl isn't here. He sleeps until fuckin' noon and doesn't come to work until three forty-five."

Still with nothing to do, Ron crossed the plaza to the chapel, stopping to watch the long-tailed goldfish in the pond for a minute. The Catholic chaplain had a library in his outer office, administered by an inmate clerk. Though overwhelmingly stocked with simplistic religious tracts, it also had some philosophical works and biographies. In an *Esquire* article Ron had seen reference to the works of Teilhard de Chardin. He found one by the existential theologian and sat reading until lunch beside the fishpond.

When Ron came through the gate he saw Earl, T.J., and a man he didn't know in the rear of the long lunch line. He was uncertain about approaching until T.J. gave a wide beckoning wave. Earl's gray stubble was longer than yesterday, and now it was on his head, too. "Get that squared away?" he asked.

Ron nodded. Earl ignored him and continued listening to a story the newcomer told, a man named Willy who had just arrived from Folsom. He was describing the murder of someone named Sheik Thompson, and the story obviously satisfied Earl. The killers had caught him stepping through a doorway and broke his leg with a baseball bat. While he was down they'd stabbed him to death. "Right in the recreation shack. The coach was there—inside—and he couldn't get past them to get out. He damn near shit his britches. He couldn't even blow his whistle. When it was over, he ran out screaming like some sissy."

"He is a sissy," Earl said. "But it's hard to believe they *finally* killed that animal Sheik. There's been a dozen tries that I know of. He was a tough motherfucker."

"Yeah . . . yeah," the storyteller said, excitedly remembering something. "When the bulls brought Slim and Buford across the yard everybody . . . everybody gave them a standing ovation. Fuckin' unbelievable. Even the guards were grinning, and he was a snitching motherfucker, too."

Suddenly the lunch line lurched forward, uncoiling the knots of talking men. The conversation ended. Ron was in front of Earl and behind T.J.

After lunch the yard was full until the afternoon work whistle. Ron found himself among nearly a score of convicts, a gathering of most of the Brotherhood. The image of a lounging pride of lions flashed to his mind. Most were in a half-circle around the man from Folsom, Willy, who had eaten with them. He told other stories about what was happening in Folsom, answered questions about how members of the Brotherhood and others were getting along. He was introduced and shook hands with those he didn't know. Earl and T.J. were outside the circle in close conversation with a splenetic small man called Bird, who seemed upset. From their poses and manner, Ron gathered they were soothing him. He felt out of place and wondered if anyone was silently questioning his presence. Then he relaxed somewhat as Baby Boy came up and slapped him on the back before listening to the new arrival.

A few minutes later, Earl touched him on the shoulder. "Let's go play some handball."

"I can't even hit that thing. I'd be embarrassed."

"Fuck all that snivelin'. I play terrible myself. I'll get you some gloves."

Ron went along without enthusiasm, waiting outside the North cellhouse while Earl went in for gloves. "Here," Earl said when he returned, handing over a stiff pair of gloves, "they'll soften when you sweat in them for a couple minutes." The work siren went off as they crossed the lower yard toward the outdoor handball courts. "Nobody'll be here," Earl said. "On weekends there's six million Mexicans on the court." He began throwing the small, hard black rubber ball at the wall in a soft, fluid motion, like the initial tosses of a baseball pitcher warming up. The muscles would loosen until he could strain them without tearing anything.

"The Bird seemed upset," Ron said.

Earl grimaced and stuck out his tongue. "Bird wanted to kill the plumber. His sink is fucked up and the guy hasn't fixed it. We talked him out of it, but . . ."

"Would he kill somebody over that?"

"Oh yeah . . . quick if he thought the guy was deliberately fuckin' him around."

Ron was less shocked than he would have been two months earlier. They played handball for an hour, much of which was spent chasing the ball when Ron missed it altogether, for it had tremendous bounce and speed. The first time he hit it, he nearly quit. It stung wickedly, even through the glove. But soon his hand ceased to hurt, and he liked the feel of fresh air sucked into his lungs because of the exertion. He was down to his floppy T-shirt and a gentle breeze cooled his perspiration. He was having fun. The sun was out, and he forgot he was in prison.

After an hour, exhaustion set in. They came to the shade of the handball court and sat down, using the wall as a brace. The damp T-shirt stuck to his body and made a dark wetness on the wall. Earl, too, was sun-flushed and sweating, though much less so. "You oughta walk around and cool off."

"Too tired," Ron answered; then patted the roll of flesh that fell over Earl's waistband when he sat down. "What's that?"

"Good jailin'."

"On this food?"

"Well . . . every night when you're in the cell, I ease into the kitchen. Nobody's there but a cleanup crew and a couple bulls and my juice lieutenant. We open the refrigerators and cook 'em up." He flipped the ball away and let it roll to a wall fifty yards away. Just beneath his left collarbone, partly hidden by chest hair, was a white scar five inches long.

"Somebody get you, too?" Ron asked.

"Yeah, when I was nineteen years old and thought I was the toughest motherfucker in the world. Now I know everybody can die. No, I knew I wasn't that tough, but I wanted everybody else to think so. We had a little clique—not like the gangs these days—and three of us were gonna bust some guy's head . . . Do you wanna hear this?"

"Sure . . . Stories of violence fascinate just about everybody."

"You'll get a full share here . . . Anyway, we trapped this guy in 'A' Section. It wasn't lockup then. He had a shiv but there was three of us. Another guy was off on the side and I didn't pay him any attention. I should have. He whipped out a shiv and put it in my chest." Earl grunted. "A couple inches lower and he would've got

116

my heart. He hit a lung and blood started coming up in my mouth. I started running for the hospital and passed out kicking on the hospital door. When I woke up, I had tubes in me and an oxygen mask. I'll say this, if they get you to the hospital alive, they'll save you. We got a couple surgeons who are the world's experts on stab wounds."

"What happened to the guy who did it?"

"Ran away . . . turned himself in and gave 'em the knife. They didn't try him because I wouldn't testify. But he knew he had to get off the yard or my partners would turn his lights out."

"Did you ever see him again?"

Earl laughed. "Not for a long time. He got transferred to Soledad, killed a guy, and went to Folsom. Our beef happened fifteen years ago." Earl chuckled. "You already met him."

"Who?"

"Friend McGee in the hospital."

"McGee! You're jivin'!"

"Un-uh . . . him for real."

"What about saving face? I can't imagine someone like you letting it go."

"How can you stay mad for fifteen years? I've been on the streets twice and he hasn't been out. He doesn't talk about it. Even T.J. and Bad Eye don't know . . . just Paul. I'm not afraid of him, and when he transferred in a couple of years ago, it went through my mind. I almost ribbed myself up, but I'm getting old and weak. I want out on the streets one more time. If something comes up and I can't get around it, I'll do what I have to do. I'm not gonna let anybody fuck me over . . . Besides, it taught me a couple of things—that everybody's mortal and to respect everybody."

Ron digested the story, looked out over the guard with the rifle on the wall to the necklace of clouds around the peak of Mount Tamalpais.

"You said you'd tell me why . . . why you've helped me."

"You really wanna hear it?"

"Yes," he said emphatically. "I'm not a punk. I'm already obligated to you, but I'm not paying off by being your kid, queen, or whatever they call it. I couldn't live with myself."

"Man, I haven't—"

"I'm paranoid. I feel like I have to hold one hand over my prick and the other over my asshole. I'm suspicious of anyone who's friendly. I see it in everybody's eyes."

"You haven't seen it in mine."

"No . . . 'cause you're a lot more slick than most of them."

Earl looked off, thinking, and then when he spoke the laconic twang and grammatical barbarisms were gone. "All right, I'll explain . . . as well as I can. There's some kind of homosexuality involved, psychological if not physical . . . if you want to call it that. It's the need for feelings—to feel—that might be given to a woman. Frankly, if you were ugly, I probably wouldn't be interested."

Ron felt an uncontrollable trembling. He disliked this; it reduced him. He started to interrupt but Earl held up a hand.

"But that's my problem, not yours. Even the little I've seen shows me you're neither stupid nor weak . . ."

"I'm just not in my element around here. This is new to me."

"And most of us grew up in it. Anyway, I need somebody . . . a friend. I love T.J. and Bad Eye and Paul, but that's a different thing. They don't fill a certain need. So I'm your friend. I'm not scheming on you. I don't intend you anything but good, and you probably need me. I'm not the baddest motherfucker here, not by far, but my friends are really bad. Prison is a separate world and you have to build a life separate from the world outside. I don't have a family, so my friends are my family. If you try to live in both worlds, you'll go crazy."

"But if this becomes your whole world, you'll forget how to cope out there."

"That happens to a lot of people, and you'll change here . . . if you survive. Maybe you can make me think about the streets. C'mon, let's go up. I have to take a shower and get ready for work . . . not that I do any."

"I can't shower until tonight."

118

"Yeah, you're still in the East block. Maybe we can get you moved over."

"That takes nine months clean conduct. I haven't been here two yet."

"But I've been here eighteen calendars and I know how to get things done. We can probably get you better accommodations in a week or two."

Gathering their shirts, they trudged toward the big yard. The vast cellhouses dominated the skyline like the battlements of castles on mountain crags. As they went up the stairs a Mexican stopped Earl and told him that someone was selling good heroin in the West cellhouse.

On the yard, Earl slapped Ron on the back and disappeared into the cellhouse. Ron felt a sense of loss, realized how swift dependency was growing, and sighed in aceptance. He found a bench in the sunlight and again read the book he'd checked out of the chapel library.

Now that he didn't have to go to the furniture factory, Ron followed Earl's example of sleeping through breakfast and coming out on the lunch unlock. He ate that meal with Earl, and sometimes with T.J. or a couple of others. He liked Earl's friends, the warm camaraderie, and yet never felt entirely at ease. The unease grew to discomfort when many of them gathered in a crowd, so he avoided them when they flocked together, finding that he had to go to the library, chapel, or elsewhere. Earl watched his nervousness and understood, but usually stayed with the clique himself. In the afternoons, after work call, they went to play handball or to sit in the lower yard and talk. The conversations were more deeply personal than any in Ron's life. He was unaccustomed to analyzing his relationships with his mother, Pamela, or why he put such an absolute premium on money, which was an obsession with him. He talked about his life outside and could tell that Earl respected him. He told one lie, thinking it would please Earl; it was in answer to the question if he was committed to crime. He answered, "Yes," but the truth was that he didn't know. His future was undecided; the clay wasn't yet hard.

Earl explained why he sometimes kept away from Ron. The unlikely relationship was bound to be viewed by many convicts as that of a jocker and his kid. "I pull 'em up," Earl said. "But I can't stop thirty-five hundred convicts individually . . . and if I did it would be, 'Methinks thou dost protest too much.' So it's best if I keep as much heat off you as I can."

"I couldn't care less what they think."

"In a way you're right, but in a way you're not. You may spend a lot of years kicking around these places. You never know. If you get a *jacket* as a punk, you'll have that wherever you go. It'll come up twenty years from now. It's the next worse thing to being jacketed as a stool pigeon. All a man in prison has is his name among his peers."

Ron thought it was an exaggeration. As long as he himself knew the truth, it didn't matter what ignorant convicts thought. In the coming months, his attitude would change. He learned that a good name was important, critically so. He saw a man with friends get slapped and do nothing about it. The friends turned their backs and the man was thereafter made to pay his canteen for protection until he finally checked into protective custody and got transferred. Any sign of weakness invited aggression, and the greatest sign was to get buggered. He saw a good-looking young man with blond hair, from a middle-class background, come in and the wolves descend. The newcomer had no friends. In a month he was wearing skin-tight jeans without back pockets. His eyebrows were blocked, and in the eyes something had died. The tough young Mexicans who had turned the blond into a queen eventually "sold" him. Ron then was glad that Earl was as concerned with appearances as with reality.

On Saturday, after two weeks of running with Earl, he passed through the yard gate late in the afternoon. A square-jawed lieutenant with billed hat cocked to the side was standing with a tall sergeant. The lieutenant called, "Hey, Decker."

The lieutenant's nameplate said "Seeman," and Ron knew it was Earl's boss. Still, Ron was embarrassed. The yard was full of convicts and it was always embarrassing to be seen talking to a guard.

"You're Earl's friend, aren't you?"

"Yes, sir."

"I talked to the North block lieutenant, trying to get you moved over. He owes me a favor and he's willing . . . but somebody's been writing the warden snitch letters about people jumping the waiting lists. But . . . there's one way." He winked. "We assign you as a tier tender . . . if you don't mind getting up at six in the morning to pour water. When you're there a while, we get you a job change. You don't have to move out once you're there. How does that sound?"

"It's fine, except I've still got two weeks on a medical lay-in."

"I'm sure you know somebody to take care of that." The lieutenant grinned.

Ron smiled back, nodded, started to leave.

"One more thing," the lieutenant said. "He tells me you're not his kid. I don't care. That's your business and his business, but don't get him in trouble. He's been clean around here and he'll get out in a year or so if he keeps it up."

"I won't get him in trouble," Ron said—and as he walked away, the statement was reinforced in his own mind. The last thing in the world he wanted was to get Earl in trouble. The older convict was already the best friend he'd ever had, like an older brother, maybe a father. It was difficult for Ron, even silently, to articulate the word "love" where it involved another man, but he managed to say it to himself.

One week later, Ron loaded his property on a flat-bedded, iron-wheeled cart and moved to the last cell on the fifth tier of the North cellhouse. By nature acquisitive, he already had more possessions than Earl, including oil paintings purchased from convict artists. One was a huge impression of the prison viewed from the Bay, the other of an East Indian barge man in cruddy turban, with distended pupils and a permanent disfiguring bulge in his jaw, the result of holding wads of coca (cocaine) leaves in there year after year. The first night he had the painting, a black came by, blinked, and went away, returning minutes later. "Say, man, what you doin', makin' fun a' da bro's toothache?" The tone was accusing. Ron explained, but resented the necessity for doing so. He understood black suspicion, but paranoia was a disease. Thereafter he turned the painting to the wall. When Earl heard about it, he laughed. "That ain't nothing. In Soledad they have a race riot over anything. One went down because the white car in a Shell T.V. commercial got better mileage than the black car."

In the North cellhouse Ron began to work as the a.m. tier tender. At 5:00 a.m. a guard woke him by banging a key on the bars. He could go to breakfast then, but he never did. At 5:30 he filled a fifty-gallon drum with hot water and pushed it down the tier on a wagon, filling the cans through the bars with a hose. He had to make three trips. When the other cells were unlocked after 6:00, he swept and mopped, and once a week picked up sheets from the bars, making a list of who turned them in. Until 2:00 p.m. he kept the heavy spike key to let men on the tier in and out of their cells, though after a few days he knew who lived where and handed them the key. Most of them worked, so the only traffic was during the lunch hour. It wasn't a really hard job, and Ron had less aversion to work than the average convict. It gave him time to read, to exercise his mind, to escape the prevailing ugliness and view the endless vistas of articulate men. In a matter of weeks he accumulated a cardboard box full of paperbacks, many brought by Earl, who shook his head in mock disdain whenever he found Ron reading frivolous entertainments. Ron quickly ceased to enjoy trash; it could not knead his mind like Dostoevsky, Hesse, Camus, and Céline, who were Earl's favorites. Ron had always assumed that Jack London wrote children's books until Earl gave him *Star Rover* and *The Sea Wolf*. He liked to listen to Earl talk about books. The older man's demeanor changed. He became enthused, his grammar precise. He had no interest in art forms other than literature, but he didn't necessarily like everything accepted as great. He disliked Dickens and Balzac, and thought Thomas Wolfe shouldn't be read by anyone over twenty-one. In three months Ron read more than he had in his entire previous life. He felt his mind widen, his perceptions become more acute, for each book was a prism refracting the infinitely varied truths of experience. Some were telescopes; some microscopes. Once Ron wanted to take his books to the Saturday-morning book swap, but T.J. was on hand when he mentioned it. "Boy," he said, "don't ya'll know we's gangsters and bullies? If we want some books, by Gawd, we'll just take 'em. You can give yours away if you want, but fuck all that nickel-and-dime shit." It was often hard to tell when T.J. was joshing, but Ron didn't go to the swap. Neither did he give the books away. Eventually he sold them for three cartons of cigarettes and a hand-tooled wallet.

One morning he passed Earl's cell and found him reading *The Happy Hooker*.

"Reading serious literature?" he said.

"Damn sure educational."

"Let me see it when you're through."

"Un-uh, too young. This lady is depraved."

"Shit!"

"Now you wanna be a jack-off idiot. That's what I've raised. You'll get warts on your hands."

"What about you?"

"I'm already crazy. Must be. I keep coming back here. I must like it, too, don't you think?"

Ron shook his head, but felt guilty, for he couldn't deny that anyone who kept returning to prison had to be a fool, or sick, or something. Even Earl. Yet Earl was his teacher, his family behind the walls, his friend. It was disloyal to have such doubts.

The tier-tender job also gave him time to write letters, two or three each week to Pamela, and one every other week to his mother. And one a month to Jacob Horvath. Pamela's replies became fewer and shorter. Vito picked up a battered portable typewriter on a debt and sold it to Earl for a fix, and thereafter it rested in Ron's cell and he used it.

Although Ron never became comfortable on the crowded yard, he temporarily lost his fear. Stabbings decreased for a while after the strike, and when they picked up again, Ron, who normally would have identified with the victim, knew that his associates were the deadliest white clique in San Quentin, and this gave him a feeling of power—until one lunch hour. He and Earl had just come from the mess hall, were walking under the shed where the majority of convicts had been driven by the hot sun. Earl was flipping pellets of crushed bread to the sea gulls and seemed completely relaxed and unaware of the flux of the yard. Suddenly he grabbed Ron's sleeve at the wrist and shouldered into him, turning him as a sheep dog would a lamb.

"Let's go . . . quick!"

"Huh?" But Ron went along, stepping lively away from where they'd been standing. From the corner of his eye he saw a flurry of movement a few feet from where they'd been. He looked more closely. A big Chicano was spinning like a dog chasing his tail, his hand clutching at his chest where the black-tape handle of a shiv jutted forth. His mouth was open in an O, as if he were yawning, but blood was flying out. The crowd was scattering from him. Ron saw a small, dark Chicano fleeing with his head down, weaving into the crowd. The big Chicano saw him and started to give chase, but after two paces, his steps weakened—and suddenly his knees gave way.

The whistles began bleating, the riflemen were aiming, guards were rushing forward, and fifty men were hemmed in. The guards began collecting I.D. cards. If Earl hadn't shoved Ron, both of them would have been in the group.

Now Earl and Ron were outside the shed in the sunlight, and Earl was angry. "Poor fuckin' Pete," he said. "Iced for nothing. *Motherfucker!*"

Now Ron remembered the big Chicano, tall, easy-laughing, who often stopped to slap hands with Earl, Paul, and T.J. Pete had been high in the Mexican Brotherhood. If a man like Pete could be murdered so casually . . . "Won't somebody get revenge?" Ron asked.

"If they can get the guy. What of it? Pete's still dead. They tore somebody off for some *shoes* . . . fuckin' shoes! And the guy didn't take it . . . probably couldn't take it. I keep tellin' our wild friends that. Eventually some sucker is going to sneak up and do *that*. Everybody can die. Everybody bleeds. And everybody can kill in the right situation."

Thirty minutes later the body was gone and the asphalt had a white chalk outline where it had lain. Soon the brogaged feet would erase that, too—the last trace of a living being.

And Ron's confidence ended. He'd never like the yard; now he abhorred it and spent as much time as he could in the cell reading. And where, contrary to Earl's advice, he'd often napped with the door unlocked, now he never did. Something else was sprouting: a hardening to violence. It was part of the human condition; men had settled matters by the sword since the beginning of time, and although it was often foolish and self-destructive, sometimes it was what a situation required. And if he felt fear, it was no longer the fear of helplessness.

Earl Copen's routine—and routine is the key to withstanding prison—changed slightly to accommodate Ron Decker's entrance into his life. Earl still slept late, but now, instead of lounging in his own cell until lunch, he usually visited his friend. Sometimes they played chess, and Earl beat him severely, but he wasn't interested because he preferred to talk. Yet he found a reserve in Ron, a belief in distance and propriety that came from his background. Earl wanted total relaxation, absolute trust. He also wanted Ron to blend better, to be more adaptable. So he charged through the decorum in the crudest prison style, patting Ron's thigh suggestively. "Oh, you must've played football," he would say. Or a San Quentin cliché: "Want some jellybeans, kid?" Or sometimes patting his ass or grabbing his crotch. At first Ron blushed furiously, nonplussed and angry, but he saw that Earl and T.J. and others often played and bantered this way, and though he never ceased to redden, he realized that such things indicated equality and acceptance rather then designs, and he began to quip back: "Keep fuckin' around and I'll pull it out."

"Put it right there," Earl would say, extending his hand.

"Oh no, I don't trust you."

Soon total relaxation came, though Ron was never as spontaneous as the others. And Earl loved him as a surrogate son. He loved T.J. and Bad Eye, too, as if they were younger brothers. Earl loved all of them the same, but he thought about Ron more. From the outset he saw the slender youth, though ill-equipped by background for San Quentin's madness, had strengths that were totally missing from the others, that he himself lacked. Ron could set goals and work toward them, whereas all his other friends lived completely for the moment, psychologically incapable of delaying satisfaction, predisposed to rage at every frustration. These qualities were strengths in situations requiring impetuosity, but a liability when prudence was called for. In many ways, Ron was already more competent than he, but Earl knew things that Ron didn't. The younger man was committed to crime—because drugs were the area where money could be made in the largest amounts in the least time. It made no difference to Earl *what* Ron wanted, but Earl wanted him to be successful, and so told him all he knew about crime and criminals—not techniques for robberies and burglaries, but attitudes and, especially, how to read personalities.

"You have fifty informers, so the police say, on the affidavit. You're not running a Safeway market. Be afraid. Be paranoid. Don't trust anyone at all unless you know them . . . under stress situations. If you're out there dealing big dope, you're a way out of jail for a lot of them. Put protection on yourself, get insulation, always assume the worst. Paranoia is a necessary trait for a criminal."

Earl outlined the organizational structure that provided as much protection as possible. On the outside, he should take one person as partner or chief lieutenant, to handle all dealers; and the dealers should only be able to reach the lieutenant by leaving coded telephone numbers with an answering service. That way, if anyone was arrested, the whole thing would dissolve and reform elsewhere. The answering service was blind; the one person who could inform on Ron would be the chief lieutenant. Risk still existed, but there was a barrier normal police procedures wouldn't get through. At the same time, it was important to keep a low profile so as to avoid arousing a major effort by the authorities.

Earl also implanted his views on life, its ultimate meaninglessness in an indifferent universe. Ron's mind was fallow ground. And even more than the pragmatics of the underworld and prison, more than a philosophical system, Earl provided a matrix that influenced—though he was not immune from Ron's criticism.

They usually ate together except when Earl was off plotting with T.J. and Paul. And in the evenings Earl sometimes came in from work to talk. Movies were shown for the North cellhouse in the mess hall on Wednesday and Saturday evenings, and Ron sat with the clique. He liked the special seats, a whole row that no convict sat in unless invited.

The days drifted into months—by routine.

Ron hadn't gotten a letter from Pamela in weeks, and although it bothered him, it wasn't the overwhelming preoccupation it would have been months before. Then came a letter with a return box number at the Los Angeles Central Jail. She'd been arrested for narcotics and wanted money. The letter gave no specifics except that it was a one-ounce possession and the bail was ten thousand dollars, but the words dripped bitter self-pity and vituperation. Ron carried it out to the plaza, watched the fish move through the water, watched the fountain spew up and gleam in the sunlight. He tried to feel some anguish. He felt nothing. He read the letter again and still felt nothing—except guilt for his lack of feeling. Time and distance had corroded love. Not only that, he now saw that most of his love was built on delusion; he'd been in love with a dope-fiend whore who was compelled to self-destruction, and from his own need he'd garbed her in white robes and put her on a pedestal. Yet did he owe her anything? He could have his mother send some money, not as much as Pamela wanted, but enough for a lawyer or the bail premium.

That evening he showed Earl the letter and asked advice.

"Whatever your conscience tells you is right . . . not what you think other people will think. If she's been a good broad, you should do it. If she's been a jive-ass bitch, fuck her in her ass."

"She's been a jive bitch. She hasn't been up here once."

"Whatever you do is right with me. If you're wrong, you're still right."

Ron tried to answer the letter. The censor sent it back. The regulations forestalled correspondence between prisoners in different institutions without special permission. He neither tried for permission nor wrote again.

One Saturday night five blacks tried to escape by going through a vent in the roof of the South cellhouse and down on ropes through a deep shadow where two cellhouses came together. They gambled that a gun tower guard wouldn't be alert. Two got down without being seen, but the third man was spotted. The alarm sent three dozen guards searching the prison property, while the surrounding water kept the escapees from leaving. All were caught within an hour and were marched back inside naked.

Earl Copen had to work typing the many reports. He missed the movie and Ron went without him, occupying the reserved space next to Paul. While the mess hall filled, they fell into conversation.

"I hear you're going to camp," Ron said.

"Maybe. I did a year of my last bit in the Sierras as a camp cook and the lieutenant wants me back. But I probably won't get it until after I go to the parole board."

"When's that?"

"A couple of months. Depends on when they meet."

"Is there any chance you'll get out?"

"Uh-huh, just about what a mouse has in a cage with a rattlesnake.

128

Three years on a safe burglary with four prior convictions is less than they need to rehabilitate. Next year, God willing and the river don't rise—unless they're trying to justify building another prison. One year they were crying about overcrowding and the need for a thirty-million-dollar institution, and the percentage of granted paroles dropped two-thirds. You've heard of practical politics . . . that's practical penology. I figured to do five or six when I got the beef. And I'm the motherfucker who can do it." Paul ended with a crooked grin.

Not many months before, Ron would have been horrified at the idea of *five* years in prison. He didn't even think of his own six years before he would be eligible for parole; he thought only of the judge calling him back. Now five years wasn't even a *long* term. Earl had served five years his first time. Bad Eye was nearly thirty years old and hadn't been free since he was eighteen. T.J. had served thirty-nine months his first time, beginning when he was nineteen, for giving his eighteen-year-old girlfriend ten marijuana cigarettes. He'd learned armed robbery techniques and put them to use within weeks of his parole. He was back for three years on an attempted robbery.

Paul said, "No matter how many years you do, when it's over, it wasn't shit. Not when you look back. Then it's over. Unless you've gone insane—and you'd be surprised how many strong men crack up and how many others just get stronger. One old man in Folsom, Charley Fitz, smashed forty-six calendar years. He was nearly ninety when he raised. You'd think somebody that old and down that long would be uptight to cope. Shit! He charged out, and sent back a postcard saying, 'Not a goddamn thing's changed. Maybe they move a little faster, but it's still the same bullshit!' He went to the zoo . . ."

Ron smiled, wondering if Paul was telling the truth. Factual truth meant little to Paul if a good lie made his point or was more interesting. And the story of Fitz made a point.

"Did you ever think about straightening up?" Ron asked. "You can't consider yourself a successful criminal . . . Earl can't either. Really, you're both disasters."

Paul reddened, touched at a sensitive point, yet unwilling to protest because he was vulnerable. He could make money, but he couldn't stay out of jail; and it took both to be a success. "Nope, not really. It's like a poker game—you sit down to win, and you don't get up while you're losing."

"That's true—for compulsive gamblers. But if you can't win—"

"I started with fifty years of life expectancy and I've blown thirty. I'm in too deep to quit. The only place I'm comfortable is among thieves. I'm a thief, and prison is the inevitable result. We don't think about staying out the rest of our lives, just how long in between imprisonments. If you do it fifty-fifty, you're a success. I stayed out four years last time, stealing every day. I shit in tall cotton the whole four years. Vegas, Acapulco, Miami, the whole tamale. So I've got memories."

Ron was silently dubious, for he saw Paul as intelligent and perhaps competent at petty crime, but so totally lacking in foresight and self-control that failure at anything bigger was inevitable. He wagered in his mind that these claims were exaggerations, embellished by time in a world where dreams had no limit. Now, however, Paul was displaying insight that Ron wouldn't have suspected.

"Maybe one in ten thousand gets out and makes it, gets back in, makes the—" he gestured with two fingers on each hand to indicate quotation marks—"'middle class.' But society never forgives and forgets the rest of us. It will let us stay free if we accept being pieces of shit. It'll let you shine shoes or wash cars or fry hamburgers. That's for white ex-cons. Think what it is to be *black* and an ex-convict, and probably uneducated. A hundred years ago you could go away. Now the computers keep you from starting over. In 1903 about two dozen men broke out of Folsom, even shot it out with a posse. A couple died right there, a couple others got hanged, but most of them got away and were never heard of again. No doubt some kept robbing, but a lot of them had to get a plow or do whatever squares did then, otherwise they'd have been caught eventually. But they could start new lives.

"The employers all want a computer printout these days. You

can't hide your yesterdays. They don't want ex-convicts—and the funny thing is they're right. A chump goes out of here and he's fucked up. Especially *this* prison. Fuck rehabilitation . . . it's a full-time job to stay alive." He finished with a shrug. "Got a cigarette?"

Ron handed him one. The mess hall was nearly full now. The denimed men filled the rows. The blacks had the entire left section. Paul chuckled. "Sometime I'll show you Earl's first prison mug shot. He looks about fourteen years old and serious as cancer."

"Yes, I'd like to see that. Did he have any . . . problems?"

"Yes and no. Anybody that young has motherfuckers speculating. But he was mean and wild. It was different then . . . no big gangs, no race trouble. If a youngster would stand up, they'd pretty much leave him alone. Now if he doesn't have friends, they just rape him and it doesn't matter how mean he is. King Kong can't stand up to fifteen or twenty men with knives who not only don't care about killing, but want to kill. God smiled on you when you found Earl. If he's your friend, it's until the wheels fall off, though he's rotten and treacherous as anybody else if you're not. It's a necessity in here. I was worried that you'd get him in some kind of jackpot . . . let your problems turn into complexes and jeopardize him. And if he gets in a hassel, T.J. and Bad Eye would go berserk, and when they do, the others do the same. But you're cool."

"Man, if I got him in trouble . . . I want to see him outside, even though I can't really imagine him anywhere but prison. But out there I'd be able to help him like he's helped me." Before Ron could go further, the mess hall lights went out and the beam carrying images flashed from the projection booth to the screen.

When spring came, it was visible only in the gardens of the plaza; there flowers bloomed—roses, zinnias, pansies. The rest of the prison retained its dead monochrome. By then, Ron stirred with boredom. He was settled but had nothing to do. His energetic nature had no outlet. He wasn't interested in gambling or narcotics, except where they led to money, though he saw how these icons were the yeast that fluffed Earl's mind. Moreover, Ron saw that it was time to build the constructive record to influence the judge.

"Yeah, chump, do something for yourself," Earl said.

"I think I'll go to night school . . . take a course in real estate."

That is what he did; also a class in Spanish. Three evenings a week he walked through twilight, in the lines of men, mostly black, to the education building. At the recess he often visited Jan the Actress in the queen's glass-enclosed office. There he met Mr. Harrell, the chubby, soft-physiqued teacher who ran the "literacy training" program for illiterates. Clark Harrell also sponsored a group called Squires that he hoped would help keep delinquents from coming to prison by showing them their future. Every Saturday morning he brought in a dozen youths to talk to the convicts. He asked Ron to join and Ron did so. He wasn't much older than most of the swaggering kids with their unkempt hair and bizarre garb. Most of them wanted to show how tough they thought they were, but Ron watched as their eyes flitted to the riflemen silhouetted on the walls, the skyline of cellhouses, the inevitable plaza loungers who ogled them as if they were young girls— and would have made them a facsimile if they had the chance.

The group met in the literacy training classroom, which was in an annex to the education building. The annex was whitewashed brick, circa 1895, and originally had been the women's prison, then the hospital, next a chapel, and finally a classroom and warehouse.

Some of the delinquents were frightened about meeting San Quentin convicts, while others looked forward to it. They'd all heard stories that were horrifying object lessons. Bob Wells, a black man who'd spent forty-two out of his last forty-three years in prison, always told of serving ten years, and coming back for car theft in 1941. He'd gotten an additional sentence for having a knife, and then knocked out a guard's eye with a spittoon and was sentenced to die. He'd spent eight years on Condemned Row, watching men take the elevator ride to the octagon chamber, waiting for the appeals to run out. Walter Winchell had saved his life by focusing publicity on his case, and finally the governor had commuted his sentence to life without possibility of parole. Now he was in his mid-sixties, suffering bad arthritis from so many years of sleeping on concrete in the hole. He was gray, gaunt, had ulcers in his stomach and circulatory problems in his legs. He smelled of age and death. Ron watched the young car thieves and burglars as they listened. Some saw what could happen to them, while others sneered.

One morning as the group broke up, Clark Harrell asked Ron to wait while he escorted the youngsters to the gate. When Harrell came back, Ron was on the ledge of the fish pond, his face turned to the sun. Harrell spoke to get his attention.

"Pretty good meeting today," he said. He fidgeted with a brass button on his blazer, an immaculate if uninspired dresser.

"Very little gets through," Ron said. "They aren't ready to learn anything."

"Yes, I know. Thomas Mann made that observation . . . that we never really *learn* anything, we just become aware of things when the time and the potential in us coincide. Or something to that effect. But now and then it reaches one or two. I've got a couple in my Sunday-school class."

Ron made a sound of mildly surprised approval.

"Where do you work?" Harrell asked.

"North block . . . tier tender."

"That's a waste of your intelligence. It doesn't take any brains to sweep a tier."

Ron shrugged.

"My assistant is going and I need somebody . . . to tutor, check tests and things. It pays thirty dollars a month, more than industries, and you'd be doing something useful."

"When do I have to decide?"

"Oh, in a few days."

Ron immediately wanted the job, knowing it would impress the judge more than sweeping tiers, and it had some prestige. Yet he wanted to consult with his mentor first.

Earl had never heard of Harrell, which wasn't unusual considering that the prison employed nearly a thousand people and the education department was not part of Earl's usual interests. The next afternoon, however, Earl knew quite a bit, including Harrell's address and the names of his wife and two children. "He's also an ordained minister. The first word I got was that he's a fruiter, but then I found out he isn't, at least not overt. He's just a boss sucker for pretty boys. Every assistant has been young and smooth, but he never makes a pass . . . And he's a mule. He won't bring dope or anything hot, but he'll pack out letters and bring in money. We can always use that kind of thing. And he doesn't have any heat because he only does it for whoever works for him. Finally, when the time comes, we can write the report for the judge and he'll sign it."

"So I should take the job?"

"Quick as a cat can lick milk."

So Ron went to work as a teacher's aide. At first sight of the class he was dismayed, for more than half of them were black and he'd been inoculated with San Quentin's racial attitudes. He expected the ubiquitous hatred to spill into the classroom. At the very least, he expected to be tested for weakness. He knew from Earl that black convicts were often masters of the bluff game. "Some got it so tight,"

Earl said, "that you don't know who's faking and who's righteously a bad motherfucker. But they don't expect Whitey to game back." Ron was ready, but it was unnecessary. Not even his youthful appearance caused trouble. The class was voluntary, and its members were dedicated, and they saw that he was interested. On the yard some of the young, usually militant blacks nodded at him or gave a modified clenched-fist salute. Some whites in the Brotherhood disliked this and he had to explain, resenting the necessity. He also got in an argument with Earl over it. "Fuck it!" Ron said. "I can't go on with this insanity. We're all locked up here, wearing the same clothes, eating the same garbage, locked in the same cages."

"Right, asshole," Earl said, "but tell *them*. When I came here, a beef was a personal matter. It might involve a couple of friends, but even that was unusual. Then came the Black Muslims and the Nazis, and as long as they just fucked each other up, it still didn't bother me. Then *they* started stabbing white convicts indiscriminately whenever one of them got stabbed, even if it was over dope or a sissy. A lot of dudes don't know when it started, but I was here. I *know*. I don't like it, but I like it a lot better than what would happen if we didn't get down. You think it doesn't involve you. It involves everybody, both sides. When the war starts, you'll be as potential a victim as anyone . . . and the dudes who do the fighting on your side don't dig fraternization. And the black warriors are even more racist. I'm not a racist . . . but it's tribal warfare. Like the Hatfields and the McCoys. You can't help being born one or the other. And if you get too friendly with the other side, your own side will disown you . . . and might kill you. And these are the dudes who will go all the way to murder *for* you because you're my friend."

It was the one time that Earl got angry, and although Ron believed the anger was irrational, he saw that the situation was equally so, so he avoided talking to any blacks on the yard.

After a week, Harrell began bringing double lunches, one for himself and one for Ron. The lunches consisted merely of what goes into brown paper bags, but the simplest things from the outside were delicacies in San Quentin—mayonnaise was unheard of, and so was soft bread from a store. Mess hall bread was kept for several days before being served. Convicts ate less that way. The tuna salad sandwiches Harrell brought were as rare as lobster thermidor on the prison menu. Ron thought that Earl might be jealous, for lunch had become the single time during the day that they always saw each other. Instead, Earl grinned and pinched Ron's cheek, a "chubby" that made him blush. "Shit, that's all right. I go grease in the kitchen every night. Now I ain't gotta worry about you."

Thus Ron ate weekday lunches with "Clark" in the classroom. He was a prissy man, very schoolmarmish. At the end of the ten-minute recess he actually stepped into the corridor and jangled a tiny bell between thumb and forefinger to tell the convicts to return to the classroom. He was nicknamed "Mother," yet he was obsessed with helping people and could get away with scolding explosive men who couldn't stand authority.

Although Ron worked for Harrell because he could manipulate the man, he also liked him, and felt mildly guilty at using him. Earl gave him two letters for Harrell to smuggle out, one to a man named Dennis, whom Earl described as his "acey-deucey partner," then hugged Ron and said, "But you're my son." The letter was a coded request for narcotics; they arrived in two weeks. The second letter was to Bobby Gardner in the Los Angeles County jail, asking him to subpoena Bad Eye to his trial if possible. The trip, even in chains, would break the grind of "B" Section, and it might give Bad Eye a chance to escape. Nothing came of it. Bobby bargained out of trial with a jail sentence. Ron addressed the envelopes in his own hand and Harrell carried them out without question.

Now and then Earl came to the classroom door, stuck his bald head inside, and beckoned Ron. Whenever it happened, Harrell was peevish afterward, though his one comment was that Ron was in "fast" company. The symptoms were of jealousy, and Ron grimly smiled inside, thinking, What a fuckin' life.

It takes between one and two years for prison's newness to wear off so its awful reality can seep in. Men who commit suicide either do it in the first geyser of shame, within days or weeks, or else after a couple of years, when all has been discovered hopeless. During the interim, no matter how much agony the man may feel, he also experiences excitement, the excitement of learning how to cope with a closed society that reflects free society as a funhouse mirror reflects the human form: everything is there, but distorted. Prison has two sets of laws, Ron learned, those of the administration and those of the convicts. In order to regain freedom, one must not get caught breaking those of the administration, which faintly resemble society's strictures. But to survive, one must follow the codes of the underworld. It is not difficult to do both if one remains inconspicuous and uninvolved. But the man who wishes to prevail wherever he is, including prison, takes to the tightrope and runs the danger. In that regard, Ron, except for his good looks, would have had it easy, for his vanities, great as they were, had nothing to do with prison values. He had decided that he was, indeed, committed to crime, but not in prison. He found nothing worth the trouble, but he understood that Earl was compelled to play whatever game was available and accept the coin of the realm—and Ron saw that his friend walked the tightrope as well as anyone. Earl was not a friend he would have chosen in other circumstances—but the friendship was nonetheless deeper than any he'd ever felt.

Spring turned to crisp early summer and Ron was settled and working on his program to utilize the remaining sixteen months when Earl brought him a tiny newspaper clipping. The legislature had passed a bill that would restrict to one hundred twenty days the authority of a judge to call back and modify a sentence under 1168 of the Penal Code.

"What should I do?" Ron asked. "The judge wanted two years and I've only got in eight months."

"You'd better do something. Fire a kite to that mouthpiece and see what he says. He has to make the motion to the judge. If he doesn't, we will. You can't lose anything."

"The judge already issued the order. Maybe it doesn't affect me."

"No, he didn't issue an order. If you wait, he won't have the power."

"Maybe he won't even call for the reports."

"Maybe not—and then you wait five more years to see the parole board. If you can't do time, don't fuck with crime . . . But we'll crank out some letters and see what's happening. You might get lucky."

That night Earl typed letters to the judge and Ron's attorney, putting a carbon of each with the other. A week later Jacob Horvath wrote that the Court was calling for reports within provisions of the proper code—work report, summary of adjustment, recommendations above the warden's signature (though a counselor would prepare it), other pertinent information, and finally, a psychological evaluation.

Earl went to work immediately. A convict clerk falsified records to show that Ron regularly attended group counseling and Alcoholics Anonymous. "But I don't drink," Ron said. "Fuck it," Earl replied. "It costs the same and it can't hurt." Mr. Harrell wrote a glowing letter about how much Ron contributed to the Squires and how good a worker he was. The psychological report worried Earl. "The shrink has been here thirty-five years and he's fuckin' schizoid himself. He's lost some cards from the deck lately."

"Man, I should get a good psych report. I mean . . . I'm the most normal person in this madhouse."

"Yeah, you *should* . . . but should and will are different things. But maybe we can make sure." And Earl did make sure. A clerk in the hospital stole the request for the report and Ron's thin medical file, which contained the graph reports of some psychological tests. These were normal. He also provided the chief psychiatrist's stationery. Earl wrote the report, concluding: "This young man represents a minimal threat to the community. I recommend a short jail confinement as part of a probation program."

"Say, I don't want to do any time in that shitty jail."

"Who's handling this? That's the clincher. It makes it look good and gives the judge another option to think about."

"But that's the world's most fucked-up jail."

"Oi vay, a sniveler I raised already. I suppose you wanna stay here . . . go to the parole board in five more years. By then I'll be long gone to Broadway."

The report with a reasonable facsimile of the chief psychiatrist's signature went out via Mr. Harrell.

"Now we wait," Earl said. "I'd say in about six weeks you'll be on the sheriff's bus back to sunny Southern California."

They were on benches against the cellhouse wall, sitting in the evening sun. It was after supper and most men were going indoors while the hungry sea gulls dove to inhale pieces of bread.

"If I get out," Ron said, "I'll be so fuckin' in debt to you . . ."

"Oh, fool, you'll forget me the first time you see some neon. That's standard shit. There's a curtain between here and out there."

The younger man's eyes turned wet. "Don't think that, bro'. You're my friend. I've never had a real friend before. When I get out, you can have whatever you want. You can shoot dope every day, or drive a Cadillac around the yard if they'll let you have it."

"The main thing I want is for you not to get busted. If you do, I'm fuckin' you when you get back. Remember that." He feinted a playful punch and then clenched Ron's hand. "I know you won't forget me. Just send the dope so I can suppress the pain."

The last stragglers were entering the cellhouse. Earl got up to go back to the yard office. "I'll bring some burritos in tonight."

"Fuck, we're doing so good I might not want to go to the pad."

"I'll bet you ain't late for the bus, what you bet?"

Earl went across the shadowed, empty yard toward the gate.

On a crystalline afternoon, while Mr. Harrell had individual members of the class reading aloud, Ron sat in reverie at his desk next to an open window overlooking the plaza. He'd finished marking papers from a spelling test, and while the stumbling voices droned on in the background, he looked out at the flowers, fountain, and convicts feeding the fish. Soon he'd be going back to court, and he had no doubt that he would go free. Although he was overjoyed, that joy was not unalloyed. He felt that he could still learn things here, that in the ten months of San Quentin he'd aged ten years, had become stronger. He smiled to himself, privately anticipating what he would do for his friend if the judge acted right. Just the forged letter from the psychiatrist was a huge debt—and it was one of so many. In this ugly place Earl had become his father—and T.J., Paul, and the still segregated Bad Eye his cousins and friends.

Mr. Harrell finished the reading lesson and it was time for two hours of educational films. Ron brought the wheeled projector from the hallway closet and set up the film. He pulled the curtains and Harrell turned off the lights. Then Ron started up the aisle toward the rear where he always sat. He felt a hand stroke his ass and a voice hissed, "You're sure fine, baby." He slapped at the hand reflexively and whirled, too stunned for immediate anger. In the darkness he could see a pale face, and he knew who it was from the location. Buck Rowan, the hulking newcomer. He'd been in the class a week, and Ron had noticed him staring, but had not given it any importance until now. He'd become accustomed to stares. Ron recalled the hillbilly twang and could smell the fetid breath.

"Are you crazy, you asshole?" Ron snapped.

"Watch it, bitch! Ah'll whup yo' ass. You're a girl an' Ah'm gonna put my dick in your ass."

Ron was paralyzed for a moment. It was too sudden, too insane. He suddenly remembered Earl's advice about not arguing with fools until things were right. He spun and walked to the rear of the room, oblivious to the images on the screen. He trembled and his face was afire. He nearly wanted to laugh. A year earlier and he would have been quaking like a rabbit without a way to run. Now the fear was tiny, and that was reined in. Everyone is mortal; everyone bleeds. As the minutes ticked away, his stunned bewilderment became a controlled rage.

When the second film started, he went down a side aisle and through the door to take a piss. He was still trying to decide what to do. In the toilet he couldn't empty his bladder. He was too tight. He rinsed his hands, splashed water on his fevered face. "A man does whatever he has to," he muttered, and accepted the possibility of killing the fool. It dismayed him, but there was no indecision. He would try for reason, but if that failed . . .

As he stepped from the toilet the classroom door opened and Buck came out, carrying a few seconds of movie sound track with him. His searching eyes said that he had followed Ron, who felt fear but was unashamed of it. Earl said that fear was good for survival and only fools were without it. Ron stepped forward to the edge of the stairs. It was unlikely that Buck had a shiv—and his hands were exposed so he would have to reach for it. By then, Ron could leap down the stairs and into the plaza. Buck was a couple of inches over six feet and weighed two hundred and fifty pounds. He was built like a bear and was too big to fight.

"You hear what I said in there?" he asked. "I wanna play from you."

"I hope it's a joke."

"Ain' a joke. We ain' gonna have no mess of trouble, are we?"

"I don't ever want trouble."

"Baby, you're *fine*. I've been watchin' you an' watchin' you an' my dick stays hard as Chinese arithmetic. I don't wanna have to beat you up, but you're gonna cooperate one way or another."

Ron's face was expressionless, but his mind sneered at the gross stupidity. "I'm not a punk. If you heard different, you heard some bad information." He knew as he spoke that the words were hurled against a gale.

"Bullshit! You're too pretty. An' Ah done seen you with that dude. I ain' Ned in the first reader. Ah been to Huntsville and Raiford. You might even be makin' tortillas with that teacher in there."

"I'm going back to court for modification. I don't want any trouble to mess that up." The situation sickened Ron, but a cold, detached part of his mind told him that Buck was accustomed to brawls with fists, feet, and teeth. San Quentin had a different ethos. Buck was a bear unaware that he was in the sights of a high-powered rifle.

"You can go back to court. The only way there'll be trouble is if your old man finds out. I'll just kick his ass. You an' me, we just meet somewhere."

Ron nodded, as if digesting the information, whereas he was really looking at Buck's shoes, visualizing the toes jutting upward from beneath a sheet.

The classroom door rattled. Ron and Buck both turned to face Mr. Harrell. The teacher's eyes flitted from face to face and he obviously felt the tension. "Oh, here you are," he said to Ron. "Would you go down to the book storeroom and pick up a box that came in?" Harrell nervously stood his ground until Ron had gone downstairs and Buck returned to the classroom.

As Ron stepped into the sunlight, he faced the yard office, thought of Earl, and vowed that he would keep his friend out of trouble. Earl had done too much already, was too near getting out himself. Ron walked to the education building, but he had no thought of getting the box. He was certain that Buck would have to be stabbed, and Ron wanted to do it—kill a mad dog—but was uncertain of himself. How did T.J. say? Underhanded and just beneath the ribs slightly to the left.

Fitz waved from the yard office, and Big Rand knocked on the glass and gave him the finger. Ron nodded, remembering that Earl had said it was almost impossible to be convicted for a prison murder unless a guard actually saw it, or unless there was a confession. For every informer willing to testify for the prosecution, a dozen would testify that the accused was in Timbuctoo—and a swearing contest between convicts never satisfies the burden of proof "beyond a reasonable doubt." And there had been several killings within recent years before hundreds of witnesses without anyone telling anything even in privacy. Too many convict clerks could find out too much.

"Yeah, we'll see who gets fucked," Ron said, turning into the education building. It was built on the slope that led to the lower yard, so that the office space was on the upper floor while the classrooms were downstairs. Ron went to the file section without speaking to the clerks. He ran through the drawers' newest numbers until he found Buck's folder. The hillbilly was "close" custody and lived on the bottom tier in the East cellhouse. That was the information Ron wanted, but he looked over the remaining data. Buck Rowan was thirty-four years of age, had a low-normal I.Q., and claimed a high school education (unverified) while scoring fourth grade on his scholastic tests. He'd served an eight-year term in Texas and three years in Florida, the first for rape-robbery, the second for burglary. He was on escape from Florida when arrested in Sacramento, California, for robbery. The picture was of a tough petty criminal, a fool asking to be killed.

For a moment Ron thought of the imminent court appearance. He could avoid trouble by having himself locked up. The thought went as quickly as it came. He could also submit, and that idea went even more quickly. If anyone fucked him, it would be Earl. The thought was sardonic, and he grinned at how he could now handle it with humor. Ron knew about southern prisons, the grinding labor in the cotton and sugarcane fields and on the roads, with stool pigeons as con bosses and convicts with rifles guarding other convicts.

They did it and lived. Buck Rowan was obviously blind to how quickly men killed in San Quentin; it had more murders in one year than all the prisons in the country put together.

It was nearly 3:00 p.m. when Ron crossed the yard and entered the North cellhouse, hurrying up the stairs toward the service alley on the fifth tier. He knew where the cache of long knives was hidden.

Earl was high on heroin and in the shower when Ron entered the building. The shower area was in view of the stairs, and Earl saw his friend hurry by. He momentarily wondered why Ron was out of work so early, but he felt no concern. Instead, he thought that his friend would soon be gone, and though there would be a sense of loss, it was a happy thought. I've done him some good, Earl thought, but he's done me good, too. I'm thinking about the streets . . . and I'm gonna get there one more time.

A minute later, Buzzard, the elderly Mexican, hurried down the stairs toward Earl. "Your friend just got a piece out of the *clavo*," he said.

Without fully rinsing off the soap or drying himself. Earl threw on a pair of pants and shower thongs and hurried up the stairs, carrying the rest of his clothes and toiletries in his hand. He was shirtless and beads of water dripped from his shoulders. Ron's cell was the only one with its gate open, and Earl was twenty yards away when Ron came out and started to close it. The younger man wore a heavy black coat zipped up and had a knit cap on his head, the standard disguise for trouble. Ron looked up and his face was drawn tight, his eyes glassy, and he seemed unhappy at Earl's presence.

"What's to it?" Earl said, stomach churning.

Ron shook his head. Earl reached out and patted the coat, feeling the hardness of the weapon under it. "Shit . . . something's sure as fuck wrong."

"Let me handle it."

"What the fuck are you talkin' about? Man, you're going to the streets in a hot minute. What're you doin' with a shiv? That's a new sentence."

"That's a secret?" Ron said, smiling sarcastically.

Earl held back his anger. This was serious, for Ron wasn't like many young cons who taped on shivs and talked murder so nobody would mess with them. Earl was afraid, not of violence but of the aftermath. A stabbing would keep the young man inside; a killing would mean at least five or six more years even without a trial. And he himself was involved. That was unquestioned, and if something happened, it would snuff out his own candle of hope. If it was unavoidable, then it had to be—but he wanted to make sure it couldn't be handled some other way. He pressed for the story and Ron told it, at first haltingly, finally without reservation. And into Earl's worry came fury. The gross stupidity of Buck Rowan, whom he didn't know, made him want to kill the man. He was mildly relieved that it was a white man; at least it wouldn't ignite a race war. And Earl knew that any white would be without backing against the Brotherhood. The man was not merely a brute; he was also an absolute fool.

"Maybe we can get around snuffing him," Earl said. "Show him what he's up against. The *best* he can get is killed."

"He's too dumb. Jesus, I hate stupid—"

"If we gotta, we gotta, but let's make sure it's necessary. It isn't as if he was an immediate threat to your life this afternoon."

"He's not trying to fuck *you*. Let me handle it."

"What! If you make a move, you'd better get ready to down me first, and then T.J. and Bad Eye will—"

"Oh, man, I don't want to get you into trouble."

"Fuck all that."

"Yeah, okay. I don't want to kill him . . . or rather I don't want the penalties for it."

"Let's check him out. Let me see if I recognize him. Then we'll plan. We'll go to the library and you point him out through the window when school lets out."

As they crossed the yard and went out the gate, Ron grabbed Earl's elbow. "Look, motherfucker, promise me . . . if it comes to trouble, don't take over for me. Don't go get T.J. and do something

145

without me. I'd hate you if you did that. I've learned how to hold up my end. Promise . . . ?"

"I promise. I can dig it."

Inside the library they waited near a front window until the school bell rang and a horde of convicts burst from the education building, many carrying schoolbooks. A minute later the literacy training class came from the annex. Buck Rowan stood out and he was alone, carrying his books. He had a clodhopper stride, arms hanging straight down, feet stepping high—as if he were pulling them from ploughed dirt.

"I've seen that fool around," Earl said. "He catches the eye. But I haven't seen him with anybody who's trouble."

"He cells on the bottom tier in the East block, close custody."

Earl's eyes narrowed to slits and the muscles twitched—but the thinking about what to do took less than a minute. "Okay, don't go back to the cellblock after chow. Hang back on the yard with the clean-up crew. Paul and Vito will be there. When T.J. comes by, tell him to wait, but don't tell him what's happening or *he's* liable to go take care of it himself. I'll meet you, and we'll catch him when he goes back to the block. He won't expect us then, and we'll have all the edge." Earl neglected to add his feeling that the problem could be handled without murder. He'd go with his allies, and if Buck's response was unsatisfactory, they would kick him within an inch of his life—but Earl was confident Buck would back down when he saw what he was up against. No man alone, no matter how tough, could win against fifteen killers.

A minute behind the convicts leaving school came the evening watch guards carrying lunchpails, hurrying toward the cellhouses to help with the main count.

"Wait a couple minutes before you go to the yard," Earl said. "When you hear the lineup whistle, go straight into the block. The mooch might be waiting. I've got to go to the yard office."

Ron nodded without enthusiasm. "Damn, I'm tired of this crap. Just . . . fuck it."

"Oh no, we can handle this. It's routine shit." Earl cuffed him on the arm.

"You have to act like an animal to get respect in here."

"Cool it. It's gonna be okay. Quit snivelin'. You've had the red carpet. I was six years younger than you and didn't smile for two years. It took me a decade to make the North block and go to night movies. And you've got as much time left as a mosquito has prick, unless you fuck it up. I need you out there to look after me."

Ron headed toward the yard and Earl went to the office. The colonel was on duty, trimly military at his desk, and Big Rand was disappearing toward the front gate. As Earl stepped in, he saw the black lieutenant known as Captain Midnight was on duty. Seeman, Earl recalled, had taken the night off to drive his daughter to the airport. Captain Midnight had a reputation for being a black racist, and whether it was deserved or not, the man was a hateful sono-fabitch—and he thoroughly disliked Earl Copen. Earl believed that the man resented any intelligent convict and despised all ignorant ones. Earl knew he would have to watch himself with both Captain Midnight and the colonel.

He thought about how to handle the situation with Buck Rowan in the East cellhouse. T.J. and Baby Boy lived on the fifth tier and ate first. He would have to get to the yard quickly and catch them before they locked up. They were necessary in case Buck Rowan needed to be stomped through the cement. Paul and Vito would be sweeping and hosing the yard. He wanted them there, too, for a show of strength. And if any of the Brotherhood were available, they could also stand on the sidelines looking mean. If he'd been planning a killing. Earl would have asked one man to come along to help and a second for lookout, but a killing was what he wanted to avoid.

The shadows of twilight deepened—and the count was very late in clearing. The colonel called control. Nobody was missing; the total was right but some bodies were in the wrong places. One tier had an extra prisoner while another had one too few, a fairly common error, but one that held back the supper unlock until corrected.

When the bell finally rang, and Earl swung his feet off the type-writer stand, Captain Midnight came from the rear office with two pieces of yellow legal tablet in hand. "Here, Copen, make an original and two copies."

"Can I go eat first?"

"Do it before you eat. Have it ready when I get back."

Earl glanced at the crabbed, nearly illegible handwriting.

"Don't make any changes," Captain Midnight said. "I'm hip to you."

"Whatever you say, boss man. I'll even leave the misspelled words if you want."

The black lieutenant froze for a second. "Just do your job, convict. And be careful. I'm after your ass."

"Oh, I know that . . . and I'm *so* careful when you're around."

"If I catch you down wrong, they'll have to pipe air into you. I know about you and your gang." He started to add something more, but clicked his teeth together and thought better of it. "Have that memo done when I get back."

"Okay, boss."

Typing the memo took longer than usual because the handwriting was hard to decipher. In addition, he pressed because he was in a hurry, and therefore made more errors than usual. When he finished, the automatic lights of the prison had gone on. He put the memo on the lieutenant's desk and rushed out. "Gonna get some chow, boss," he said.

"Best hurry, lad. It's nearly time for the mess hall to close."

The last tier—Buck Rowan's tier—had long since entered the mess hall, and men were straggling back across the yard to the East cellhouse from the exit door. The North cellhouse doors were locked, though they would open after the meal for night school and other activities. He circled in that direction, looking for Ron—but Ron wasn't there. At the far end of the yard, in the overhang of the canteen roof, stood several figures silhouetted against the canteen lights. The night yard crew, among them Paul and Vito. Earl moved quickly in that direction, unable to run because it was against the rules and the rifleman would blast his whistle. Paul and Vito were both leaning on broom handles.

148

"Where's Superhonky?" Earl asked.

"Him and Baby Boy went in. They're both drunk," Paul said.

"I was gonna try and fuck him while he was out," Vito said, "but the big motherfucker might wake up."

"Shit!" Earl said. "I needed him to stand around and look mean. I gotta drive on some fool."

"Who is it?" Vito asked.

"Some lop fuckin' with Ron."

"Ron just went in the East block," Paul said.

"I told him—" Earl began; then wheeled and nearly ran toward the square of yellow light filling the open door. Vito and Paul threw down their brooms and hurried after.

The vast cellhouse hummed with the accumulated voices of trapped men. The tiers were packed with inmates waiting for lockup, and around the door were men jammed waiting for night unlocks to begin. Earl pushed through, turned around the corner and put an arm up beside his face as he passed the sergeant's office. The rifleman was on the other side of the cellhouse. The crowd was much thinner on the bottom because the space was much larger, going all the way to the cellhouse wall.

Earl immediately saw Ron and Buck facing each other halfway down the tier. He increased his pace. Paul and Vito were twenty feet behind him, moving more slowly and trying to appear unconcerned. Earl was both proud of Ron's courage and angry at his foolishness. I'll let him handle it as long as he can, Earl thought when he was ten feet away, but that thought was instantly erased when Buck saw him over Ron's shoulder and said. "Here's your daddy," he sneered. "Or maybe he's a sissy, too. Or a rat."

Nobody had ever been so disrespectful. Earl's mind reeled with the burst of fury. He leaped past Ron and swung—but his rage made him start the punch from too far away, with too much warning. Buck evaded the blow and Earl's momentum sent him crashing into the big man. He instantly saw that Buck was too big and too strong, clumsy but quick, his hands swinging like a bear swatting bees. Earl was slammed back as they went around. Buck drove him back under the tier, into the cell bars with such force that Earl's wind was knocked out. He couldn't get leverage to punch. Buck's hands went around him, grabbed the cell bars and tried to crush him. The big man's cheek was next to Earl's face. He grabbed the head, sunk his teeth into the top of Buck's right ear and bit it off, the blood running instantly.

Surprised, Paul and Vito were seconds late—for Ron had pulled the knife from his waistband and come forward with the quick steps of a matador. Without hesitation, he struck with all his strength, burying fourteen inches of steel in the wide back. "Die, you mother-fucker!"

The big man collapsed instantly, falling straight down like a dynamited building. The spinal cord was severed. He nearly pulled Earl down on top of him until Vito's brogan thudded into his face. Then he screamed, a terrible, bellowing sound that cut through the cellhouse hum and brought a sudden hush as hundreds of eyes looked for signs of another murder.

"Cut his throat," Vito said, "so he can't snitch." And he reached for the knife when Ron hesitated.

A police whistle shrilled alarm.

"Split!" Paul said. "The gun bull's coming."

The whistle came again. The guard was rushing down the catwalk, levering a cartridge into the rifle's firing chamber. He couldn't see under the bottom tier. Earl shoved Ron and they started running toward the rear of the building, keeping under the tier so only their feet were visible. Paul and Vito were behind them. The cellhouse bulls would come from the front. When they reached the back stairs, Earl and Ron went up, disappearing before the rifleman could come around on the catwalk. Paul and Vito stayed on the bottom, circling the cellblock. The whistle still bleated, but it was falling behind.

Ron still had the shiv. Convicts on the tier fell back from them, giving them passage.

"Throw it," Earl said.

Ron reached through a cell's bars and dropped the weapon. Someone would get rid of it. They pushed along the third tier, heading toward the front stairs.

"They'll lock that door in a minute," Earl said. "We've gotta get out of here before that."

No guards were in front. They'd rushed toward the scene of the stabbing. Ron and Earl leaped down the steel stairs three at a bound, and in seconds were through the rotunda and in the dark yard. A hundred yards ahead of them Paul and Vito were already turning into the mess hall where the night yard crew was allowed to drink coffee. To the right, convicts were streaming out of the North cellhouse on evening unlocks.

"Go to education," Earl said. "We might be okay. It was under the tier and not many saw it. Maybe we won't get snitched on."

"I never thought I could do that—and it was easy. It just went in."

Earl draped an arm around Ron's shoulder. "If an asshole ever got his issue, it was that one."

Ron nodded, suddenly unable to speak, beginning to feel the squeezing fingers of fear in his stomach. If the act had been easy, the possible repercussions were not.

When they neared the gate, Earl patted him on the back and stopped. "Keep going. The colonel will see us together if we go much farther."

While Ron hurried on, turning through the lighted door into the school building, Earl loitered under the gate. Then he saw Captain Midnight and the third watch sergeant hurrying toward him down the road, en route to the East cellhouse stabbing. Earl sauntered toward them, passed with a nod to the sergeant, ignoring the lieutenant. He went into the yard office, glad to be hidden by darkness, for he was trembling from nervous tension. The colonel sat in the shadows. "Another stabbing in the East block," he said.

"Who was it?"

"Don't have his name yet. But it's a good one."

"Is he dead?"

"He was on a gurney when I got the call . . . so he's still alive."

Earl grunted, not wanting to appear too interested. He sat in his own chair, looking out at the prison night, wondering if they would get by. Five minutes later a cadaverous-faced doctor hurried across the plaza from the front gate, going to the hospital. He was a legend among convicts, especially with knife wounds. He'd saved men stabbed in the heart.

Earl stood up, too tense to sit still. He wanted to go somewhere, see Ron.

"Better hang around," the colonel said. "There'll probably be some reports to type when the lieutenant gets back."

"That won't be for half an hour. I'm going to the cell for some cigarettes. Call over there if you need me."

"Just so we know where you are," the colonel said.

"I can't go too far," Earl said, stepping out into the night.

As Earl neared the doorway of the education building, he met an older convict coming the other way. Red Malone was a friend, though they seldom saw each other. Red worked outside the walls in the employees' snack bar as a night cook and lived in the elite West cellhouse. Red stopped as Earl approached, obviously wanting to talk, and although Earl's mind raced on other things, he stopped and grinned. Then, as Red stuck out his hand, Earl remembered that the man was going home—after a dozen calendars behind the walls.

"When is it, Red?"

"*Mañana.*"

"Good luck, brother."

"I'm scared shitless. I've gotta make it. I can't stand another jolt. My teeth are gone and my hair is going."

"You'll be okay. Just keep your shit together."

"We're getting old."

"We're younger than springtime, sucker." He slapped Red affectionately on the back and clenched his hand.

When Red was gone, Earl stuck his head through the doorway to education. Half a dozen clerks were behind their desks around the room. Three teachers were picking up their roll call sheets. Ron was in the glass-enclosed office of the supervisor of education, sitting on the edge of the desk talking to Jan the Actress. Mr. Harrell was also there—and Earl wondered if the man ever went home. It was best not to go in. They might provide Ron with a partial alibi if

153

they thought he'd been there five minutes earlier than he was. He wanted to tell Ron not to say a word if he was picked up—not even a lie. He decided Ron probably knew that; silence cannot be impeached, whereas a lie can sometimes be refuted.

Earl continued to the yard. The mess-hall doors were locked and he didn't know if Vito and Paul were inside. The years of prison told Earl that it was likely he'd be picked up for the assault. Someone would fink privately, though it was most unlikely that he would testify. It was a good idea to get ready for the hole. He headed toward the North cellhouse, ducking through the door just before the guard locked it after the night unlocks had finished.

Buzzard had the cell key for the fifth tier. Earl found him working on a leather purse in his cell. "Unlock my cell, Buzz, and keep a watch on the door downstairs. I think the pigs might be coming for me."

They went quickly, and as Buzzard inserted the key, he said he'd heard something about a stabbing in the East cellhouse. He didn't punctuate the statement with a significant look; the words were enough. Earl didn't reply, but took off the pillowslip and began filling it with property that he could have in "B" Section—cigarettes, toiletries, paperback books. He took three twenty-dollar bills from the hiding place in the gallon can, rolled them up one at a time, and inserted each in a tube of shaving cream through the top. The guards checked the bottom of tubes for tampering, but not the hole. It got messy to squirt everything out, and the convict who had nothing could complain loudly about it. He looked at his cell furniture, the oil painting shutters, the lampshade, the glass-topped desk. "Give it all to T.J.," he said; then handed Buzzard the pillowslip. "If they slam me, give the sack to Lieutenant Seeman. He'll see that I get it."

"What about those cigarettes I'm holding for you in my cell?"

"Consider them a present."

Earl glanced over the tier and saw Captain Midnight and two other guards come through the door, carrying nightsticks. Earl momentarily thought of hurrying to one of the two hundred and fifty cells and hiding. They wouldn't find him until the last lockup, or later than that if he wanted to risk a charge of attempted escape. Instead, he went to the stairs and started down, feigning surprise when they ganged around him. "What's the trouble?" he asked.

Surprised, they hesitated, hefting the clubs nervously, and then Captain Midnight had him turn and lean against the wall for a weapons frisk. Then they jammed him close and the group went down the stairs where the cellhouse guard had the door open for them. One of the guards, an old-timer and a favorite of Lieutenant Seeman's, wrinkled up his face to show he was doing something distasteful in arresting Earl. The convict nearly smiled, thinking that after enough years in prison, everybody's values were distorted. The old guard didn't care about the stabbing; he was sorry to pick up a convict he liked.

The colonel's face was hidden in the darkness behind the window when the quartet went by; the old Army man didn't move his head. As they passed the chapel, nearing the custody office, Earl heard the voices of the choir. It had to be a tour, for the lights were also on under the fountain. Captain Midnight opened the door and Earl went in ahead of the two escorts. The large room with half-glass offices along its walls was deserted except for two convict clerks and the sergeant in the control booth; and Ron was on a bench outside the associate warden's office, a young guard beside him.

Captain Midnight motioned Earl to keep going, wanting him as far across the room from Ron as possible. Earl stopped and the guards nearly bumped into him. "What's happening?" Earl asked.

"They won't tell me," Ron said.

"Keep moving and be quiet," Captain Midnight said, reaching for Earl's sleeve. Earl jerked away.

"Keep your hands off me, chump." He turned to Ron. "If it's serious, demand to see a lawyer."

"Knock it off!" the lieutenant said, raising a can of mace with his thumb on the button.

"Man, fuck you! What're you gonna do? Kick my ass? Assholes have been doing that ever since I can remember. You can't kill me

". . . and if you do, you can't eat me . . . it's against the law." He threw his head back, the personification of defiance, and everyone froze for half a dozen seconds. "You ain't nothing," Earl said.

They sat in silence except for the clicking of the clerks' type-writers. Earl smoked and tried not to think about the future. Finally the warden came in, a big man almost never seen inside the walls. Now he wore slacks, sweater, and a ten-gallon hat, an unlit cigar between his teeth. He glanced at the two convicts and went into the associate warden's office, followed by the black lieutenant. Ten minutes later Captain Midnight leaned out and beckoned Earl. The guards stayed with him until he reached the door, and the lieutenant told them to wait outside.

The warden was behind the wide desk, his hat off and one cowboy-booted leg propped across the corner. He had a cup of coffee. His face was droopy at the jowls and his eyes were big behind his glasses.

"Have a seat," he said, waving expansively toward a chair across the desk. Captain Midnight stayed behind Earl's right shoulder, moving as the convict moved.

"No, I don't think I'll be here that long."

"Want some coffee?" the warden asked.

Earl shook his head, smiled softly.

"Boy, you shore got a mess of trouble," the warden said laconically. "That ol' boy Rowan says you stuck him . . . an' he's willin' to go on the witness stand . . . from a wheelchair, I might add."

"Who's Rowan?"

The warden flushed momentarily; then regained his fellowship. "Oh, he's a sorry ol' thing . . . and you know him. He probably had it coming."

"I don't know what you're talking about."

"I really didn't think you did. You're an ol' smartass . . . don't even know how to help yourself . . . tell your side of the story."

"I'd have to talk to my lawyer before I make any statement. Besides, you didn't warn me about my constitutional rights."

"Might as well put him away in the shitcan," the warden said, still not displaying anger—certain of his power.

156

When Captain Midnight ushered him to the door and opened it, the lieutenant said to the guard, "Make sure he's in a boxcar. Bring his clothes back to see if there's any blood samples on them, especially his shoes."

Earl looked at Ron seated outside the door. The young man was pale and drawn, but his eyes radiated strength. "You weren't in there long," Ron said.

"I didn't have anything to say. They think I stabbed some guy."

"They better watch what they're smoking."

A guard nudged Earl and the trio went out. He sucked deep on the clean air, looked up at the dome of night cluttered with stars, knowing he might never again be outdoors at night—even in prison. Certainly not for a long time.

When they crossed the yard they stopped while the keys to the South cellhouse rotunda were passed down from No. 2 Wall Post. At night the keys were taken from the cellhouses so it would do the convicts inside no good to overpower their keepers. Moments later they opened the door to "B" Section and the bedlam of the damned rolled forth. The yelling voices were an unbroken roar in the shadows of the honeycomb. Trash was ankle deep the entire length of the floor, and the stench of excrement and urine was overpowering. The cells broken up nearly a year before had still not been repaired. Earl looked up at the fence that sheeted the outside of the tiers. Two "B" Section guards were waiting for him, apparently having been called by Control.

"We want his clothes," an escort said.

Earl stood against the wall and stripped, handing over his clothes and going through the poses of a skin search. When he finished, they returned his shorts and motioned him to walk to the rear of the cellhouse. He kept far out from the tier and walked softly, carefully avoiding the shards of glass from jars discarded over the tiers. He could see shadowed faces behind the bars.

"Hey, Bad Eye!" someone yelled. "Earl Copen just came in!" The voice had to rise above the uproar, but Bad Eye heard, for in seconds an arm came through bars on the third tier and Bad Eye yelled,

"They finally got your slick ass!"

"They think so!" Earl yelled back, still pussyfooting along, slowly.

"What they say you done did?"

"Some fool got stabbed!"

"I know you're innocent!"

They reached the "boxcars," five cells at the rear. They'd begun as regular cells but then concrete blocks had been extended between each out to the walkway above. A solid door was added, and when it was closed, a man screaming inside the cell was just a squeak outside of it. A tiny light, dimmed by the wire over it, was in a niche in the ceiling between the cell gate and the door.

Earl stepped into the cell, noting that the cast aluminum toilet and washbowl were still in place. Apparently, the occupant during the strike hadn't been able to break them. A grimy mattress and two blankets were on the floor. Wadding a blanket into a pillow, Earl flopped down. The smell was bad, like mildew. Water was leaking somewhere, perhaps in the service alley, maybe from the seal on the toilet. The floor under his bare feet was both gritty and sticky. "Just like home," he muttered. "I love it." He was still keyed up, his mind jumping and unable to focus. He knew from other situations that eventually the despair would eat through into consciousness. Hope would become an uncertain flicker, the candle wax melted, the wick bare. He'd know that suicide was really the one answer to the miserable futility of his existence, but he'd lack the courage of his knowledge. He worried about Ron, hoped the younger man would not feel obliged to confess to take Earl off the hook—and he wished he knew precisely what Buck Rowan had said. It would be very bad if he testified, especially from a wheelchair. Vito had been right: the fool should have had his throat cut. It certainly would have been no loss to the world.

The musings were broken by a rhythmic thumping through the concrete ceiling. He was wanted on the "telephone." He signaled back by standing on the toilet and pounding with the heel of his hand.

Quickly he folded both blankets into squares, put them over the mouth of the seatless toilet, sat down and began jumping—forcing the water out. He scooped the last of it into the sink and kneeled at the toilet, his face in the bowl. "Hello!" he yelled. "Who's on the phone?"

"It's Rube Samuel . . . your man! The old ass sure looked smooth when you went by."

"Only 'cause it was dark. It's all wrinkled and hairy." Earl liked Rube, the half-Mexican who'd served twelve of fifteen years in the hole at both San Quentin and Folsom. Rube had come to prison for mistakenly entering the wrong apartment, while drunk, but when accosted by the irate resident, Rube had beat him up. The charge was first-degree burglary. Rube had then picked up new convictions for a stabbing and an escape and seemed to be getting wilder and more frenzied as the years went by. Earl liked Rube, even though they seldom saw each other. "Where's Bad Eye?" Earl asked.

"Too far away. You could probably hear each other if you blew your voices, but I'll relay messages."

"Are you above me?"

"I'm on the third tier, a couple cells from Bad Eye. That's Wayne, T.J.'s home boy, above you. He just came from Soledad."

"I heard about him."

"What's with you? I thought you were too slick to get busted."

"They say something about a sticking in the East block." Earl was aware that others could have their toilets empty and be listening. "Did they bring my partner in?"

"Who's that?"

"That youngster I fuck with."

"I heard about him. They say he's pretty."

"Nothin' happenin' there, sucker."

"You sure you ain't eatin' him up? You know how you old convicts are."

"You've been here a long time yourself. I ain't got caught if I am, so you'll never know if you should be jealous."

"How bad is the dude hurt?"

"He's paralyzed . . . everything but his mouth."

"Snitchin', huh?"

"Does a dog have fleas?"

"Who is he?"

"Some hillbilly fish. Been here a couple months and wanted to be a bully."

"Hold it! I'm signin' off. Bad Eye's calling me, these fools are screaming . . . I'll talk to you in the morning."

"Send some smokes and something to read."

"Got you covered."

"If you can send word out, tell our friends about how that fool is snitchin'."

"We'll send word first thing in the morning. I'll see you if they let you out to exercise."

"Right on!"

When Earl flopped back on the mattress, he expected to spend the night turning things over and over in his mind. He called it "squirrel-caging," the compulsive repetition of thoughts without conclusions. He felt the gritted dirt imbedded in the mattress and was chilled because he wore no T-shirt. He pulled the second blanket over him. In three minutes he fell asleep, both because he was utterly drained and because his unconscious said sleep was a means to escape reality.

Ron Decker was in a more modern cell—in the adjustment center. It, too, was at the very rear, but on a solid floor rather than a tier, and instead of a toilet there was a hole in the floor beside the mattress. It was the floor where militant revolutionaries were usually kept, nearly all of them black, and when Ron had walked by with the guard they had stared out with silent, hostile faces. He could hear the sounds of voices beyond the double doors but could not decipher the words. Here he was doubly an alien, and he wished they'd put him in "B" Section where he might communicate with Earl. Buck Rowan apparently believed that Earl had stabbed him in the melee, and Ron was being torn apart by the situation. He was astounded that he felt so indifferent to Buck Rowan's condition; it was the death of something in himself, or perhaps the beginning of something new. But he was also crucified by guilt that Earl was in trouble because of him when he was basically innocent. Ron had gone into the building alone to avoid just such a situation. The warden had promised that he, Ron, would get favorable action from the judge if he turned on Earl. It was an insulting offer and he'd sneered, refusing to make any statement whatsoever without an attorney—but it also raised hope. Maybe they needed corroboration. Whatever happened, he wouldn't let Earl be convicted of the assault—fuck what Earl said. Yet his own freedom, which had been firmly in hand, was in danger of oozing between his fingers. Either Earl or himself convicted of the crime would face a life sentence or the death penalty, depending on what the jury decided. Even without that, if the judge in Los Angeles found out, he would deny sentence modification, which would mean five long, bitter years before he was *eligible* for parole, and the chances of getting it would be small even then. He'd already seen too many men psychologically maimed by the indefinite sentences of California. If one year made him capable of plunging a knife into a man's back, what would a decade do?

Actually, there was nothing for him to decide, not yet. He would simply wait until things became clearer. Maybe both of them would skate by—unlikely as it now seemed. He could take a few weeks in a bare cell. When it gets too tough for the average motherfucker, it gets the way I like it, he thought, grinning at one of Earl's expressions.

Earl came awake when the key turned in the outer door and the light stabbed through his eyelids. It took him a few seconds to recall his predicament; his mind fought to ignore it.

He stood up slowly, his mouth tasting foul, as the guard stepped aside for the convict to enter with a paper plate of food, the wooden spoon upright in the oatmeal.

"Hey, don't I get a tray?" Earl demanded of the guard over the convict's shoulder.

"Not in the strip cell," the guard said.

"I wish your mother was in a strip cell," Earl said clearly, not caring if the guards—and they were capable of it—came in and whipped him. That would be *something*. But the guard was going off duty in five minutes and chose to ignore the insult.

When the first convict stepped out, a second entered the dark alcove with a Styrofoam cup in one hand and a bucket of coffee in the other—and a grin on his face. The man's name was Leakey, and Earl disliked him because he knew he wasn't a friend, though he was always friendly to Earl's face. Once Earl had bruised the man's ego, challenging him not in so many words but in undisguised anger. Leakey had backed down, though he was in the hole for a killing (with two others helping him). Since then Earl had gotten word that Leakey made snide comments behind his back. Now Leakey's teeth shone. He didn't say anything, but he jiggled the cup as he set it on the bars. His body shielded the move from the waiting guard. He filled the cup and went out. When the door was locked,

Earl separated the two cups, one inside the other, and took the tobacco and matches from the bottom one.

Earl wasn't hungry, but he forced himself to dab the soggy bread in the hardening oatmeal and take a few bites. The flat wooden spoon was ridiculous. He picked the stewed prunes up between thumb and forefinger and downed them. Then he rolled a cigarette and smoked while drinking the coffee, which was at least hot. While he sat, he turned his mind's eye inward, probing his thoughts and feelings, scanning his own attitude toward the awful situation. On the surface was a sheen of calm, even of indifference, but he could sense that deep within was a volcano of despair waiting to erupt. Indeed, that had been the real motive for his quick cursing of the guard minutes ago. Because he couldn't handle despair, it would become nihilistic rage; it always happened when he was trapped, and he had never been so completely trapped as now. Always before he'd had youth to draw upon. The years of the future were there if he lost some now. Now the reservoir was nearly gone. He wondered why he was so detached.

The end of the hand-rolled cigarette was flushed and the makings put in a hole in the mattress. Next he searched the cell, the few niches around the toilet and under the bars where something could be stashed. Beneath the top of the mattress he found a year old *Reader's Digest*. If he stayed in this boxcar for many days, he would have to arrange for Bad Eye to smuggle in reading material. He could handle whatever happened for however long, but it would be much easier with tobacco and books.

Finished with the search, he momentarily thought about doing calisthenics—it was always a *thought* in the hole and never went any further. He decided to masturbate as a reasonable substitute, and wished he had a magazine with photos of women in high heels and stockings to stimulate his imagination. His memories of the real thing were turning yellow. He lay down on the mattress and pulled the blanket over him. It would be embarrassing to have the door open while he was loping his mule. In a crowded reform school dormitory he'd learned to masturbate on his side without moving the blankets. A thrashing was the penalty for "self-abuse." Now he fondled himself, sorting through the images of memory as if selecting a woman in a whorehouse. He found Kitty, a series of pictures beginning with how her dancer's legs had looked as she sat in miniskirt on a car seat, chubby and smooth, and then bare-breasted in blue jeans, the aureoles pink against the white, the globes white against the suntan. She was the younger sister of a girlfriend, and he'd never made a pass at her, but Jesus he'd wanted to, and he speculated on what it would be like with such clarity that it was now almost as if it had happened. Different women aroused different fantasies in him. Some had round, firm asses so he wanted to place them on their sides and fuck them from the rear, his belly against their butt. Others had big strong legs that he wanted to feel wrapped around him—but with Kitty ... he wanted to tongue her, while cupping the cheeks of her ass in his hands, her legs spread. He wanted her standing up, braced against a table or dresser. Now he conjured her in bikini panties and high heels. He stroked her butt through the sheer nylon—that was in his mind, while in reality he spat in his hand for slickness and stroked himself. He slipped the panties down and she stepped from them while his tongue worked from her belly button down to her inner thigh. She raised one leg. About this time he had an orgasm. He wiped the result from the mattress with toilet paper and threw it in the toilet, wondering how many others had jacked off on this dirty mattress. "Shit! What else is there to do in the hole? Ah, sweet Kitty, you'll be an old lady when I get a chance to give you some head. Old and cold."

Now he propped a folded blanket as a headrest and webbed his fingers behind his neck, waiting for whatever might happen next. A lifetime of conditioning to bare, dirty cells had given him the ability to endure without letting his mind scream in silent futility at the walls. Such conduct as that was the path to mental break-down. He didn't care about *that* either, except that it would give the enemy too much satisfaction. He knew how to be still within his own being. His one worry was Ron, who obviously wasn't in "B" Section and therefore had to be in the adjustment center where eighty percent of the occupants were Whitey-hating blacks, many of whom had killed guards here or in other prisons in the system. Nobody could get out of their cells, but they could make life miserable. Yet nothing could be done about it, not yet. When the smoke cleared, it might be possible to have him moved over here through Seeman—and there was the matter of his court appearance, too. It was no use thinking about it, about anything, not without more facts. Not a goddamned thing could be decided or done. He picked up the *Reader's Digest* and read about someone's most unforgettable experience.

Following lunch, Earl had to quickly stifle a cigarette when he heard the key hit the lock. As he turned from the toilet, two guards stood outside the bars. "Okay, strip on down," one said. "The associate warden wants to see you."

"I don't know if I want to see him."

"They sent us for you. Either you come or we bring the stun gun and the gurney."

"You fuckers discovered technology," Earl said. He stepped to the rear of the cell and stripped off his shorts. When he was naked he went through the dance while one of them held a flashlight on him. "I feel like Liza Minnelli," he said, moving to the bars to get the white coveralls with the zipper. They were baggy on him. Then, through the bars, they put a chain around his waist and fastened his wrists in handcuffs holding his arms tight to his hips. One unlocked the door and he stepped out. Several feet of extra chain were put between his legs—front to rear, from the belly chain—and one guard held it. He could be jerked off his feet with one hard tug. It was how everyone was taken from the hole since guards had been slain in recent years. Men even went to visits that way.

Somehow T.J. and Paul had known that he was being brought out, for as soon as the procession hit the yard, which was still packed because the work whistle hadn't blown, the two men were there. T.J. jerked his head toward the hospital, clenched his fist, and then turned his thumb down in the classic gesture of the Roman arena.

Earl knew instantly that Buck Rowan was either already dead or soon would be. A guard would be seated by his door, but Earl's friends had found a way to get around that.

"You look like a Christmas package in all that shit," Paul said.

"They're overrating me," Earl said. "They think I'm tough."

"Knock it off, Copen," one guard said while the other waved the two convicts away.

Following the procession from a parallel catwalk was one of the yard's riflemen. After another stabbing, the suspect had been under escort when someone knocked the guard down and killed the assailant. Now the officials took no chances.

The crowd parted, and several convicts called his name and waved, their faces blurs in the gray light. He kept his face hard under the scrutiny of so many eyes, but inside he saw the humor of such excessive drama. As they passed the yard office, Fitz stuck his head out and asked, "Need anything over there?"

"Some high-grade heroin," Earl called back, grinning.

The custody office was now full of people, with a dozen clerks and half a dozen lieutenants and several guards, all behind their desks. One lieutenant—his face permanently lumped and reddened by booze—glared at Earl. He'd spent twenty years in this office, going from guard to sergeant to lieutenant from one desk to another, and never going out among the main-line convicts. Lieutenant Seeman thought the man was afraid of convicts, and Earl had mused at the time that it was indeed tragic for a man afraid of convicts to spend his life working in a prison. It showed that he was also afraid of life.

Stoneface was behind his desk, the drapes behind him opened to expose barred windows and the panorama of the bay. The associate warden got his nickname from the ravages of acne that had scarred and removed the flexibility of his skin—that and his long, square jaw. Earl remembered when the man's hair was black; now it was streaked heavily with gray. A movement to the right turned Earl's eyes to the man sitting there, a chubby young man with pudgy mouth and modish tattersall suit.

"You can wait outside," Stoneface said to the guards.

When they withdrew, Stoneface introduced the man as Mr. McDonald from the Marin County district attorney's office.

"How you doing, Copen?" Mr. McDonald asked, reaching down beside his chair to flip on a tape recorder, and then, perhaps because he was thinking of that, he stood up to shake hands, blushing when he saw how Earl was chained.

"I'm fine," Earl said. "How's your mother?"

The matter-of-fact question stopped the man cold for a few seconds; then he took a card from his pocket and read, "I'm advising you of your constitutional rights. You have a right to remain silent. If you choose to give up that right, anything you say may be used against you. You can have an attorney present before you're interviewed. And if you can't afford an attorney, one will be provided free of charge. Do you understand?"

"Run that by me again."

Earl smirked while the red-faced man repeated the litany. When he finished, Earl looked around the room, bent over, and feigned peering beneath the desk. "Where is he? The lip?"

Stoneface had been sneering with his mouth and staring with his eyes during the charade. "I told you this one was a smartass. He'd think it was a joke until he walked to the gas chamber. Only we'd probably have to carry him with shit running out of his pants."

Earl flushed, momentarily considering spitting in the man's face, but realizing he'd be beaten to a pulp if he did so. He looked down at the carpet.

"Rowan's a paraplegic," McDonald said evenly. "He's signed a statement that he had an argument with Decker over some schoolwork, and you took it up. He's ready to testify. He thinks it's the only way he can get revenge. We found traces of blood on your shoes, O positive, which is his blood type."

"It's mine, too. I cut myself shaving."

"We've got corroboration that you were in the cellhouse, too. Now if you make it easy for us, I promise we won't ask for the death penalty."

"Just a natural life sentence, huh?"

"Better than death."

"I think I'll pay my money and take my chances . . . especially since I'm innocent as a baby."

"Don't say I didn't give you a chance. And if you change your mind, it'll save us money."

"I'll give it some thought, but don't hold your breath." Earl's voice dripped disdain. It wasn't bravado. It was knowledge that no jury would vote death for this, and if one did, no execution would take place. Only once had a convict been executed for a nonfatal assault, and he had demanded it.

"You'd be smart to tell us your side of the story," Stoneface said. "I looked at Rowan's record and he's no prize citizen. You probably had a good reason . . . that sweet boy of yours."

"No, it was your mother." The response, though certainly not a witty retort, came reflexively, delivered with venom, and Stoneface puffed up. "Man, send me back to my motherfuckin' cell. I don't have anything to say. I don't know anything, and if you've got a case, put a dozen in the jury box and convince them." He turned for the door and both men jumped up. He stopped. "Don't get nervous. I'm just getting the bulls. Whaddya think, I'm goin' somewhere in all this hardware? You sure are scary assholes." He kicked on the door and the guard instantly opened it.

"Get the car, Jeeves," Earl said.

The confused guards looked to the associate warden. Stoneface motioned for them to take him. "And if the bastard opens his mouth, kick his teeth in."

The yard was now nearly empty, but when he was marched down the bottom tier of "B" Section, several friends yelled out words of ribald encouragement. Rube was the loudest, but Bad Eye was not far behind.

As soon as the cell gate and outer door were locked, the bravado was darkened by clouds of despair. What real difference was there between the gas chamber and a life sentence; both ended hope. And even if he wasn't taken to trial, or acquitted, the parole board would make him pay, five, six, eight years . . . For a moment he wished that Ron would confess, but cursed himself for the idea. It was beneath what he thought of himself. And he was legally guilty anyway. Pacing the cell, he thought of T.J.'s signal in the yard. Someone was going to somehow kill Buck Rowan, or try. The signed statement would be no good in court; it wasn't a dying statement. It would leave the parole board, but, Jesus, that was better than a conviction. Yet Earl was ripped apart inside about the killing, too. If T.J. got in trouble . . . that would be an unbearable burden to be the cause of a friend spending years in the hole and perhaps never getting out of prison. Nor was there any telling what T.J. would do. Earl hoped it wasn't what some blacks had done in a futile attempt to get an informer. They'd murdered a guard outside the door who didn't even have a key. They were still in boxcars in the adjustment center after three years. T.J. certainly had the nerve for it—for anything—but he also had brains. And Paul would be an influence. They apparently had a plan . . .

If the grand jury indicted him, Earl would need an attorney. No doubt Ron would have his mother cough up some money, not the thousands necessary for a top lawyer, but anything was better than the public defender. The one chance for acquittal was on insanity. Earl grinned, realizing that he knew precisely how to go about it.

During the afternoon he heard the shuffle of feet going by. The upper tiers were being let out in the small "B" Section yard for an hour of exercise, watched by two riflemen. Someone knocked once on the outer door and several magazines slid under it, one at a time, vintage *Playboys* with missing pictures. He used a blanket to fish them in.

At 4:30 the door opened for a second as a guard peeked in to count him. A minute later the stamping foot from the cell above indicated that he was wanted on the phone. The toilet was already empty. He kept it that way, except when he used it.

"Yo, here I am," he called.

"That dude in the hospital croaked," Rube said.

"Where'd you hear that?"

"The bull just told Leakey."

"Any details?"

"Naw . . . just that he kicked off."

Earl was silent, face in the toilet, wondering how he should feel, worrying about T.J. and Paul.

"Did you get that?" Rube called

"Yeah, I got it."

"Bad Eye wants to know if you need anything."

"Some narcotics."

"Naw, that's dead."

"Some coffee and something to heat water in . . . a metal cup."

"We'll get it down at chow."

The rattle of the key in the lock brought him spinning away from the toilet. Before the door fully opened, silhouetting Lieutenant Seeman in the spilled light, Earl was on the mattress and acting as if he was just getting up. Seeman began extracting packages of cigarettes from various pockets and threw them on the mattress. "If they catch you with them, forget where they came from."

"You don't have to say that."

"I'd have been here half an hour ago, but they found that Rowan guy dead in the hospital."

"Not from the stabbing," Earl said, thinking that the signed statement might be admissible under that circumstance; it might be considered a dying statement, hence an exception to the hearsay rule.

"Not from the looks of him. They won't know for sure until the autopsy, but he had an I.V. tube in his arm, and the bottle smelled like a mix of embalming fluid, cleaning solvent, and God knows what else. He was supposed to be getting saline. Somebody must've made a mistake." Seeman's weatherworn face was so masked with naïveté that it expressed a knowing smirk. "The mortician might have trouble. The body is nearly black."

"Jesus," Earl said, truly shocked by the image.

"I'm the investigator on both the stabbing and the murder. My reports say the word is that he was hit by some blacks . . . and there's no suspects for the radiator flush he got. It won't convince the disciplinary committee, and it isn't admissible in court, but it'll be in your file and might help at some future time. The parole board members change every few years. It's a speck of doubt for you to argue about."

"Thanks, boss." But inside himself Earl knew the help was nearly meaningless.

"Off the record," Seeman said, "I *know* what happened. I've never committed a crime and I'm a law-and-order man all the way. But I know the rules of society aren't the rules in here, and only an idiot would try to apply them."

"You know I ain't copping to anything . . . not even spitting on the sidewalk."

"I just wanted to tell you."

"Can you do anything about getting me out of this boxcar . . . and moving Decker over here?"

"Not right now. Wait until the front office won't notice it. There'll be another killing in a few days to get their attention."

"What about going to see my friend in the Adjustment Center. Tell him that his mother might have to cough up some bucks for a lawyer. See how he is."

"That's no problem."

"Cleaning solvent and embalming fluid! Stoneface is gonna be mad at that."

"He is already. He was at home when they called him. He was ready to bite anybody in his way when he came in . . . I've got to go supervise the mess hall." He banged the heel of his hand on the crossbar as a gesture of farewell.

"When'll you be back?"

"Maybe this evening . . . tomorrow for sure. You're going to be locked up for a year or two at least. I'll need another clerk until you get out. Take it easy."

"A choice I've got?"

"You were going to get a parole, too."

"Parole! Fuck parole! I like it here. No work, no taxes . . ."

171

When Seeman was gone, Earl tore open a pack of Camels and lay down. The geyser of lostness came suddenly, and with it his eyes turned wet, not really tears but the expression of an ache to the marrow of his being. What a total waste his life was. Yet he felt— no matter what others or intellect said—that there had never been any real alternative, that each terrible step of his life had grown inevitably from what had proceeded, so that it had never been a matter of real choice. As for this, what else could he have done? Let Ron go alone? Let the late Buck Rowan shit on him, on both of them?

Fuck the post-mortems. Now what?

And he knew the answer was escape, and it was the only answer. Now that had to be his goal. How to do it was another matter, but he'd have months to plan. It had been done half a dozen times during his era—and twice that many had tried and failed. At least he knew what wouldn't work and could formulate principles to examine possibilities. Nobody knew San Quentin any better. One worry was a possible transfer to Folsom. Nobody escaped from the main security area there. The new idea, whether or not it became a reality, was a raft buoying his spirits. Hope may spring eternal, but it needs an idea to feed upon.

The days passed and nobody came to see him. He wasn't questioned. A guard opened the door to take him to the Disciplinary Committee but didn't press the issue when he refused to go. He knew the committees were a charade. Later that afternoon he was given the result. He'd been found guilty in absentia of the assault and assigned to segregation. The committee would review the action in six months. That, too, would be a charade with equally foreseeable results.

Word came from the yard via the toilet bowl that Ron had gone back to court. It removed a burden—and also increased his loneliness. He wished he'd been able to see his friend and wondered how long it would be until he heard something.

Nobody was locked up for Buck Rowan's death; it was another

unsolved San Quentin murder, the investigation forgotten when two other murders, unconnected with each other, happened the same day. Baby Boy was a suspect in one, but there wasn't even enough evidence to keep him locked up.

Seeman brought word that a transfer to Folsom was being considered, and although it wasn't yet a decision, it caused Earl's mind to pound at the walls. The next day he realized how he could stop the possibility. Folsom had no psychiatrist. If he feigned a breakdown and got under the psych department it was unlikely the transfer would go through. He knew a way to attract attention and get to the hospital, and it might also provide a defense in the unlikely circumstance that he was indicted for the stabbing. He would play crazy—a friend had been acquitted of a robbery-murder with the same act, though he'd served twelve years in a mental hospital and was actually insane when it was over—but he had to make sure he wasn't ignored. Breakdowns in "B" Section were too common to merit attention. He'd feign a suicide attempt, opening a vein at the elbow joint with a razor blade, putting the blood in a cup and mixing it with water, and splattering it everywhere. The frosting would be the "eating shit" routine: he'd take the morning oatmeal, mix it with instant coffee until it was the right shade of soggy brown, and have it on a magazine inside the toilet. The shocked guard would *see* shit because that's what came from toilet bowls and was brown and wet.

Earl looked at his arm. What difference did a scar make? Yet he hesitated to commit himself. Some convicts, like Leakey, who lacked mental agility and disliked him anyway, would see such behavior as weakness. They would backbite to others who believed in image and appearance rather than substance and reality. He hesitated another day, and then wrote Bad Eye a note in precise detail, asking him to send down a razor blade and tell Paul and T.J. what was going on. Rube delivered Bad Eye's reply through the pipes: "Bad Eye says you're a crazy old coot, but he loves you." And that evening a magazine came under the door with the razor blade inside. The next morning he saved the oatmeal and a cup of coffee and mixed them together.

As lunchtime approached, he frenzied his mind, for slicing one's own veins open is not an easy thing to do. He was ready when he heard the food cart rattling down the tier several cells away. He wrapped a T-shirt around his bicep, grimaced, clenched the razor blade between thumb and forefinger, and cut hard and short where the vein rose at the inner pit of the elbow. The flesh fell apart like open lips, the inside white for a moment until it welled with blood. He saw the vein encased in white fiber and chopped again. This time it squirted, a thin stream flashing up about eighteen inches. He filled a third of the cup, added water and poured it over himself from the top of his head. He filled the cup again and flung the mess onto the walls in a sweeping motion that coated them. A third cup went on the ceiling, where it immediately dripped. The floor was coated with the slippery liquid.

Hearing the food cart right outside his door, he hunkered at the toilet, turning his head away because he wanted to laugh. He had his body between his arm and the door and pressed a thumb on the wound, which immediately stopped bleeding except for a trickle.

The key turned, the door opened, light flooded in on the gore. It looked as if Earl had lost several pints—and might be drowning in it.

"God-damn!" the guard muttered in shocked disbelief, slamming the door and yelling for someone to call the hospital and bring a stretcher. Then he opened the door again.

"Copen, hold on! Jesus H. Christ!"

By now Earl was on his knees, only half-feigning the wooziness, and he was beside the toilet where the magazine sat with the mound of oatmeal colored by coffee.

"Fuckin' radiation everywhere," Earl said.

"The what . . . where?"

"The motherfuckin' radiation, chump. Gotta protect myself." He reached into the toilet, scooped out the mush and slapped it on his face like a mud pack; then stuffed a handful in his mouth.

"Oh my fuckin' God," the guard moaned. "Don't . . . don't eat shit." Then he leaned out and yelled down the tier. "He's eating shit!"

Earl hurled a handful of mush at the door and the guard ducked away. Earl took the magazine and dropped it on the bloody floor.

Then came the sound of jangling keys and running feet. The convicts on the upper tiers, aroused like monkeys by any excitement, began screaming and pounding the bars.

An old sergeant who'd known Earl for many years came into the alcove. "What's wrong?"

"It's the radio in my brain . . . I warned 'em about Pearl Harbor in thirty-seven and they didn't believe me." He sang, "They didn't believe me . . . they didn't believe me . . ."

"He's off his bloomin' rocker," the sergeant said; then yelled, "Hurry up that goddamn gurney."

The medical technician used a tourniquet instead of a compress, and the blood squirted again. They puffed and bumped and got him on the gurney. Behind closed eyes Earl could hear someone say, "Looks bad." He had his other arm flung over his face and grinned behind it, knowing he could get up and fight ten rounds. Also, he knew that they wouldn't put him back in "B" Section until he regained his sanity.

Three hours later he was watching television on the psych ward, his arm sutured and bandaged. The Valium and Demerol made him feel quite good.

The next day when the psychiatrist made his rounds, Earl was forewarned. It was lunchtime. All psych patients were fed on paper plates. The psychiatrist found Earl with the plate on top of his head, spaghetti hanging and sauce dripping. Earl claimed it was his Chinese hat. The psychiatrist agreed that there was a resemblance and increased the medication.

Earl settled down on the hospital's psychiatric ward, an isolated sanctuary behind a barred gate on the third floor. Guards could enter only to count and if called on in an emergency. The freeman nurse came in to pass out medication, but otherwise convict attendants were in charge of the three or four patients. The attendants wrote on the medical chart whatever Earl wanted, an official hospital record that could be subpoenaed to court to prove that he was insane—if that became necessary.

The other patients usually stayed in their rooms, turned into fidgety zombies by Prolixin. Earl was supposed to take Thorazine three times a day, but he held the pills under his tongue until the nurse turned away; then he flushed them down the toilet. He needed his wits about him.

The steel doors of the rooms were unlocked until 11:00 p.m., but even then could be picked, so Earl usually watched television until the wee hours of morning and slept late. It was nearly impossible for him to be caught out of his room; the elevator could be heard when it left the bottom floor, and anyone coming up the stairs could be heard unlocking doors far away.

The morning after the fake suicide attempt, Ivan McGee delivered a pillowcase bulging with cigarettes, coffee, pastries, and toiletries. T.J., Paul, and Vito had taken up a collection from the clique. That afternoon the trio sneaked into the hospital and up to the third floor. They couldn't get through the gate, but called him to it. They shook hands through the bars, grinning and shaking their heads. Then he learned how Buck Rowan had been killed. It wasn't Ivan McGee, as he'd thought, but someone he didn't know. Ivan had told them who could get into Buck's room, an anonymous convict in the West Honor Unit. Vito, Baby Boy, Bird, and T.J. had gone there with long knives. The convict was aware of the Brotherhood, but threats weren't necessary. The attendant hated stool pigeons as much as anyone; it was even his idea to do the job with the I.V. bottles.

Earl listened silently, surging with gratitude tinged with horror, though the latter was soon stifled by the former. Nevertheless, he simply nodded and smiled; thanking someone for committing murder seemed inappropriate.

The sound of keys jangling as the hospital's sergeant came up the stairs sent the trio scurrying down a right-angled corridor away from the psych ward grill gate.

Several evenings later, Lieutenant Seeman came up to tell him that the district attorney wasn't filing charges, and that Ron Decker had been picked up that afternoon by deputies from Los Angeles. "So why don't you knock off the act, do your time in segregation, and come back to the yard?"

"I'll think about it, boss," Earl said.

The gust of joy about the district attorney, and the mixed feelings about Ron leaving, turned to melancholia that evening. Dutch Holland was the attendant on duty, and they were watching the first Monday night football game of the season, a dull game where the halftime score was outlandish.

"Rams, my ass!" Earl said, getting up. "My prick is stronger than Gabriel's arm. They oughta call 'em *Lambs*. Want something to eat?"

"Naw," Dutch said without moving his eyes from the screen. His massive arms were crossed on his chest, exaggerating their tattooed bulk.

"What about coffee?"

"Can't sleep if I drink it this late."

Earl stretched and jiggled his shoulders to unkink the muscles, meanwhile looking at Dutch's thick neck with its rolls of fat. Dutch was a legend even before Earl first came to prison. Many convicts thought he might be the greatest wrestler in the world; but he liked good booze and bad checks and in his sixth decade this was his sixth imprisonment. With his pancake face and cauliflower ear, Dutch epitomized the brutal convict in appearance, but in reality was a gentle man who needed intolerable provocation to become violent, provocation that seldom came because of his appearance. Nobody challenges a man who looks like a grizzly bear.

The first room had been converted into a small kitchen with a refrigerator and hotplate—and stolen steaks were sent up to Earl from the butcher shop. He usually shared them with Dutch, who like most athletes was committed to the high protein of meat. Now Earl didn't feel like eating, but put the water pitcher on the hotplate and stepped back into the hallway where big windows overlooked a fence and the blackness of the Bay. Lights of cities beyond the water sparkled brighter than the stars above them. The lights danced in the crystalline air, and the Oakland Bay Bridge was a bright arc disappearing in the brilliance of the Oakland skyline. Earl could see the flash of taillights and neon. The quiet psych ward was conducive to reflections and bittersweet aches. He looked out and wanted freedom; it was so close—and yet so fuckin' far.

He missed Ron, worried about him. It could go all right in court, or it could fall apart if some prison official sent a report about the stabbing and murder. But there was no use worrying, nothing could be done. For himself, escape was all he had to hope for. He looked out at the dark silhouette of the gun tower on the edge of the water. Though he could see nothing inside it, he knew it was occupied. And the towering banks of vapor lights turned the perimeter into a surreal dayscape. Tower guards often fell asleep, and men in fenced prisons had sometimes managed to cut or climb the wire without being seen. More frequently, they were spotted and shot down. It was a pure gamble, a cast of the dice, and the odds were terrible. Even if he was willing to gamble, San Quentin's walls were not vulnerable to that move. Earl thought of two successful escapes he knew about; ten years apart men had used dummies during the main count while hiding out in the industrial area. When the count cleared, the riflemen on the walls of the industrial area went home and it was easy to go over. It all hinged on the cellhouse guards counting the dummy. Fool the guard and it was a cinch. If not, it was the hole and new indictments. The guards tended to become lax every few years, ignoring the rule that everyone was to stand at the bars for count. Yet that was also a gamble.

Hostages? Not worth thinking about. Nobody had made it out that way in forty years. It was against the law to open the gate for an inmate with hostages, no matter who they were. In Folsom, three of Earl's friends had grabbed a visiting choir in the chapel, mostly teen-aged girls, killing a convict who tried to stop them. (He'd gotten a posthumous pardon.) They'd demanded a car. They were told they'd get a hearse. They surrendered and got life sentences. If the gates weren't opened when a girls' choir was the hostages, they wouldn't be opened for anyone.

Equally futile was the "hideout," used by fish who didn't know better. They planned to hide until the search was over and then climb over the wall. Hunger was all they got. The search continued until there was definite evidence the missing convicts were outside. Otherwise they were presumed to be within the walls. One search had gone on for two months—until a dog found the missing body buried in the lower yard. It wasn't an escape but a murder. After a century the guards knew the prison better than the convicts. Records were kept of every possible hiding place.

Nearly every successful escape from inside the prison was in a truck.

Dutch called out that the second half was ready to start, breaking into Earl's fierce reverie. Earl made the coffee and walked back toward the television, noticing Dutch's seamed neck and the stubble of white hair on the round skull. Dutch was an old man. His life was over. Fear curled through Earl. Everyone gets old and dies, and it doesn't matter afterward, but it was frightening to be old and facing death without memories of having lived.

I'll get out, Earl vowed, one way or another. Then he thought of

Ron, wondered what was happening in Los Angeles. If Ron came back, he would have to be included in any plans for escape.

Beyond having more graffiti penciled and carved into its walls, the courtroom bullpen hadn't changed, nor had the human debris jamming it. The puffed, doughy faces and dirty clothes were those of the helpless and poor, not of criminals. But where Ron's attitude toward them had once been pity flecked with contempt, now contempt for weakness was uppermost. Also missing was the slight sense of fear that he'd known before. He leaned against a corner, legs extended along a bench, not letting a trembling wino sit down. When a husky young black began cursing the world, the rage trembling in his voice, Ron half smiled and felt bemused. Once the sight of such fury would have caused his stomach to knot up; now he knew it was probably a defensive bluff, noise to hide fear, and even if it was real, it was no threat. He'd learned that physical toughness didn't make for real dangerousness. Being a tough guy was in the mind, in being able to steal someone's life without a qualm. He now knew he was capable of that. What was it Earl said? "Rattlesnakes give off a noise, but cobras are silent."

On the heels of these nihilistic thoughts came realization that they were a reaction to the devastating news Jacob Horvath had brought to the jail's attorney room last night. Horvath's drooping lower lip and pained eyes signaled the reality even before he spoke. He'd gone to see the judge in the afternoon, to get the feel of the situation, but expecting no trouble. The judge had shown him an incident report about the murder (Horvath hadn't known), and a letter signed by the associate warden and the warden, saying that Ron Decker was a member of the notorious White Brotherhood, which group was responsible for at least half a dozen murders in California prisons within the past two years. Although the evidence was insufficient to prosecute for this latest killing, a number of anonymous but reliable inmate informants had linked Decker to it. Jacob Horvath's voice had risen from sad concern to near indignation, as if Ron had somehow failed him. Ron's first sense of deflation had been replaced by cold anger and contempt. He would meet the defeat with scorn; it diminished pain. And that had been his attitude all night long. He didn't even want to appear in court; it was all a ritual sham. The matter was already decided and he wasn't going to give anyone the satisfaction of showing that it hurt. He could be precisely what they thought him to be. Life was all the playing of roles anyway. All games; all bullshit.

When the deputy sheriff acting as bailiff called Ron to the gate and fastened the bright steel bracelets over his wrists, Ron felt a mild scorn, and a bizarre sense of pride or power, for if they were fetters, they were also symbols of society's fear.

The courtroom was totally without spectators. Just the clerk and court reporter were there, and Horvath behind a seated deputy district attorney. Horvath was leaning over, talking into the man's ear. Both of them laughed softly, but it sounded loud in the empty stillness. Ron felt a tug of anger. Not long ago he would have been benignly indifferent to such friendliness between competing attorneys, but now he thought it was traitorous. The prosecutor was the enemy, and war was never friendly.

Without being told by the accompanying deputy, Ron pushed through the low gate and sat on a chair inside the railing. The deputy hovered next to him. The clerk, a pudgy man in rimless glasses, saw the arrival of the defendant and went through the door at the left of the bench. This was the only case being heard this afternoon and he was notifying the judge that all was ready.

Ron was wearing khaki pants and shirt and prison shoes, the issue given men going to court. Once he would have felt self-conscious; now it didn't matter that he was branded as different. Horvath waved but seemed ready to continue talking to the prosecutor until Ron beckoned with a peremptory gesture. Then Horvath came over, putting his attaché case on top of the counsel table en route.

"Anything new?" Ron asked.

"Nope. Nothing. I tried to talk to him in chambers, but his mind is made up. I don't understand what the hell happened to you up there. You knew—"

"Quit it. What's done is done."

"I'm going to make a pitch, but—" He shook his head.

"Don't waste your breath. I've got some things to say. In fact, just tell him I'm making my own statement. You don't have to do a thing."

"Instead of me?"

"Right."

"You can't do that."

"Bullshit! Just tell him—"

Before more could be said, the clerk came out, banged the gavel, and intoned, "Please rise. Department Northeast B. Superior Court of the State of California, County of Los Angeles, is now in session, the Honorable Arlen Standish, judge presiding."

It was the same as before, the few people getting to their feet as the black-robed jurist came out and gained majesty as he stepped up to the bench. That is, everyone stood except Ron. When the deputy tugged his arm, he leaned forward and raised his ass three inches from the chair. He wouldn't have done that much except complete refusal might have brought a later ass-kicking. He managed thus to comply while showing how he felt. The judge, however, didn't look up until everyone was again seated.

"People versus Decker," the clerk said. "Hearing under Eleven sixty-eight of the Penal Code."

When Ron stood beside Horvath, he was assailed by the fragrance of the lawyer's aftershave; his awareness was magnified by a year of smelling nothing fragrant except farts.

"I suppose we have to . . . uh . . . have discussions on this matter," the judge said. As before, he shifted unseen papers. He put on glasses, read something; then looked over the glasses toward Horvath. "I imagine you have something to say, Counselor."

"Yes, Your Honor."

Before Horvath could say more, Ron poked him with an elbow and hissed from between clenched teeth, "Tell him."

"Rrr-uh," Horvath stuttered, his articulate circuits jammed.

"Your Honor," Ron said loudly, even more loudly and more shrilly than he wanted, "I'd like to address the Court in this matter."

"No, no, Mr. Decker. You will speak through counsel. That's what counsel is for."

"In that case, Your Honor," Ron said slowly, "I wish to remove Mr. Horvath as counsel of record and invoke my right to proceed in *propria persona*."

The judge hesitated. "Are you dissatisfied with Mr. Horvath?"

"That isn't the question. I simply want to represent myself at this hearing . . . and according to decisions, I have an absolute right to do so if I can make an intelligent waiver of my right to counsel. I believe the standard is that I know the elements of the offense, the defenses, and the penalties. It isn't necessary that I be a trained attorney. The first two are moot at this point . . . and I obviously know the penalties." As soon as he began speaking, the tension went away, and he knew he sounded articulate. It surprised him.

"Do you have any comment, Mr. Horvath?"

"It's a surprise . . . I . . . I've done my best. I have no objection. Mr. Decker is far from illiterate and he knows what's at stake."

The judge looked to the youthful deputy district attorney. "Do the People have anything to add?"

The prosecutor came to his feet. "The People would like to make sure this is an intelligent waiver . . . that the defendant doesn't double back later with a petition for habeas corpus claiming the waiver was invalid."

"I don't think that the record will reflect incompetency," the judge said mildly. "If we were in a critical proceeding where legal training . . . I would certainly make a lengthy inquiry before allowing a defendant to abandon the protection of counsel. But, as I recall, the decisions indicate the right to self-representation is absolute if the waiver is intelligent . . . and this defendant has recited the proper standards." The judge nodded to Ron. "Proceed, Mr. Decker. You are your own attorney as long as you maintain decorum."

Confronted with permission to speak, Ron was temporarily unable to. He'd intended to express disdain for the sham, but the avuncular judiciousness of the judge had ignited a flicker of hope. Perhaps it wasn't already decided. Yet he didn't want to show weakness, didn't want to snivel. He would take the middle course and play it according to the response elicited.

"Your Honor, there's no question that I sold a lot of marijuana and cocaine, but that means there were a lot of people buying it. In fact, millions of people don't see anything wrong with it. It's pretty well established that it isn't any worse than cigarettes, and less harmful than alcohol. I don't feel any guilt about doing it. I didn't hurt anyone. Getting caught was . . . like getting hit with lightning. Not justice or retribution. Just an act of God.

"When you sent me to prison, I was afraid of it. But I didn't expect prison to change me . . . not for good, not for bad. But after a year I have changed, and the change is for the worse . . . at least by society's standards. Trying to make a decent human being out of someone by sending them to prison is like trying to make a Moslem by putting someone in a Trappist monastery. A year ago the idea of hurting someone physically, hurting someone seriously, was abhorrent to me—but after a year in a world where nobody ever says it's wrong to kill, where the law of the jungle prevails, I find myself able to contemplate doing violence with equanimity. People have been killing each other for eons. When I was selling marijuana, I pretty much had the values of society, right and wrong, good and evil. Now, after a year—I'm being honest—when I read about a policeman being killed I'm on the side of the outlaw. That's where my sympathies are turning. Not completely yet, but with seeming inevitability.

"What I'm trying to say is simply that sending me back isn't going to do anything. Prison is a factory that turns out human animals. The chances are that whatever you get out of prison will be worse than what you send in. I'll have to serve *at least* five more years before I'm even eligible for parole. What will that do? It won't help me. It won't deter anyone else. Look around. Nobody will even know . . . so how can it deter?

"I don't know what I'll be after half a dozen years in a madhouse. And I've already lost everything outside. I think I've already suffered enough punishment—" His voice trailed off. His mind searched for more words, but he could find none. "That's all," he said finally.

When he sat down, breathless and flushed from his loquacity, the judge nodded to the deputy district attorney. "Do the People have any comment?" As he finished the question, the judge's eyes swiveled almost pointedly to look at a clock on the opposite wall.

The prosecutor, who was pushing back his chair to rise, let his eyes follow those of the judge. "Uh . . . the People . . . uh . . . concur with the letters from the prison officials and submit the matter."

The judge faced Ron again, and the visage of kindly patience seemed to harden, or maybe it was the timber of his voice that made his face seem like granite. "Mr. Decker, you originally came before this court and were convicted of a serious offense. Because of your youth and background, I tried to leave an opening to avoid sending you to prison for a *long* term. I wanted to give you a chance both to see what the future could hold and to help yourself. From the information sent me by the prison officials, you are a dangerous man. Whether you were already that or became so in prison is immaterial. The ultimate factor is not whether prison will help you, nor whether your imprisonment will deter anyone else. The main thing is to protect society. Anyone who can kill another person in cold blood—and you nearly admitted that you can—isn't fit to live in society. I know society will be protected for *at least* five years. After that the parole board, if they wish, can let you out. I'm not going to modify the sentence. Motion denied."

"Then fuck you!" Ron said loudly, unexpectedly, scarcely believing it himself. "Right in your old wrinkled ass!"

The deputy's fingers digging into his arm and tugging him stopped the words. "Watch yourself," the deputy said, his voice quiet but taut. "That's a judge."

"Yeah, okay." Ron was up, his eyes flicking over Horvath's astonished face. Then he was going up the aisle, the deputy reaching for the handcuffs. He stopped at the doors and put out his wrists. By head gesture and a hand on his shoulder, the deputy told him to turn. The outburst caused the handcuffs to be put on behind him, making him more helpless. He turned and complied, the shadow of a sneer on his face. He was wondering how long it would be before he got back to San Quentin.

The sanctuary of the psych ward was also a gilded cage. Earl luxuriated in the solitude, but he also fretted at the inactivity. Now that the murder charge was no threat he was ready to go back to "B" Section and do whatever punishment the officials wanted. It was a gauntlet that had to be run before he could get back on the big yard. The psych ward time didn't count toward the segregation term. And if he stayed too long in his "nervous breakdown," they would transfer him to the Medical Facility, where he might be given shock treatments—and rumors of lobotomies were sifting back. The old-fashioned brutality of "B" Section was preferable. Moreover, only two successful escapes had been made from within the Medical Facility during the fifteen years it had been open; both escapees had used the gamble of cutting cell bars and going over double fences in the shadow of gun towers.

Still he hesitated until word came that Ron was back from court and in "B" Section. The next morning he told the doctor that he was feeling better. Dutch and the other attendants marked the charts to show an end to his delusions. After a week, the doctor diagnosed a Ganzer syndrome, a form of psychosis that convicts call going "stir crazy." The following Monday the doctor discharged him. He knew the paper was signed within minutes and had his gear packed when the guards suddenly appeared.

"Get your shit together, Copen," one said. "The vacation is over."

When the "B" Section door was unlocked and the noise and the stench poured out, Earl's stomach turned queasy. Fuck it, he thought stoically. You've gotta know how to take a loss or you can't enjoy winning. He walked in, carrying a pillowcase with all his worldly possessions.

The chunky sergeant in charge of "B" Section was an old-timer who liked Earl. "How's it going?"

"I'm okay."

"I thought you might not make it when they took you out."

"I wouldn't cheat the state out of a minute."

"There's a cell near your friends up on the third tier. That's where you want to go, I'd guess."

"Is Decker up there?"

"Two cells from Bad Eye. You'll be on the other side. You'll all be close enough to talk."

"You mean close enough to scream." Earl jerked his head toward the tiers where the voices were a magnified babble. "We exercise together, huh?"

"Same program, one tier at a time."

Because they took Earl upstairs at the end and then down the third tier rather than along the bottom floor, nobody noticed his arrival. He looked into the cells as he walked by, especially those near where he was going, but everyone seemed to be asleep. As the sergeant turned the huge spike key in the lock and motioned for the bar to be dropped, Earl threw his pillowcase on the bare mattress on the floor and looked around. One wall was charred and blistered from a cell fire, but the toilet and sink were still on the wall; and the mattress and blankets seemed cleaner than usual. He began setting things in order; this would be his residence for a long time.

Not until lunch, when the hurricane of noise slackened temporarily, did he call out to make his presence known to Bad Eye and Ron. Even then it was necessary to yell, and it was impossible to hold a real conversation. He was glad the doctor had continued his Valium prescription. He hated noise and this was the World Series of chaos twenty-four hours a day. It was never entirely quiet, though near dawn only two or three men held screamed conversations. Every few months someone committed suicide by hanging, and half the men were on the edge of insanity. Bad Eye had been in here for nine months and awaiting transfer to Folsom, seething with hatred at the world. Earl remembered when Bad Eye had been merely a wild kid; now viciousness and evil had permeated the marrow of him.

"B" Section had its own exercise yard, actually outside the walls of San Quentin. A doorway had been cut into the outer cellhouse wall—facing the Bay. The hospital ran beside it, an area one-hundred yards long with a fence topped by concertina wire, outside of which was a gun tower. Another rifleman was perched just over the door from the cellhouse. Nobody was going anywhere. Except for an intervening headland a mile away, the Golden Gate and Alcatraz would have been visible.

Each tier had a special classification and was unlocked separately for two hours twice a week, morning or afternoon. The bottom tier was the hole, men serving short punishment sentences, most going back to the big yard afterward. The second tier was militant blacks. The third tier was for militant whites and Chicanos, mostly members of the White and Mexican Brotherhoods. The fourth tier was a mix, men locked up for rules violations who weren't affiliated or expected to start trouble. The fifth tier was protective custody, full of queens and informers, and very few of its occupants came out to the yard to exercise, for as they passed the other cells they were cursed, spat upon, and splashed with piss and shit.

Most of Earl's friends were on the third tier, some of them having been locked up for years, and during the first exercise period, a bright, cold morning, he was engulfed at the outset by a dozen men. There was laughter, embraces, handshakes, pats on the back. Bad Eye was the most effusive, squeezing Earl in a bear hug and lifting him off the ground. Bad Eye was going on the next bus to Folsom and was glad to be able to say goodbye in person. He was happy to leave, hoping that he could get a parole in a year or two. "I'll never get out if I stay here. I need a new ballpark. I've been down so long a snake's belly looks like up to me. My fuckin' crime partner has been out for six years . . . and he was five years older'n me when we got busted."

While the rites of camaraderie were going on, Ron Decker stood aside from the throng, smiling softly. He liked watching Earl handle people, enjoyed the knowledge that Earl changed façades easily, being whatever his particular audience wanted. Nor was it merely to manipulate them; rather it was because Earl really liked them and wanted to make them at ease.

Soon the group broke up, Bad Eye going to play handball on the small court where the winners kept playing challengers until beaten, the others of the crowd having nothing more of importance to say. Then Earl slapped one on the back and said that he had things to discuss with his partner, indicating Ron with a nod. It was understood and accepted.

"Man, I'm sorry about Court," Earl said as the two embraced. It was the first time Ron had used the gesture without embarrassment.

"It's a bummer," Ron said, "but what the fuck . . ."

"We didn't handle that move the best way."

"Hindsight is always wise. I don't feel bad about it."

"Naw, that asshole had a good killin' comin' to him. Still . . . you would've been on Broadway, and he wasn't worth that."

Ron shrugged. The pain was gone, the wound turned into a scar that sometimes itched but didn't hurt.

"Let's walk," Earl said.

Nearly all the two score convicts on the small yard were near the looming cellhouse where the handball court was. The fenced end was open to the wind, occasional gusts of which shivered it. The dark water of the Bay had tips of white. Ron had on a coat and turned up the collar, but Earl was in shirtsleeves and jammed his hands down inside his waistband and hunched his shoulders, jerking his head to indicate that they should walk the twenty yards along the fence.

"What'd your mother say?" Earl asked.

"She couldn't believe it . . . and she's ready to go broke if it'll do any good."

"Been to the Disciplinary Committee?"

"Uh-huh. They gave me a year in here. Jesus, it's an insane asylum. Nobody would believe a place like this."

"If I found a way out of here, out of San Quentin, would you want to split?"

Ron contemplated just a few seconds. "If you had a way out—I don't really want to do five more years to the parole board . . . and then not even be sure they'll let me out. Do you have a way?"

"Naw, not right now, but I can find a hole somewhere. I know that. The secret of busting out of one of these garbage cans is to keep your mind on it all the time, keep thinking, watching. I do know what won't work, and all the ways that've worked before. But even if we get out, that's just part of it. It's a bitch staying out. We'll need somewhere to go, someone to help—and really a way out of the country. Everybody in this counry is in the computer. The only place a fugitive is safe here is herding sheep in Montana or something. Shit! That's worse'n being on the yard."

"If you get us out, I can get us some help. My mother . . . and I know some people down in the mountains of Mexico—Sinaloa—who run things. They've got all the guns in the hills. The authorities don't go in with less than a battalion. I know some people in Costa Rica, too. If you get us out . . ."

They stopped at the corner of the fence and looked out to where cloud-mottled sunlight danced across the tops of Marin's green hills. A highway came between two of them, angling in a slight grade, the myriad windshields sparkling like jewels. "Yes," Ron said, "I like some of what this place has done for me, but I don't like what a lot of years will do."

Earl slapped him on the back. "Yeah, you'll start jackin' off over fat-butted boys." He laughed loudly as Ron made a wry face and shook his head.

Their attention was attracted by Bad Eye calling for Earl; then waving for him to come play handball. They had the next tally. Earl held up a hand and gestured for him to wait. "I'd better go. You know how sensitive he is. Anyway, we damn sure can't escape from in the hole—though a couple of game fools did it a few years ago."

"From 'B' Section?"

"Yeah, just cut their way out of the cells; then cut their way out of the cellhouse—and nobody saw 'em. Not the gun bull in the cell-block, not the gun tower outside, nobody. Naturally they got busted in a hot minute when they started running amok outside. Anyway, we'll just cool it in here, do the hole time, and get back on the yard. A sucker doin' time has to be patient . . . but not too patient when it comes time to move."

"I've noticed that," Ron said. "After a man gets a few years invested, he's afraid to move, and even if he isn't afraid, there's a sort of inertia that's hard to overcome."

Bad Eye had now moved fifteen feet from the spectators at the handball court and was calling and gesturing. "Better go," Ron said. "But I don't see why he wants you . . . bad as you play."

"Fuck you," Earl said, wanting some horseplay but remembering the riflemen at each end of the yard. Horseplay was forbidden, and fights were broken up with bullets, and sometimes the guards couldn't tell the difference. As Earl walked quickly—even playing the clown by skipping a few times—he thought about Ron's words concerning the changes wrought by San Quentin. He himself was already permanently maimed, but Ron wasn't. It was important that he not serve a long sentence.

"We're next," Bad Eye said. "Wanna play the front or the back?"

"Front. I can't play the back."

Two Chicanos from the Mexican Brotherhood, both friends of Earl's, had won the previous game; they stood waiting in sweat-dampened T-shirts. "C'mon, old motherfucker," one called. "You can't play either place."

Earl was taking off his shirt. "You might have to turn in your Mexican card when this *old* peckerwood runs you off the court." He borrowed a red bandanna and wrapped his hand in it in lieu of a glove.

Earl and Bad Eye lost, but the game was close and they would have won except that Earl was winded long before the last point. The stripped cell and the inactivity of the psych ward had taken its toll.

While he was cooling off, the steel door opened and a guard banged a large key against it, signaling that it was time to go back to the cages. The convicts formed a ragged line and filed slowly inside. Within the door half a dozen guards waited in a row, frisking each convict to make sure no weapons had been tossed down from the hospital windows.

*   *   *

Earl and Ron settled into the routine of "B" Section. Bad Eye was in the cell adjacent to Ron's, and when he was transferred (despite three guards he started at one end of the tier and stopped to shake hands with all his friends), Earl moved into the cell. They could talk without yelling most of the time. At exercise unlock they were closest to the stairs, hence first on the yard to get the handball court. Earl talked Ron into playing, and they invariably had the first game, invariably losing for the first month, but then beginning to win at least half the time. They'd play until they were beaten and then walk and talk until lockup was called. Though the method of escape was still unknown, they talked about what they would do. Despite Ron's assurances that his mother would give them refuge and money and transportation out of the country, Earl wanted to make some robberies to be independent. He knew two banks ripe for heisting, and he had a simple type of armed robbery, one that didn't require planning, that had been successful in the past. "It's as easy as stickin' up a fuckin' liquor store, and you're a lot less likely to get blowed away by some asshole in the backroom with a shotgun. Just pick a high-class jeweler, not Kay's or a junk place, but something like Tiffany or Van Cleef. Go in and ask to see some Patek Philippe's or unset two-carat diamonds. When the clerk brings 'em, just open the coat and show 'em the butt of the pistol. Workin' alone, without much planning, a dozen two-grand watches is a pretty sweet sting."

"We don't have to do that," Ron protested, voice rising in exasperation, wondering if Earl had an obsession with taking risks that would bring him right back.

"*You* don't have to. Maybe I don't either. But I ain't leanin' on nobody. I carry my own weight, brother."

"Okay . . . okay. We'll see what happens when we get out—*if* we get out."

"Have some confidence in me, kid."

"Then show me something."

The "B" Section clerk went to the San Quentin main line and Earl got the job. From 7:00 a.m. until evening he was out of his cell, doing a little official typing and running the tiers. When drugs were smuggled in from the yard, he invariably got an issue no matter who received them. In another week he used his influence to get Ron assigned as "B" Section barber. It was shaky for a few days, Ron scarcely able to tell the difference between clipper blades and shears, but the solid convicts simply refused to get haircuts until he'd practiced on the fifth tier protective custody inmates. Necessity is a brilliant teacher; in a week he could give a passable haircut.

As the months of winter passed, two events broke the basic routine. In February, Earl was near the door to the exercise yard when the second tier, filled with militant blacks, came out. His usual caution had lapsed, because there had been no race wars for nearly two years, and he was "all right" with several blacks on the tier. Suddenly one leaped from the crowd and stabbed him with a sharpened bedspring, a piece of wire similar to an icepick, though not so straight or sharp. Thrust into the stomach, it could have done considerable harm, but the blows were overhand and Earl got up an arm; the rude weapon punctured his bicep and then, as he ducked away and ran, sank into the flesh above his shoulder blade and was stopped by bone, causing superficial holes. The gun rail guard saw the flash of movement, blew his whistle, and loosed a shot that sounded like a cannon inside the building. The guards closed immediately on the black.

As Earl sat on the hospital gurney while peroxide was poured into the holes, he told Captain Midnight that he had nothing to say about anything or anyone. He was told by other blacks that the assailant was deranged, and thought that whites were trying to put a radio in his brain. When word came from the yard that the White Brotherhood planned to retaliate by indiscriminately stabbing blacks, Earl sent T.J. a long note, telling him that such stupidity would make him want to stop talking to them; that it would start a race war needlessly; that just one crazy man was responsible, and Earl wouldn't even take revenge on him because he was crazy. Though he didn't add it, Earl had never approved of race war—and when he accepted that fighting was necessary for survival because the other side had declared war, he still disapproved of indiscriminately murdering people because they were available. Indeed, both sides did it, and the uninvolved were usually the casualties; the warriors watched themselves and stayed out of bad situations.

For several days the blacks in "B" Section were wary, knowing who the riflemen would shoot if trouble started, disbelieving Earl—who went to the cell of the Muslim minister and told him there would be no repercussions—until the tension oozed away, leaving just the normal degree of paranoia. Then he had the respect of some of the leaders of the blacks, they knew that although he would "get down" in a war, he was not an agitator.

The second important incident was Stoneface's retirement and the arrival of "Tex" Waco from Soledad as the new associate warden. When Earl got the news, he began popping fingers and doing a dance. Ron, seated in the barber chair, asked him what was up.

"Well, bro'," he began in a heavy Southern accent, the kind where every phrase becomes a question, "this heah new 'sociate warden? He was a rookie heah? He was a-goin' to University of California at Berkeley? Well, this ol' convict heah did that ol' boy's term papers for him? In other words," he dropped the accent, "I've got long juice with this dude."

"Think he'll help us escape?"

"No, smartass motherfucker! But I'll bet that I—me—get outta the hole in the next couple of months. You better act right if you want out."

"No, you can't give me no head and you can't fuck me."

Earl leaped forward, put a one-arm headlock on Ron, and then rubbed his knuckles hard across the scalp. "What about beatin' the shit outta you?"

"C'mon," Ron protested; he really disliked horseplay. "Quit fuckin' around and find us a way out of here."

Earl was searching through his knowledge of San Quentin for exactly that, and in anticipation of the discovery he let his hair grow out. A shaved head would be conspicuous when they escaped. He discovered that he was gray at the temples.

194

Lieutenant Seeman also had influence with Associate Warden Waco, having been a sergeant when Waco was just a guard. The new A.W. agreed to review both Earl and Ron as soon as he got settled.

It was a month, and Ron was released to the general population one day ahead of Earl because of a paperwork mixup.

Bedding under one arm, shoebox of personal possessions in the other hand, Earl Copen came out of the South cellhouse rotunda into the big yard. A dozen friends were waiting, though some of his closest were gone. Not only Bad Eye, but also Paul Adams, transferred to camp, and the Bird to another state where he had a detainer. But T. J. Wilkes was there, grinning like a Jack o' Lantern (complete with missing tooth) and stretching a huge sweatshirt taut across his chest and arms. Vito was also on hand and took the bedding from Earl so T.J. could hug him and pat him on the back. "Ol' thing," T.J. said. "I was sho' nuff worried they wasn't ne'er gonna let you outta there."

"I was scared to come out. Hellfire, there's tough guys out here."

"Boy, I ain't gonna let nobody mo-lest you. 'Cept me." He reached around and squeezed Earl's rump. "Still firm."

"Easy on the hemorrhoids, chump . . . and show some respect. I'm the senior citizen since Paul split."

The gathered convicts laughed. Baby Boy shook hands and patted him on the back, as usual less effusive than the others. "Need anything?" Baby Boy asked. "I've got a full canteen draw."

"I'm all right. Thanks, bro."

Next Vito gave a "brotherhood" handshake, interlocking thumbs so it was two clenched fists—and whispered, "I've got a paper of stuff for you."

"That sounds like a winner."

T.J. put his arm around a square-jawed, lean convict that Earl didn't recognize. "This is my home boy," T.J. said. "Name of Wayne."

196

"We talked through the shitter," Earl said as he clenched hands with Wayne, knowing that he'd been convicted of killing a black with a roofing hatchet during a Soledad race war—and that he was in prison for a crime he hadn't committed. A car was identified as being used in a robbery, and the car salesman identified Wayne as having bought it. Actually, it was Wayne's brother who had purchased the car and committed the crime. So Wayne had parlayed a miscarriage of justice into murder and a life sentence.

"Ronnie's working," Baby Boy said, reading Earl's sweeping glance. "They assigned him to the textile mill."

"Aw, fuck!" Earl said in disgust; but he was confident that he could arrange a better job for his friend.

"Where'd they put you to work?" Vito asked.

"Sheeit! You know I don't do nuthin' but work for Big Daddy Seeman."

"He's already got a clerk."

"Well, I'm the *ex officio* clerk."

"Ah don't know what that is," T.J. piped in, "but it goddamn sure sounds good."

"When you goin' back to the North block?" Vito asked; it was a sardonic question; the regulations called for a year of clean behavior.

"It'll take a couple of weeks," Earl said, winking broadly. "But me, I've got a single cell . . . even if it is in the ghetto with the riffraff."

"Let's get your shit into the ghet-to," T.J. said, taking the bedding from Vito. "You can't get in. You don't live there."

As they crossed the yard, heading toward the barred gates to the East cellhouse, T.J. confided that the parole board had given him a release six months away, but he kept that fact hidden except from his closest partners. A man scheduled for parole was vulnerable; enemies would be all too happy if he did something to have the parole taken away—and others might figure they could take advantage of him in some manner because he wouldn't want to lose the parole. He wanted to know if Ron would send him to people across the border so he could start trafficking in drugs at a good level. "I can make a lot of money in Fresno, believe it or not. And I've got to stop robbing people. The fuckin' parole board told me that they'll bury me if I bring back another robbery. They're serious about robbery."

"About dealing dope, too."

"Yeah, I know. I'd go to work, 'cept you know how lazy I am. Fact is, they make you lazier in here. Hellfire, when I was a sprite I could pick cotton—"

"Quit lyin'! Goddamnit, if someone listens to you for five minutes, you gotta start lyin'. You talked to Paul too much."

T.J. gaped his mouth and saucered his eyes in a parody of innocence; then became serious. "Why don't you talk to him? If I could deal for six months, I'd buy me a cocktail lounge and retire."

"I'll run it to him. Are you gonna have any bread to invest or do you want it fronted?"

"I could pull *one* robbery."

They were on the fourth tier and the sound of the security bar being raised broke the conversation. A guard was coming down the tier with the spike key to unlock the cell gate. The floor was gritty with dirt and the fluorescent tubes had been torn out for some other cell. Otherwise it was in good shape. Earl's gear was put behind the bunk where it couldn't be fished out. The guard locked the gate and dropped the security bar behind them.

When they exited the cellhouse, Earl decided to go to the yard office. T.J. walked him as far as the yard gate; then turned down the stairs toward the lower yard and the gym. Earl felt good walking down the road between the library and education building. The warm sun was out and the air was fresh. Coming from the hole to the main line was similar to going from prison to the streets; he experienced the same exhilaration.

A week later the Catholic chaplain needed a clerk. The old-line convict who had had the job had always been "solid," but one night he was secretly taken out to testify at a grand jury about a Mexican Brotherhood killing. Word got out immediately, and he foolishly went about his business. Late the next afternoon, while the priest was visiting Death Row, a pair of Chicanos slipped into the chapel office with shivs and began carving. Miraculously, the victim lived despite thirty stab wounds. He was never again seen in San Quentin (and he didn't testify at the trial).

Ron Decker got the job. He had talked to the chaplain often when getting books before the Buck Rowan stabbing, and Lieutenant Seeman was a staunch Catholic and recommended him. Ron was happy to escape the cotton textile mill (every day he came up the stairs with cotton lint stuck to his clothes and his hair and the rhythmic noise of looms ringing in his ears), but he really wanted to escape from San Quentin. Earl had implanted the idea, and it grew to dominate everything else. A smuggled letter to his mother brought a reply—in veiled words—that she would be on hand whenever he needed her; she would hide them and help them get out of the country, whatever the cost. This was kerosene on the flame of Ron's desire. And because he had arranged for the all-important outside help, he felt no qualms about hounding Earl to find the way out. When Earl asked him if he wanted to move back to the North cellhouse, Ron answered that it was all right for now, but he really wanted to move to Mexico.

As for Earl, the more they hashed it over and the more he reflected, the more certain he was that they needed a truck. He excluded other ideas. He'd hoped that they could use the laundry truck, a route taken fifteen years earlier without the officials learning how the man got out. The laundry foreman watched while the panel truck was loaded with bundles of free personnel clothing, and then he rode it to the sallyport gate and gave it clearance. But there was a thirty-second weakness. After the truck was loaded at a vehicle entrance, the foreman locked that from inside and walked fifteen feet to come out of the building through a pedestrian door. Then he got in the truck. While he covered the fifteen feet, there was time to burrow under the bundles being taken out to the prison reservation. The scheme required cooperation from the convict truck driver—and when Earl checked on this one he found, to his chagrin, that the man was suspected of being a stool pigeon. Earl contemplated having the driver bashed in the head with a pipe—hurt but not slain—to get him out of the way. He decided against it because nobody knew who would get the job and because he didn't want to get any of his friends in trouble.

False gas tanks and false seats were also run through the mental grinder. The former could be made in the sheet metal shop, the latter in upholstery. They *might* work, especially a false-bottomed gas tank, but just one body could go out.

The trucks easiest to use were those loaded with products, mainly furniture, in the industrial area. A guard stood on the loading dock watching everything and then locking the truck. It was good security. If the procedure was followed diligently, nobody could sneak into a truck and through the walls. The flaw was human nature. After months or years of uneventful routine—what could be more dull than watching trucks be loaded, unless it was sitting all night in a dark gun tower watching a wall?—any guard lost his concentration, and many could be distracted for the few seconds needed to duck into a truck. Earl knew of two successful escapes from San Quentin under exactly those circumstances. Naturally they were years apart, for after one happened, the security was intense for a year, two years. It had been eight years since anyone had used it. Besides having a phenomenal success percentage, this particular way required no commitment until the actual moment. The guard was "turned" or not turned. It was different from cutting the bars or digging a tunnel (the last was impossible because the prison was on bedrock and the walls went nearly as deep into the earth as up into the sky) where the convict was committed the moment the hacksaw blade made a groove.

The insurmountable problem in using industrial area trucks was an inability to reach them. Even Earl couldn't go there without a pass or a phone call to the guard on the industries gate. Even industries clerks couldn't loiter day after day on the loading dock. Just a few convicts—those on the dock itself and, perhaps, those working in the shipping room—could wait and watch for the chance. If he,

Earl Copen, got a job change to loading trucks in the furniture factory, he might as well announce his plans in the *San Quentin News*. And if Ron also got a job change . . . sheeit! Even if it was possible, the chance to go might be months away, and Earl's life was much too easy to exchange it for blisters, splinters, and a sore back.

Easy as his existence was by convict standards, something happened to herald that it could become even easier. One afternoon he was crossing the plaza toward the chapel when Tex Waco came out of the custodial offices en route to the front gate. The new associate warden was as plump as Stoneface had been cadaverous. His not-quite-fat physique was the same as the last time Earl had seen him, but the hair was thinner and fashionably longer, and where his uniforms had once been patched and his shoes resoled, now he was garbed more fashionably than any other official. It was something convicts talked about; and as a group they gave a few points to a sharp dresser. Earl nodded and smiled. Why not? He'd known the man for a dozen years, had even covered for him on New Year's Day when he came to work still reeking of gin and staggering, his thermos full of scotch for his keyman (it was a while before he learned that he couldn't trust convicts and couldn't afford to be too "good" without being betrayed). New Year's Day was a show in the mess hall; nearly every nightclub in the Bay area sent its show. Those who didn't go to the show could watch the Bowl games in the gym. The few who wanted to do neither had to stay locked in their cells. The cellhouse tiers were empty. Earl was the South cellhouse clerk, Seeman was cellhouse sergeant. Correctional Officer Tex Waco had sneaked into a mattress storage room for a drunken nap. A lieutenant came around, asked for the officer. Earl told a lie that Waco was on the fifth tier searching a cell, and when the lieutenant said he wanted to talk to him, Earl had volunteered to get him, waked him, and straightened him out. The lieutenant's nostrils flared and his eyes narrowed, but nothing was said. Nor did Officer Waco ever mention it. He'd gone up the promotional ladder quickly, moving from institution to institution, and now was associate warden where he'd started. He recognized Earl and beckoned him. "When the hell're you gonna stay out, Earl?" he asked.

"When they stop catchin' me."

Tex Waco shook his head and made a clucking noise. "My clerk is going on parole in four months. If you want the job, you can have it."

When Earl mentioned the offer to Seeman, who still had a good clerk so that Earl actually did no work, the lieutenant told him to take the job. Seeman grinned, "Hell, I need a friend in high places. And it could just get you out in a few years—even with that unfortunate incident."

Earl wanted the job, knowing Waco was a poor writer in an executive position that required lots of reports, memorandums, and administrative orders. The associate warden would be dependent on his clerk. Earl could take up the slack, just as he'd done with the term papers years ago, and by doing the work, he would have access to some of the power. Even under Stoneface, the associate warden's clerk was treated respectfully by lieutenants and deferentially by lowly guards who didn't want to spend a year in a graveyard-shift wall post. The clerk could arrange cell moves simply by asking the control sergeant to do the favor—a dozen a week at five cartons apiece was a nice income. Job assignments were even easier to arrange. Even getting a man—all other things being equal—a transfer to a minimum prison or camp wasn't impossible. Waco was easygoing, had a conscience, and could be manipulated. Earl would certainly be a whale in a fishpond. He'd be able to patronize Lieutenant Hodges, the Christian, and Lieutenant Captain Midnight, the undercover racist. The average clerk working so close to officials suffered the suspicion of yard convicts. They might ask and pay for favors, and the mere fact of the job wasn't enough to brand a man, but usually there was a question mark after his name. Earl wouldn't even have *that* problem, except to fish and fools. His friends were the most notorious white clique in San Quentin, he'd known the leaders of the Chicano clique since reform school, and the meanest blacks respected him. Everything in the prison world would be his, and it was neither more nor less hollow a triumph than anything else—especially considering that it was all Vanity, or so said Ecclesties (sic). And what had Milton's Satan said when God hurled him from heaven to the abyss? Something about it being better to reign in the pit than serve in heaven.

But when Ron heard, the younger man made a flatulent, disparaging sound with his mouth. "Earl, brother," he reproached. "Let's get out of here."

"We're gonna do that. I'm just runnin' it down. What the fuck. You want we should just go kick on the gate and say, 'Let us out, cocksucker?' Is that it?"

"Don't ridicule me with that phony country twang. You're the one who said that people want to escape when they get here, and then settle into a routine and the fever dies. They get too comfortable, don't want to put it together, don't want to take the risk." Ron shook his head for emphasis. "I'm not going to let myself get like that . . . and I'm not going to let you rest until we're sipping Margaritas in Culiacán."

"Fuck! I raised a monster. Maybe we should think about having somebody subpoena us out to a small county jail. The gimmick is to take the tools with you from here—handcuff key, hacksaw blades between the shoe soles. We can get it done in the shoe shop."

"Do you know anybody to subpoena us?"

"Not offhand."

"The principles—or theories—are wonderful. I agree about the trucks. I agree with what you just said. But let's put theory into practice. Can you dig it?"

Earl sighed. "Yeah, I can dig it. Say, why don't you find the hole?"

"I'm trying, but I wasn't born here."

"Thanks, smartass motherfucker."

They grinned at each other.

The revelation came two nights later when Earl was somnolent on heroin. He was on his back, naked, a sheet over him, a cigarette in one hand while he lackadaisically scratched his pubic hair with the other, savoring the ultimate euphoria. He wasn't really thinking, but images of the day's event floated through his mind. Big Rand had looked from the yard office window; then said he'd like to put troublemaking niggers in the Dempsey Dumpster. Earl had grunted and looked. The huge year-old trash truck was halted in front of the education building. The swampers were dumping barrels of trash in it. The guard sat in the cab of the flat-nosed vehicle. Earl had already thought about and discarded the dumpster for the same reason that the guard could sit in the cab instead of watching. Where the old truck had been double watched, and probed with stakes at the gate, and watched while dumped, the new truck protected itself . . . anyone climbing into the dumpster would be committing suicide: a crusher inside applied tons of pressure. Earl didn't know how many tons, but probably enough to turn a convict into a pancake.

Except . . .

If . . .

His heart pounded with his excited thoughts. He tried to calm himself by looking out at the night and the lights twinkling in the hills across the Bay. It looked so easy that an inexorable pendulum of doubt swung back through the certainty. Yet doubt had no facts, while his inspiration seemed to have all the facts. Ruthlessly he throttled enthusiasm, and stifled his impulse to wake Ron and tell him as soon as the cell doors opened. Earl would check it out first.

Too excited to sleep, feeling too good because of the dope, he smoked cigarettes until his mouth was raw. Near dawn he dozed off without expecting to. And dreamed of escaping from Alcatraz, or trying to; he was running up and down the shoreline, unable for some reason to plunge into the water and swim for freedom.

When Earl came awake, the cell doors were open and everyone else had gone to the mess hall. He dressed quickly, not bothering to wash or comb his hair, wanting to get into the mess hall before it closed.

A guard was starting to close the steel door, but held it when Earl called. Once inside, he went through the line, but abandoned the tray the moment he reached the table. Instead, he went back up the aisle into the kitchen. It was out of bounds, but convict cooks, pot washers, and other workers were everywhere and provided cover. The free stewards paid not one glance to yet another convict. He circled the huge vats, tiptoed through sudsy water, and turned down a short corridor toward wire double doors. This was the vegetable room, its air heavy with the odor of peeled potatoes soaking in barrels, of grated carrots and onions. When Earl entered, the crew of half a dozen Chicanos was shucking corn, chattering Spanish, and listening to Mexican music on a portable radio. They were a clique of *braceros* who spoke no English and stayed together for mutual support. The vegetable room was their domain. When one left, they selected another of the brethren to replace him. They looked at Earl expressionlessly, neither questioning nor hostile. He motioned that he wanted nothing from them and went to a large double door at the rear, made sure it was unlocked, and peered out through mesh wire at a small yard behind the kitchen. It was the loading zone for trucks. Empty crates were stacked against a wall next to empty milk cans. Two convicts in high boots and heavy rubber gloves and aprons were using a steam hose to rinse garbage cans. The road to the small yard came up a ramp through an archway in a wall—though beyond the wall was only the lower yard. A guard tower sat on top of the wall. This was the first stop the trash truck made every morning, the beginning of its route, and Earl knew it was also the most secluded. It was the best place to see if what he thought was true, and if it was true, it would be the best place to make the gamble.

A quarter of an hour later the truck came up the ramp, its flat snout high until it reached level ground. It swung around and backed to the loading dock—ten feet from the vegetable room door— where the trash barrels waited. Two convicts stepped off the rear and began dumping them. The guard stayed inside the cab. The convict driver waited until signaled by a swamper and then threw a lever. The compressor whined the crushed trash.

Earl bounced and popped his fingers in a dance. It'll work. "It

... fuckin' ... will ... work," he said, and actually felt dizzy. He'd seen a prayer answered with a miracle. He and Ronald Decker were going to break out of San Quentin.

The work whistle had blown, the yard gate opened, and convicts were streaming out when Earl went against the flow toward the North cellhouse rotunda. Ron was coming down the steel stairs, still bleary-eyed, when Earl leaped at him and squeezed his neck in a headlock. "Gimme some asshole and I'll tell you the way out of here."

"Naw, you'd burn me."

"If I tell you, you'll burn me."

"That's the chance you take." Then Ron saw the elation glowing on his friend's face. "You jivin'?"

"Not jivin'. It's the trash truck." He started shadowboxing, bobbing and weaving and throwing hooks into thin air. "Hear me, brother! It's a winner. They don't watch it 'cause they think a chump would get killed. But ... the play is to dive in with some kind of brace, like four-by-fours, or a couple of Olympic-size weight bars. Put them against the back wall. Believe me, that motherfuckin' crusher ain't gonna bust no weight bar."

Ron was incredulous. "It *can't* be that easy."

"I checked it out this morning."

"How could they be so dumb?"

Earl shrugged.

"Or nobody else noticed it before this?"

"They weren't looking. Like the bulls. The crusher stopped them."

"When can we go? Tomorrow?" The last was obviously in jest.

"C'mon, fool. We gotta find out where it goes, where they empty it, and arrange for your mother to pick us up ... or somebody. If she can't make it—"

"She can—"

"—we'll wait until T.J. goes out in a couple of months. We can't just wander around like lost sheep. We wouldn't last three days. Man, you've got *heat* when you split from *inside the walls*. It ain't like runnin' off from a camp."

"I'll get on my end right away. The padre will let me make a phone call home. I'll get her out here."

"No, no. You don't want a visit. That'll put heat on her. We'll smuggle her a letter. She's gotta make it look like she never left home."

"How long is it going to take?"

"Two weeks. We've got to check out the swampers . . . make sure they aren't stool pigeons . . . and get 'em out of the way if they are. I know it uses an outside dump somewhere. We might have to run when we get out of the truck. I think I'll start jogging to get in shape."

"When I see *you* jogging, *I'll* have a heart attack."

"Maybe I am being too extreme."

The preparations to escape, once begun, went swiftly. A clerk in the maintenance office found the truck's manual and confirmed that the crusher would never break a four-by-four, much less an Olympic weightlifting bar; and there was enough room for several men within the truck. The reputation of the two swampers was okay among convicts. Earl then had Seeman look at their files to find out if there was a recorded taint in their backgrounds. He told the lieutenant he needed to know to stop some trouble and Seeman didn't question further. The records showed no prior snitching, and one had an unidentified crime partner still loose, which really indicated staunchness, for both the police and the parole board exerted pressure and threatened penalties in that situation. Ron talked to his mother on the chapel telephone and got the reassurance; then they smuggled the letter with detailed instructions and she confirmed with a telegram. She would rent a car, change the license plates, and follow the trash truck on three consecutive days from the moment it left the prison reservation, ready to rescue them whenever they made their move. She would have money, clothes, and a second car. Ron knew where to get phony I.D., but preferred to get it himself when they were out. She balked at having firearms waiting, which both Earl and Ron had expected, but Earl had insisted on asking. It didn't really matter. He knew where to get shotguns and pistols as soon as they reached Los Angeles. Baby Boy, in paint-splattered white coveralls, pushed a handcart up the ramp to the kitchen yard. Under a tarp, amidst buckets of paint and thinner, were two weightlifting bars, and wrapped in dirty rags were two shivs. T.J. had stolen the bars from the gym. It was after lunch and the vegetable crew was gone for the day. Baby Boy climbed on top of sacks of potatoes and stashed the equipment next to the wall. Despite the promise from Ron's mother, they gathered civilian shirts stolen from the laundry and sixty dollars in currency—just in case.

The escape was set for Tuesday. On Monday evening Earl was so tense that he couldn't eat. Pains squeezed his chest. He spent twenty dollars of the escape money on two papers of heroin and they erased the anxiety.

Just before lockup in the South and East cellhouses, T.J. and Wayne cornered one of the trash truck swampers, Vito and Baby Boy the other, and told them what to expect and how to react—by acting normal and going on with their job. Telling them so late wasn't to forestall them from snitching, but to keep them from gossiping to other convicts, who would gossip with yet more, until somewhere down the line a stool pigeon would hear.

After lockup, both Ron and Earl finished disposing of what was in their cells, giving away cigarettes, toiletries, bonaroo clothes, and books. Ron tore up letters and legal papers and put his photographs in a large manilla envelope that he would carry inside his shirt. Earl kept two packs of cigarettes, a spoon of coffee in an envelope for morning, and one squib of toothpaste on the brush. All he was taking with him were three snapshots in a shirt pocket. "Sheeit!" he muttered. "I travel light as Mahatma Gandhi." He was soundly asleep before midnight, while Ron never really got to sleep. Ron had quit smoking months before, but that night he puffed nearly a pack.

The moment the security bar was lifted and North cellhouse convicts came out for breakfast, Ron went to Earl's cell and found him snoring. The honor cellhouse door was unlocked and Ron pulled it open, tugging his friend's foot through the blanket. Earl's eyes opened immediately.

"Hey," Ron said, uncertain if he should laugh or be indignant. "What're you doing still asleep?"

Earl nodded in slow, dramatic patience. "Look, this is the first cellhouse out. The swampers and driver don't even leave their cells for half an hour. It's at least an hour before the truck starts rolling. What should we do, go to the vegetable room and cut up string beans until it gets there?"

Laughter won inside Ron. "Okay, but sometimes I can't believe you. Sleeping!"

"Ain't nothin' better to do. But I'll get up if you get me some hot water for coffee."

When Ron came back from the hot water spigot at the end of the tier, carrying a steaming jar of water wrapped in a towel, Earl was buttoning the blue jail shirt over the candy-striped civilian one. Ron sat down on the end of the lower bunk, back against one wall, feet on the other, while Earl brushed his teeth, drank coffee, and hacked up the gummy phlegm of a heavy smoker.

Through the tall barred windows they could see the yard, the prison's drabness even more monochromatic in the gray morning light. A line of convicts was starting to emerge from the East cellhouse at the far end, while below them North cellhouse residents were coming back.

"Shouldn't we go say goodbye to our friends?" Ron asked.

Earl looked at him, smiled. "Yeah, we should—and I didn't even think of it."

They went downstairs, against a flow of convicts, and out into the still nearly empty yard—empty except for the long line of convicts stretching from mess hall to cellhouse. The yard would fill as the mess hall emptied. Now only a dozen convicts were standing around or pacing back and forth. Ron and Earl walked through and scattered a flock of pigeons waiting to be fed, and went to the concrete bench along the East cellhouse wall.

Moments later a pair of convicts came from the mess hall line—T.J. and Wayne, the former hugging Earl and shaking hands with Ron, the latter shaking hands, in reverse order, with both of them—and wishing them good luck.

"Yeah, good luck, brothers," T.J. said. "We took care of that with that fool on the truck last night. He's all right."

210

"I'll see you out there in a couple of months," Earl said. "I've got your people's address. I'll get in touch when I think you've raised."

"If you don't make it," Wayne said, "we'll send you a care package into 'B' Section, smokes, coffee, and shit."

"If we *don't*," Ron said, "send *me* some arsenic."

"Ain't that bad round here," T.J. said. "Hell, there's lots of excitement." Then to Earl: "Send us a package of dope as soon as you can."

"I'll run off in a Thrifty drugstore for you."

From the corner of the South mess hall, Vito and Baby Boy appeared, cutting through the lines and angling over.

"Glad we caught you," Baby Boy said, shaking hands. "Sure wanted to say goodbye and wish you luck."

Vito was more demonstrative, goosing Earl and giggling. "Say, man," Earl said, slapping the hand away. "I'll be glad to get away from you."

The last of the mess hall lines was nearing the door.

"We gotta go," Ron said.

The clique gave quick pats on the back, and then they crossed the yard and got in the end of the line.

"When we get inside," Earl said, "follow me about ten feet behind."

As they stepped within, Earl bypassed taking a tray and stepped out of the line, walking along the rear wall where off-duty kitchen workers were standing. They gave cover. He glanced back and Ron was following.

It was the same in the confusion of the huge kitchen. Nobody even looked curiously at them.

Just two of the *braceros* were still working when Earl opened the vegetable room door. They were using hose and squeegee to clean scraps from the tile floor. They glanced up and kept working; they were nearly done.

Earl held the door until Ron ducked through. Then Earl told him to keep lookout down the hallway and scrambled onto the sacks of potatoes, retrieving the weightlifting bars and shivs. The *braceros* still said nothing, but hurried to scoop up the scraps and get out of the room.

Earl handed one shiv to Ron and put the other under his shirt.

He propped both weight bars next to the loading dock door and leaned forward, staring out at the kitchen yard and the top of the ramp. Ron stayed, watching the corridor.

The sound of the truck came before it was visible, but the time lapse was just a few seconds. Ron heard, and felt as if something that should have been in his chest had worked up into his throat and was trying to gag him. He could hear the truck growling loud as it strained in low gear; then it stopped and the gears shifted. He could hear it backing up.

Earl watched the gun tower on the wall against the gray sky. The guard had his back turned, as usual. The truck backed in less than ten feet away. The swampers bounded off, going for the trash barrels.

"C'mon, Ron," Earl said, his words punctuated by the crash of the first barrel.

As Ron moved, the tension dissolved—burst and went away. He was as calm and detached as at any time in his life, and so keyed up his senses captured every impression intensely. He even noticed that Earl's cheek was twitching.

They each held one of the long bars, pausing just momentarily at the door. "You get in first," Earl said. "Push the bar ahead of you . . . and don't drop the fucker." He opened the door and Ron went out onto the dock, nearly bumping into a barrel, causing Earl to step on his heels.

The swampers looked at them with wide eyes and stopped work, stepping back to give them room.

Ron put his head down and plunged into the hole, running into a stench like a wall and instantly starting to breathe through his mouth, thinking that he had to get a handkerchief out to breathe into as soon as he was seated. His knees waded through the trash, and he pushed the bar ahead of him.

The moment Ron's head and shoulders went in, Earl heard the truck's cab open and he knew the guard was getting out. He couldn't stay where he was, and he wouldn't have time to follow Ron. Both of them would be caught. All of this took one second to register, and then he stepped around the rear of the truck and jumped down from the loading dock, angling as if heading toward the other kitchen door, appearing just a few feet from the old guard. "Hey, Smitty," he said as if mildly surprised.

The guard's head came up but there was no suspicion as he recognized Earl. "Copen. You're a little out of your usual run, aren't you?"

Earl held the weightlifting bar. "Yeah, somebody carted this out of the gym to the kitchen—who knows what for—and Rand sent me to get it." As Earl finished the sentence, he heard a barrel being dumped and knew Ron was safe.

"Goddamn convicts would steal false teeth," the guard said.

Earl nodded, said nothing, and walked away.

In the darkness Ron heard the voices, recognized Earl's without the words. The fact of *any* talk was terrible. Ron's hopes withered, he *knew* they were caught. Then a barrel of trash flew in, sending dust toward him, and he dug for the handkerchief. Another barrel came. There was no alarm. His thoughts and feelings were tangled. Something had made Earl back off. He couldn't think further because the truck's motor started and he heard the clunk of the crusher. He braced the bar against the wall and held it with both hands like a lance. The trash crept over his feet, but when the crusher hit the steel brace it stopped. Everything held for a few seconds that seemed like minutes, and then the crush receded and the square of light reappeared.

Ron's confusion and terror evaporated in soaring elation. He was going to be *free* in a few minutes. The half-dozen stops were routine; he was over the hurdle. In the smelly darkness his thoughts had already left prison and were on life.

In the shadows of the kitchen doorway Earl Copen watched the high, ungainly truck roll down the ramp. His lips were pressed together but drawn as far back as possible, and his eyes were squinted into slits to suppress their stinging. His friend was gone and he was left behind, but it was better that one should be free than neither. Still, the hurt was deep—but when the truck had disappeared, Earl turned away, then snorted an ironical laugh. "Aw, fuck it. I run something around here. I'd probably starve to death out there."

It was as good a way to look at it as any other.

To find out more about Eddie Bunker you should read,

Mr Blue:
Memoirs of a Renegade,

his autobiography, but followed here is an article by *Crime Time's* Charles Waring, the master of the retro-spective, on a life like no other . . .

BORN UNDER A BAD SIGN—
THE LIFE OF EDWARD BUNKER

Charles Waring

Inauspicious Beginnings

Despite assurances from scientists about the nature of earthquakes, supernatural beliefs regarding the significance of seismic land-upheavals still persist in some parts of the world. Of course, in ancient times, natural disasters were often perceived as punishment from an angry deity. Although now, in the late twentieth century, we live in the epoch of the global village and at a time when science is regarded as an infallible avatar, superstitious notions are still harboured by many of the world's inhabitants. One such person who didn't accept earthquakes at face value was Edward Bunker's mother, Sarah.

A sense of profound foreboding (call it superstition if you will) affected the troubled mind of this young woman who, during the 1930s, had worked in vaudeville theatre and been a chorus girl in Busby Berkeley's extravagant Hollywood musicals. She sensed some portentous event had occurred at the moment of her son's conception. That was March, 1933, in Southern California. A major earthquake—resulting in fatalities and extensive damage to buildings—terrorised Los Angeles's inhabitants. It also mortified Bunker's parents, who were coupling at the exact moment the first tremors of the earthquake struck. To make matters worse for Bunker, at the time he made his unpropitious entry into the world (at Hollywood's Cedar Of Lebanon Hospital on December 31st, 1933), Los Angeles was in the grip of a torrential downpour of almost Biblical proportions with trees and even houses being swept away by dangerous currents. The alarming synchronicity of both cataclysmic events confirmed in his mother's mind that Edward would be trouble. For her, there was no denying that Bunker Junior was born under a bad sign, and sadly, she instilled this belief into him when he was an impressionable youngster.

Formative Years

Well, for young Edward and his parents, it was not long before the seeds of that pair of bad omens seemed to bear substantial fruit. At the age of two, Edward wandered off from a family picnic in a local park but was eventually located after a search-party of two hundred men had combed the area. Then he accidentally set fire to a neighbour's garage! On the face of it, young Ed may have seemed the toddler from hell but it's more likely that these incidents resulted from his parents' abject lack of super-vision rather than any innate inclination on his part to do harm. Indeed, Bunker's abiding memories from this period focus on the deteriorating relationship of his parents, who fought and argued with an intensity that resulted in the police frequently being called out to intervene. Bunker's father, incidentally, Edward Snr, like his wife, worked in Hollywood. Principally he was a stage-hand although occasionally he worked as a grip (a specialised technician who builds film sets). He was almost fifty when his only son, Edward Junior was born. As the marriage became increasingly acrimonious (fuelled in part by alcoholism), so young Ed was left to his own devices.

Fight and Flight

Bunker was only five when his parents' troubled marriage was finally dissolved. A consequence of the divorce proceedings was that he was sent to a boarding/foster home. Profoundly unhappy, he ran away for the first time and found himself roaming the city streets at night. For this, the foster home rejected him and Bunker then went through a succession of draconian institutions which attempted to curb his defiant, rebellious nature with harsh discipline and sadistic, often brutal practices. He attended a military school for a couple of months (where, through peer pressure, he took to theft). He ran way from here, boarded a train and found himself four-hundred miles away in a hobo camp. The authori-ties were alerted and Bunker was accosted but this chaotic, peripatetic lifestyle persisted throughout his formative years. Shoplifting and the theft of ration coupons eventually landed Bunker in a heap of big trouble and he was sent to an institution known as a Juvenile Hall, a kind of borstal or reform school. Here, Bunker became acquainted with hardened young criminals and quickly realised that if he wanted to survive this experience or at least avoid being somebody's punk (being sodomised) he had to learn the rules of the jungle. Although younger and smaller than most of his fellow inmates, Bunker was smart (his IQ had been estimated at 152), highly literate, streetwise and recalcitrant. He soon became fearless and inured to the dog-eat-dog brutality of the place. After a fight with a fellow inmate, Bunker was sent to a state hospital for observation from which he soon escaped, living rough on the streets. He was caught by the cops after a car he hot-wired crashed. He was then sent to an insane asylum to be assessed and was almost beaten to death by an attendant. Fortunately, Bunker was declared sane, and was allowed to leave with his life just about intact. It was not long before he escaped reform school and was back roughing it on the streets. Three months later, he was apprehended by the cops living in an a old car in someone's backyard. He was then shunted on to the Preston School of Industry which was designated for older teenagers. Bunker was still only fourteen. Eventually, he was paroled to his aunt. By this time his estranged mother had remarried and his father (now sixty-two) languished in a rest home because of premature senility. While with his aunt, Bunker continued to keep bad company and late hours. It was only a matter of time before he fell foul of the law again, this time for an outstanding parole violation. But Bunker's reputation as a troublemaker had catapulted him beyond the remit of California's Youth Authority. Despite his age, he was in the big league now. This time it was serious. This time it was prison.

Crime and Punishment

While most teenagers were still at high school, Edward Bunker was a veteran of California's stern custodial institutions for young offenders. From his earliest days, his life had been hurtling on a relentless trajectory towards a life in crime that would ultimately lead to lengthy incarceration in prison. And that's where he found himself at sixteen years-of-age. But it didn't chasten him one iota. To the proud, hardened Bunker, prison was an underground university of life. He gained the acquaintance of some of America's most notorious criminals and from this experience gleaned knowledge which not only helped him to survive on the inside but inspired schemes and scams when he was back on the outside.

But back on the inside, Bunker was hard and vicious and proud of it. He stabbed a mass murderer in the showers while at L.A.'s notorious County Jail. He was feared and he was respected (some regarded Bunker as a little crazy but in *Mr Blue*, he stated it was a protective mechanism on his part so that people would leave him alone). The last vestiges of civilisation's thin veneer had been scraped away in prison, leaving the inner core of one's being. In prison, men reverted back to animalistic behaviour: the predator and the prey. In spite of his youth, Bunker made it patently clear he was not in the latter category. If anyone messed with him, they'd find themselves either dead or in hospital (in truth, Bunker was not a cold-blooded killer but would not hesitate to ruthlessly defend himself). Furthermore, he knew the consequences of his lifestyle, heedful of the old prison adage "if you do the crime you do the time." It was a simple equation that Bunker understood implicitly and accepted without question.

Hollywood's Helping Hand

During his rampant teenage years, Bunker made an important acquaintance with an affluent fifty-something woman who was to help him change his life. She was Louise Fazenda Wallis, wife of the legendary Hollywood movie producer, Hal B. Wallis, the mogul behind such cinematic classics as *Little Caesar*, *Casablanca* and *Gunfight At The OK Corral*. Louise Wallis had been a movie star herself in the 1920s, a slapstick comedienne starring in some of Max Sennett's riotous silent reels. In the 1950s, when she met Edward Bunker, she was involved in helping out those less fortunate than herself. When Bunker left L.A. County Jail she gave him work. Initially, Bunker was perplexed by Mrs. Wallis's interest in him and was under the impression that her motives were less than honourable: he imagined she might want a teenage gigolo or else wanted to hire him to kill her husband. But Bunker's suspicions were soon allayed by Louise Wallis's warm, ingenuous nature and zany sense of humour. She really did want to help him and gave strong words of encouragement without reproaching him for his past. Bunker was more fortunate than many of his peers in having such a magnanimous benefactress. He spent many pleasurable hours in her company, not only doing chores for her but also lounging in the swimming pool at her mansion. He also met many of that period's celebrities, including the boxer Jack Dempsey, the writers Aldous Huxley and Tennessee Williams and even the media magnate, William Randolph Hearst (the inspiration for Orson Welles' *Citizen Kane*). By this time, Hearst was infirm and wheel-chair bound. Bunker actually was taken to Hearst's palatial residence at San Simeon and was there, dipping in the old man's swimming pool, the day the mogul died.

But apart from his friendship with Louise Wallis, Bunker continued to hang-out with low lifes: pimps, whores, dope-addicts and boosters. He tried heroin and then began selling crudely-harvested marijuana. While out on a delivery a police car pulled up alongside him, indicating him to stop. Bunker drove off but crashed into a car and a mail truck. Apprehended by the law, he was sent to L.A. county jail. Fortunately, Bunker didn't have the proverbial book thrown at him (he was charged with violating parole and put on probation) and ended up at a parole centre from which he escaped, returning to drug-selling. He was eventually caught again and was charged with assault with a deadly weapon. It was 1951 and Bunker was seventeen. The exasperated authorities finally sent him to his destiny: the notorious San Quentin prison.

San Quentin—Blood and Books

At that time, in 1951, seventeen-year-old Edward Bunker had the dubious honour of being San Quentin's youngest ever inmate. While banged up in solitary (aka "the hole"), Bunker could hear the incessant clicking of a typewriter. It came from the cell of death-row inmate, Caryl Chessman. Chessman, known as L.A.'s notorious "red light bandit", had written a thinly-disguised autobiographical novel about prison life called *Cell 2455 Death Row*. Bunker already knew Chessman from an earlier meeting. Chessman sent over to Bunker's cell (via a sympathetic guard) a copy of *Argosy* Magazine in which the first chapter of his book appeared. Bunker was inspired by Chessman's example. He also identified with the writers Cervantes and Dostoyevsky, both of whom had written while incarcerated. Later, Louise Wallis (who kept Bunker on her mailing and visiting list) procured him a typewriter. Learning the fundamental mechanics of writing as he went along, over the course of the next eighteen months Bunker would eventually produce a novel which was smuggled out to Wallis who showed it her friends and declared that although it was unpublishable, Bunker evinced a nascent writing talent. But it would take a further seventeen years before a book of Bunker's reached publication (that book, *No Beast So Fierce*, would actually be his sixth completed novel). Bunker, who had a voracious appetite for reading books since a child, spent much of his time acquainting himself with the contents of the prison library, accruing, as a result, a vast and encyclopaedic knowledge. Louise Wallis (who by this time Bunker addressed in his correspondence as "Mom") gave him a subscription to the *New York Times Book Review*. Bunker even sold his blood to pay postage costs and the fees for a university correspondence course.

Cars and bars

Bunker was twenty-two when he was finally paroled. It was 1956. He had served almost five years inside San Quentin. The important thing was that he had survived (and without becoming anyone's punk!). But survival on the outside was a different matter. In fact, it seemed a far harder task to do it by honest endeavour, despite the many doors that Louise Wallis opened for him with her altruism. She wanted to assist Bunker in helping himself and pointed him in the right direction by finding him work and accommodation. But Bunker, as a former con, felt ostracised by a society which never truly felt comfortable with convicted criminals in its midst. And besides, after his being banged up for half a decade, the temptations were just too overwhelming.

For a time, Bunker stayed clear of trouble. However, his benefactor, Louise Wallis, evinced increasingly erratic behaviour and seemed at the point of recklessly giving all her wealth away. Although she bought him a car and kitted him out in expensive clothes, Bunker never tried to take advantage of her good nature. After a drunken outburst at her home, Louise Wallis was diagnosed as having a nervous breakdown and while she went to hospital to recuperate, her husband Hal Wallis alienated her network of old friends and acquaintances, including Bunker. He had harboured ambitions of becoming a screenplay writer but overnight had become a persona non gratis in the Wallis household (Louise Wallis would die not long after, in 1962). So he tried his hand at selling used cars for a short time and then worked as a salesman at a small garage owned by an English ex-patriot. It wasn't long, though, before he descended into

...A.'s seamy underworld and returned to crime to make ends meet: orchestrating robberies (though not actually taking part himself, he took a percentage for the planning), forging cheques and involving himself in extorting protection money from pimps.

Within a couple of years, Bunker found himself back on the inside again, having been found consorting with known felons (he happened to be travelling in a car owned by two burglars who had their tools in the boot of the vehicle). Details of Bunker's misdemeanours together with a damning report by his hard-ass probation officer conspired to give him a ninety day jail sentence which included being sent out on work detail to the county farm (where low risk prisoners were sent). Bunker escaped almost immediately by climbing over a poorly guarded fence. He was a fugitive from justice once again and stayed on the run for over a year, despite a couple of close shaves with the police. Robbed of his cash while staying in an hotel during a road trip to New York, Bunker resorted to armed robbery out of desperation for immediate funds.

Inevitably, the agents of justice caught up with Bunker, but not before a failed bank heist and a wild car chase had ensued.

Bunker tried to get out of going back to prison by pretending to be insane. He gave a convincing performance (faking suicide and declaring that the Catholic Church had inserted a radio inside his head!) and was declared criminally insane. Bunker was shunted back and forth between Atascadero State Hospital and the California Medical Facility at Vacaville (where he edited a prison newspaper). Although Bunker was eventually freed, he could not keep out of trouble. His notoriety as a criminal mastermind put him on the FBI's Ten Most Wanted list. In San Francisco in the early '70s, Bunker ran a profitable drug empire. He was eventually caught after the cops had put a tracking device on his vehicle and followed him to Los Angeles where he boosted a bank (in fact, the police couldn't believe their luck—they were under the erroneous impression that a drug deal was going down). With a helicopter and five cop cars on his trail, Bunker was apprehended after a car chase. He expected the book to be thrown at him for the robbery, anticipating at least a twenty-year sentence. Miraculously and largely due to the solicitations of influential friends and a lenient judge, he got only a five year custodial sentence.

Back in prison, Bunker focused on improving his writing skills. His perseverance (he produced six novels and fifty short stories between

1953 and '72) was rewarded by encouraging words from an genuinely interested literary agent. By 1972, Bunker had finally produced a novel *No Beast So Fierce*, which, after some judicious pruning was accepted by the publisher, WW Norton. At the same time, Bunker's essay "War Behind Wall" about San Quentin's internecine race wars was published in the prestigious *Harper's* magazine.

Straight Time

When Eddie Bunker was released on parole in 1975, he had spent eighteen years of his life in prison institutions. Despite his new career as a writer, for a time, a life of crime still had its temptations, particularly when money got tight. But once Bunker was earning money from his writing and film appearances, he had no need to resort to crime to survive. His own view of his descent into criminal activity was that it was dictated solely by circumstances and necessity—once those circumstances changed for the better, the criminal impulse died in him.

A second published novel, *Animal Factory*, appeared in 1977 and articles followed in *The New Yorker* and both the *New York Times* and *LA Times*. Happily for the ex-convict, the actor, Dustin Hoffman, who had bought the film rights to *No Beast So Fierce*, in 1975, made a favourable deal with First Artists which allowed him not only to direct the movie but also supervise its all-important final cut. But taking on the mantle of director as well as starring in the main role as convict Max Dembo proved too much for Hoffman, who persuaded his old pal Ulu Grosbard to take over directorial duties. To Hoffman's dismay, First Artists reneged on their earlier decision to allow him the final cut and tampered with the film's editing in such a way that Hoffman sued for damages. Controversy aside and despite disappointing critical and commercial responses, *Straight Time* was a good movie and a faithful representation of life in the U.S. penal system. Bunker collaborated with Alvin Sargeant and Jeffrey Roam on the movie's screenplay. The film was also significant for Edward Bunker in that it represented his first acting part in a movie. It would be the first of many fleeting cameos that Bunker would play over the next two decades, including playing the part of a cop (Captain Holmes) in *Tango and Cash* (1988) and culminating with his famous role as Mr Blue in Tarantino's acclaimed *Reservoir Dogs*. Indeed, Bunker's minor thespian exertions even made him eligible for a Screen Actors Guild pension.

In 1979, Bunker claimed that he found true salvation in an attractive young lawyer, Jennifer, whom he married (despite a difference in age and background they are still together and have a young son, Brendan, born in 1994).

In 1981, Bunker produced a third novel, *Little Boy Blue*, which contained some of his most impressive and eloquent writing. In 1985, Bunker wrote part of the Academy Award-nominated screenplay to the film *Runaway Train*, starring Jon Voigt as a fugitive con (Bunker mainly wrote the opening half-hour of the movie depicting prison life).

In 1991, Bunker was cast by wunderkind director, Quentin Tarantino (at the suggestion of Chris Penn) in *Reservoir Dogs* as Mr Blue. Tarantino, in fact, had apparently studied the movie *Straight Time* while attending a course at Robert Redford's Sundance Institute for young film-makers. A couple of years later, in 1994, Bunker was hired as a consultant on the film *American Heart*, starring Jeff Bridges as the con Jack Kelson, who has just been released from the slammer and is hoping to go straight by cleaning windows. In Michael Mann's slick 1995 thriller, *Heat*, starring Al Pacino and Robert De Niro, some of the cast picked Bunker's brain about the nature of the criminal mind (Jon Voigt's character, in fact, was made to resemble Bunker in appearance).

In 1996, Bunker produced his fourth crime novel, the action-packed *Dog Eat Dog*, based upon a story a fellow con had related to him while in prison. His latest book, *Mr Blue*, a candid autobiography, has just been published with the possibility that one of his earlier, previously unpublished novels, a sort of Jim Thompson-esque, noir novel, will follow shortly afterwards.

Ironically, Edward Bunker continues to make a living from crime—but for the last quarter of a century, he's only been writing about it. After having begun life in somewhat unfortunate circumstances in Hollywood some sixty-six years ago, Edward Bunker has returned to whence he came to reside in tinsel town as a model citizen. No longer the human equivalent of an earthquake, Bunker (though still unrepentant about his criminal exploits), lives in relative serenity after many turbulent years evading the law.

Edward Bunker titles can be obtained from

NO EXIT PRESS

978-1-84243-264-8	Stark	£6.99
978-1-84243-266-2	No Beast So Fierce NE	£7.99
978-1-84243-267-9	Animal Factory NE	£7.99
978-1-84243-268-6	Little Boy Blue NE	£7.99
978-1-84243-269-3	Dog Eat Dog NE	£7.99
978-1-84243-270-0	Mr Blue NE	£9.99

Please send orders to;

HIGH STAKES BOOKSHOP
21 Great Ormond Street,
London WC1N 3JB

Add fifteen per cent P&P. Cheques payable to High Stakes in Sterling drawn on UK bank or pay by credit card (Visa, MasterCard, Maestro) quoting card number, expiry date, 3 digit security code and valid from date and issue number where appropriate

Tel 020 7430 1021
Fax 020 7430 0021

Or order online at www.noexit.co.uk/bunker